KỌ̀LÁ ÀKÀNBÍ

AND THE HEART OF MIDNIGHT

MARIA MOTÚNRÁYỌ̀ ADÉBÍSÍ
ILLUSTRATED BY SIMONE DOUGLAS

Orion

ORION CHILDREN'S BOOKS

First published in Great Britain in 2023 by Hodder & Stoughton

1 3 5 7 9 10 8 6 4 2

A CIP catalogue record for this book is available from the British Library.

ISBN 978 1 510 11143 1

Typeset in Sabon by Avon DataSet Ltd, Alcester, Warwickshire

Printed and bound in Great Britain by Clays Ltd, Elcograf S.p.A.

The paper and board used in this book
are made from wood from responsible sources.

Orion Children's Books
An imprint of
Hachette Children's Group
Part of Hodder & Stoughton Limited
Carmelite House
50 Victoria Embankment
London EC4Y 0DZ

An Hachette UK Company
www.hachette.co.uk

www.hachettechildrens.co.uk

**To my sister Emmanuela Olúdárà
who listened first**

'We can redream this world and make
the dream come real. Human beings
are gods hidden from themselves'
– Ben Okri's *The Famished Road*

MAP OF OLÓRÍ

ÒRÌṢÀ GODS
AND GODDESSES

Olókun:	The Goddess of Darkness
Ògún:	The God of Iron and War
Ṣàngó:	The God of Fire and Lightning
Òṣun:	The Goddess of Love
Ọya:	The Goddess of Wind
Rùnmí:	The God of Wisdom and Divination
Aganjù:	The God of the Wilderness
Babalú:	The God of Diseases and Healing

Night Creatures

Lègbá
Leader of the Night Creatures and
guardian of the dead.

Mami Wata
Water spirits in the shape of beautiful
snake women, sometimes
known as mermaids.

Àbíkú
Soul swapping spirits who swap places
with children while spiriting their souls
to the forbidden jungle known as
Jujuland. They also have the power to
turn invisible at will.

Àgbákò
Part scorpion, part elephant and part
snake monster that roams the Jujuland
jungle, consuming any living
thing in its path.

CHAPTER ONE

The Museum Incident

I thought the museum school trip was going to be dead, but it was actually sort of interesting.

Our class had to go down a creaky staircase to the basement, where there was a wooden sign with faded letters on it that read *The Victor Frobenius Africa Collection*. While the rest of the museum was showing off with its super high ceilings, crisp white walls and blinding lights, our room was small, dingy and cramped.

But I'm not gonna lie – this tiny exhibit had some cool stuff.

There were strips of patterned ankara cloth, glistening cowrie shells, gleaming coral necklaces, brass amulets with roaring leopards' faces, ultra sharp flat throwing knives, beaded orange terracotta pots and menacing masks all arranged behind sheets of glass. The guy who jacked this stuff – Phineas, or whatever – had pretty good taste.

It looked kind of sick and, unlike the Roman stuff upstairs, it was made by people who looked like me.

It was super loud, though, cause there were thirty kids but only four teachers, all running after ponytailed girls with lip-gloss, and footy guys doing Messi impressions all over the place.

I was tryna ignore the noise cause I was actually getting interested in something for once, when a shivery feeling crawled up my spine and lit my insides on fire. I have this condition called sickle-cell anaemia. My blood cells have a weird shape which makes them rubbish at carrying oxygen, which is their job. It makes me tired all the time and super sensitive to temperature changes: when I get too cold, I get this painful crisis.

The museum air con was doing madnesses to my insides.

I shut my eyes tight and tried to ignore it. I hoped it would go away soon. All I needed was quiet. Then I felt a shove out of nowhere.

Atticus Sharp. He's this moist kid in our class that runs around thinking he's Draco Malfoy or something. He sticks out like a sore thumb with his fluorescent ginger hair and pasty, flaky skin that makes him look like an uncooked sausage roll.

'Do you want to see something strange, Cuckoo?' Atticus said, poking at a glass box that contained a weird, skinny, wooden doll. It had curved horns on its rectangular forehead, which was painted black and red.

I kissed my teeth without bothering to answer back. Then I tried to read a large sign on the wall to distract me from the pain in my ribs.

'A British explorer named Victor Frobenius collected the artefacts on display here from a tribal nation in West Africa,' Atticus read out loud in his toady, posh voice. 'Frobenius was last seen in a jungle where he was embarking on a quest to find a legendary black diamond known as the Heart of Midnight. This jewel was thought to contain the heart of a vengeful goddess, and it was said that its possessor would become the richest, most powerful person in the world.'

Atticus jabbed his swordfish nose in my direction. 'Oi, Cuckoo,' he said, trying to get my attention.

He knows my name is Koku. Like a can of Coke, with an extra 'oou' at the end.

'Shut it, Abacus.' I gritted my teeth as another jolt of pain ran through me. I took a swig of water, cause I know I gotta keep hydrated to stop things from getting even worse.

'Are you alright?' he asked.

'I'm fine,' I said, trying not to be too bait. None of the other kids had noticed, and I was planning on keeping it that way.

'Hmph . . . you've gone all grey.' Atticus narrowed his dishwater-grey eyes at me. 'You're not scared of this tiny doll, are you?'

'Are you dizzy, fam?' I managed to squeak out, even though I was the dizzy one. The pain squished my lungs together and I was having trouble standing up straight.

'That doll with the horns has an absurd look on its face, see?' Atticus said, pointing at the doll figure again.

I looked at its holes for eyes and charred black stumps for teeth. It had shells around its neck and three lines carved into both its cheeks, like whiskers. Looking at it made me feel strange, like static electricity was washing over me. I'd never felt this during a crisis before.

'It's supposed to have an ancient demon sealed in it from the Oh-low-ree tribe,' Atticus continued, pressing his nose against the glass. 'Apparently just looking at it can summon its spirit.' He turned and rolled his eyes. 'I can't believe these people actually believed in stuff like that.' Then he looked at me. 'That's where you're *really* from, isn't it?' Atticus said, pointing at the label underneath.

According to my uncle, my mum died during a war in Olori when I was three years old. I didn't like thinking too much about it cause it was just a land of ghosts for me – it took all the people that were supposed to be mine, and left me with no one.

I shrugged.

'There's an uncanny resemblance,' Atticus added. 'It's so tiny and weird-looking . . . sort of like you, don't you think, Cuckoo?' He sneered.

'I'm not a chicken leg, so why are you roasting me, fam?' I said.

Atticus had no sauce. Everyone knows I'm freakishly small for my age. What they don't know is that my puberty is delayed cause I don't get the oxygen my body needs to develop.

Atticus was giving me stress – it was making the pain worse. The pain had travelled to my knees now, and I had to focus on how dandruffy my guy's neck was to stop myself collapsing on top of him.

'Especially this part,' Atticus sniggered.

I followed his finger to the tiny crumb between the figurine's legs.

That did it. I got so mad it was almost spiritual.

This tingly feeling started building up inside me. It was giving me energy – even though I still felt pain from the crisis – like I had downed a thousand Lucozades or something. Since I've been ill my whole life, I know exactly what a crisis feels like – and this wasn't it.

I couldn't stop staring at the doll. Staring at it made the electric feeling grow stronger. A yellow sun appeared in the doll's hollow wooden eyes. The faint light kept flickering on and off in the darkness. It made me want to reach out and grab it.

'Did you see that light?' I asked.

Atticus squinted at me like I had lost the plot. I probably had, cause as soon as I touched the glass a sharp jolt of energy shot into me. One moment Atticus was flapping his chapped lips at me, the next he was flying into the glass front of the exhibit case.

The glass shattered into a thousand pieces, catching

the light at weird angles, making everything look ultra bright.

An alarm sounded as the figurine rolled towards the edge. I caught the doll before it fell, clutching it in my left palm.

I get all hypersensitive when I'm going through a crisis. That's how I noticed that the dark wood had been brushed with a musky-smelling oil. It made it feel a bit warm and wet. I stroked its horned head gently with my thumb. Its yellow eyes were still flashing.

Atticus didn't have a single scratch on him, but that didn't stop his high-pitched screaming getting everyone's attention. I guess his private opera lessons paid off big time.

The nicest girls in my year were saying, 'Poor Atticus! That Koku kid has serious anger issues . . .'

'Do you think there's trouble at home or something?' Miss Adams whispered loudly enough for everyone to hear.

'I always knew there was something wrong with Cuckoo . . .' Mr Stokes, my head of year, replied.

I was in loads of trouble, and I couldn't even defend myself. The teachers had called a bunch of hench security guards on me.

'We got a situation over 'ere!' One of them yelled

into a crackly walkie-talkie. 'One of the little devils has broken into one of the displays in the Frobenius exhibit!'

I wasn't concentrating on the big guys. I was in a state of pure shock. The only thing that helped was focusing on the tiny sculpture in my hand.

Then Miss Adebayo, the only teacher who could actually say my name right, came over. Her big brown eyes were magnified by the tortoiseshell frames of her glasses. 'Koku, I know you must have some explanation for this. But we need our history intact so we can understand our past.' She held out her palm expectantly. 'Please return the figurine to me before you get in serious trouble.'

A normal person would've handed it over. But sometimes I just don't think things through. And I feel stuff too hard. Harder than most. That's where all my problems start.

I kept stroking the horns on the doll gently – like a numpty – till it suddenly splintered and cut my thumb.

I looked as a tiny trickle of red ran down my hand – and a thousand silvery whispers slithered into my ear. I shuddered as raspy, wet voices whispered my full name: **'KOKUMO, *E GBA MI O!*'**

I knew the last part was Yoruba, the language of

Olori. Apparently I spoke Yoruba when I was little and I used to live over there, but now I had no clue what it meant.

My fingers loosened on the oily wood, and the little figure slid right out of my palm. The doll shattered into pieces on the cement floor.

My heart started beating like crazy as shadows seeped out of the broken pieces, dividing into shapes that looked like decapitated people. Others were just floating faces, or backwards legs, or wispy arms with fingers bent all the way back. And then these smoky shadow tendrils began to gather into one colossal, human-like shape.

SMASH

The dark shadow moved to seat itself on top of the exhibit stand it had been trapped inside.

The rest of its body looked human enough – it wasn't naked like the doll it came out of – thank God – but it was skinny, like it had been starving for decades, and covered in burnt leaves and white painted spots all over. But its face was something else, man. It made Atticus Sharp look like a supermodel.

Smoke curled around its massive head. I barely came up to its hips. It had streaks of black and red on each cheek that were starting to flake off and long black teeth that were as long as my fingers set in a lopsided grin. Its yellow eyes burned right through me to the back of my skull.

The creature gave me a look that felt like a wink, but its yellow eyes did not move. Even when a dark cloud that looked like a bunch of chewed-up faces settled around its shoulders it didn't even blink or nothing. The faces stretched their mouths in silent screams: '*E gba mi ooo! E gba mi oooo!*' the voices whispered desperately.

Centuries-old dust blew right into my face, throwing me into a mad coughing fit. I blinked the stinging wetness from my eyes.

When I next looked up, the creature and the ghostly

faces were gone. Just like that.

Replaced by the furious faces of my class screaming my name wrong.

CHAPTER TWO

Back to Olori

I was marched back to school by the army of teachers like I'd blown up the museum or something.

As soon as I opened my form-room door, I saw that my uncle was already there, waiting for me. He was wearing his cheap silver suit – it glistened like foil when it caught the light, making him look like an out-of-season Christmas pudding.

'Mr Tunji!' Mr Stokes exclaimed. 'How on earth did you get here so quickly? I was just about to give you a ring and discuss what happened at the museum today.'

'Ah, don't worry yourself, sah!' Uncle Tunji announced, boldly. 'I knew this day would come. The priest with the power to see into the days of new told me that a spirit would enter this boy in a museum and cause confusion in my life.'

He was just waffling. I bet one of the other teachers rang him when I broke the dumb doll. I slid into the nearest seat – it happened to be Mr Stokes's fancy desk chair – knowing we'd be here for some time.

'Right . . .' Mr Stokes blinked at my uncle and cleared his throat. 'Well, Mr Tunji, we're going to have to discuss a suitable punishment for the young man.'

'You are very right, sah! I will make sure this boy learns sense,' Uncle Tunji agreed enthusiastically.

'Cuckoo needs to learn how to control his temper,' Stokes added, not even bothering to hide his slimy grin. 'This was meant to be a treat for the children before their summer holidays.' He shrugged. 'I'm sure Cuckoo didn't mean to harm poor Atticus. He's a well-meaning boy, although he tends to get easily distracted.'

He was nodding after every sentence, like he was expecting me to agree with him. Mr Stokes loved talking down on me. Maybe if he spent the same amount of time on his receding hairline, he wouldn't look so clapped.

I wished Miss Adebayo was there: she was the only teacher who actually believed in me.

My uncle tugged his right earlobe down and leaned into me. 'Koku, your head is not balanced, *ee-o*.'

I moved back, cause his breath kicks like rotten crayfish and I'm not about that life. When I didn't respond, he yelled: 'Ah-ah! Your deafness is first class! Did I send you to school to scatter other people's property?' he asked.

Who cares? I thought. *It was stolen anyway – how do you think the explorer guy got hold of it?*

I just ignored my guy and focused on building a yellow Post-it Note pyramid on the teacher's desk. Doing anything art related normally calms me down.

'Gods have mercy on me, *ee-o*!' Uncle Tunji said, grabbing his bald head in fake shock. My eyes peeled back like a tangerine whenever he spoke. His screaming was drawing attention – my entire year was pressing their noses up against the glass tryna get a look in.

I sank down in my seat to avoid their glares.

'You shameless goat!' My uncle swiped at my Post-it Note fortress, making the papers flutter to the ground. 'Koku, you are trying to kill me with nonsense upon nonsense, eh?'

I had no idea why my uncle always thought his life was under threat; if anything, he was the one who was always trying to kill me.

'I am in soup! *O pari o!* I am finished!' Uncle Tunji's forehead-sweat dripped into his eyes so it looked like he was crying.

'Sorry to interrupt, but I'm afraid I have no choice but to suspend Cuckoo for the entirety of the next week,' Mr Stokes said. 'And you can take the boy home now, as we don't need any further disruptions today.'

My uncle was scarily quiet on the walk back. The high street was a long, depressing slab of concrete that smelled like chicken, dotted with shops that sold fakes of pretty much anything. Most of them had the audacity to add 'Premium' and 'Luxury' to their peeling names, like that would somehow make them legit.

We followed the greasy trail all the way home to our flat.

As soon as we got in, Uncle Tunji collapsed into his favourite brown leather recliner chair, which he had positioned right in front of the TV. 'The time has come for you to spend the summer in Olori,' he said, bluntly.

It's not like our cramped flat above the QFC chicken shop (I reckoned it stood for Questionably Fried Chicken) was anything special, but it was the only home I'd ever known.

'I don't wanna spend summer there. I'm begging you man, please let me stay!' I pleaded with him, trying not to be disgusted by the way he kicked his sandals off, revealing his curling toenails. As annoying as he was, my uncle was the only sort of family I had. He wasn't even my *real* uncle – he's a friend of my family who agreed to adopt me and bring me to the UK after my mum died during the war in Olori.

I only have one, faint memory of Olori: of some annoying, lanky kid who used to flick my ears. I can't even remember what their face looked like.

'I'll do anything! I'll even do my homework and . . . and I'll never make you into a meme again!' I begged.

'What is "meeemumu"?' my uncle yelled.

'Well, it's—' I tried to explain.

'Stop this nonsense!' he interrupted. 'Listen, and listen well, Àbíkú.'

I braced myself as soon as he called me 'Àbíkú'. He only said that when he was properly mad. He once told me that Àbíkús are demon spirits that trap the souls of kids in a dark forest so they can terrorise their parents by inhabiting their bodies. Àbíkú kids are supposed to be more annoying than regular ones cause they're mischievous and got attitude problems and all that. Apparently, if an Àbíkú substitutes for your real kid, there's nothing you can do until the soul-stealer swaps back.

Uncle Tunji thinks everyone has got some kind of evil magic in them. According to my man, his last boss was possessed, which is how he lost his last job, and before that his first four wives were all witches with crazy powers, which was why it didn't work out with any of them.

I ain't like my guy. I know those are just excuses for his lameness. I don't believe in magic.

Like, yeah, for a moment I wondered if the ghostly spirits I saw in the museum were real. But there's no way, cause if magic was real, I could just use it to get rid of my sickle cell or something.

'Kokumo, since you were a small cockroach I knew this day would come. I started making preparations for your visit to Olori long long ago.'

I shuddered at my whole name being said aloud. It reminded me of the voices whispering in the museum. If someone uses your full name, it means they are ready to rip you a new one – and my name means, 'Don't die any more,' in Yoruba.

It's actually peak. Before the ghost mandem started calling out my name, the last time I remembered being called anything other than Koku was when I was in the hospital for the longest time.

The thing is that everyone, even the hardest guys, are scared of dying. But most people don't have to think about it till they get all wrinkly. My life ain't promised, though, cause my own body tries to kill me on the daily.

'We can inform the plane of your condition so they can help you,' Uncle Tunji added, more softly this time, as if he could read my thoughts. 'Now pass me the remote control!' he demanded, gesturing to the device on his armrest, which was *literally* one inch away from his fingertips. As soon as I handed it over, he turned on his show with the shouty preacher guy on it and sent me away.

Wasteman.

CHAPTER
THREE

Ghost Fridge

Cause I was suspended from school, I was chilling at home while my uncle was at work.

Ever since I can remember, I've never been anywhere the 97 bus couldn't take me. You can get all around London from my yard to the big Westfield Shopping Centre. That's where they got the arcade, and the cinema with the biggest screens and the pengest blueberry slushies.

But skipping school is kinda dead when you got no mates to bunk off with. It would've been alright, if I couldn't hear the air whispering, **'KOKUMO, *E GBA MI OOOO*,'** whenever my sickle cell randomly flared up.

I still had no clue what the Yoruba word *e gba mi*

meant. I would've asked my uncle about it, but I wasn't really talking to him since he was actually sending me to Olori for the summer. He's told me he has booked my flight for Friday the thirteenth, which is tomorrow. You'd think a superstitious guy would avoid that day, but they were having a sale so he copped the tickets no long ting.

I still don't know if I believe him – I hope he's just bluffing like all the other times he threatened to send me back there.

It had been a week since the museum incident and something inside me had changed. I got a whole new sickle-cell symptom: hallucinations. It put me on edge, cause my greatest fear is getting super sick again like when I was a kid. If you think I'm skinny now, back then I was, like, two-dimensional or something. I don't want to end up in hospital for so long ever again – I missed out on the whole of Year 7 cause of my illness, which is why I got no friends now.

A memory from way back seeped into my mind. It was the doctor's warning from the day I was diagnosed: 'Look, Quackoo, I'm going to be honest with you,' the guy said, although he was addressing my uncle and staring right through me. 'You have sickle cell. That means you're not like other kids.'

He had droned on, scratching his patchy black moustache. 'You won't be able to play sports or go on crazy adventures. You'll have to take it easy from now on . . .'

His words had forced me awake like someone had dashed ice water on my head.

'Red blood cells are supposed to be circle shaped, but yours are shaped like a crescent moon. When they pass through your blood vessels they get all sticky and clump together. This causes a pain crisis.'

'So, what can I do to get better?'

'You'll have good days, bad days and some downright awful days. But it's not going to get better. It's a lifelong illness that's likely inherited from your parents.'

Suddenly breathing had felt impossible until I felt a gentle rhythm on my knee. It was Uncle Tunji. 'Don't mind this man, Koku – when do you ever do what you are supposed to do, eh? Your stubbornness will come to your aid. You will beat this thing one day.'

I'd been tiptoeing around my condition ever since.

And now I hear voices and see horrible ghostly things during a crisis, as well as experiencing the pain.

It made me scared to open the fridge door, cause the chill coming out of it can sometimes trigger my condition. But it's not like I could get away without eating till my uncle came back from work.

Time seemed to slow down as I gripped the cool handle of the fridge door. As it jerked open, frosty air droplets blew out, sending a prickly sensation over my arms.

Something like a fever slowly rose inside me. Hideous shapes that stared at me with no eyes began to rise out of the kitchen floor. Some of them were just arms and legs; others were heads bouncing about with no bodies attached.

They limped towards me, their broken transparent bodies reaching towards me as if they were after me. **'KOKUMO, *E GBA MI O!'*** they kept saying, over and over. Grey phantom claws scratched at my joggers. My throat squeezed tight as clammy hands passed through my skin.

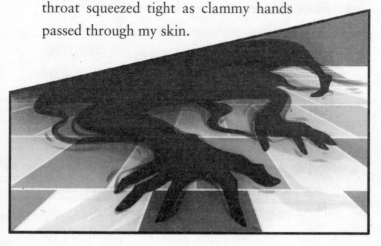

I gritted my teeth and pulled the rice out of the fridge before it could get worse. As I slammed the fridge door shut, the sludgy shapes disintegrated into a thin mist. I blinked a couple of times and they all disappeared into thin air.

I wasn't hungry no more.

I tried to take my mind off things by sorting out Jollof's food instead. Jollof is my cat, sort of. He followed me home from school one day and I felt sorry for him, cause he's weird-looking like me.

I might grow into my looks one day. I really hope so, cause I really don't know what I'm going to be doing out there with my pointy ears, my cheekbones so sharp that they could shank you, maroon eyes that freak people out and a white comma birthmark on my chin, which makes my whole face look like an unfinished sentence or something. I don't look like what I'm supposed to, I think. Same with Jollof. He has puddle eyes and a dopey face, like he would say 'Five' if you asked him what two plus two was. But I love Jollof anyways. He's my best mate. I was going to miss him if I really was getting sent to Olori.

After Jollof was done with his food, I led him to my room. I had to hide him away before my uncle got back. He thinks cats are possessed by spirits or something. I patted Jollof behind his ears just the way he likes, then I stared at my reflection in my bedroom mirror.

I missed the way my uncle's last wife, Aunty Bola, used to do my hair – shaving it neatly at the sides with a crisp fade and adding small twists at the top that looked like tree branches.

I still keep it longer at the top with a fade at the sides, cause Uncle Tunji hates it that way. But I can't be bothered to do all those little twists. So, I get two sections and I twist them up, so they stick up like curved horns.

Uncle Tunji says it makes me look like the devil – or worse, a rapper. I think it bangs. It's my signature look.

After I sorted my hair, I sat on my bed, which still has faded red Lightning McQueen bed sheets from when I was tiny. I tried to keep happy thoughts in my mind, like crisp white Air Force Ones and brand-new iPhones without the sticky bit peeled off. But I actually deeped it.

I was going to Olori tomorrow for the whole summer holidays. And there was nothing I could do about it.

I hate Olori. I didn't remember nothing about it.

I ain't even got a memory of when my parents were around. All I knew was my Mum was dead and my dad wasn't nowhere to be found. So I ain't got nothing and I don't come from nothing. The only thing that was passed down to me was an incurable disease. Some legacy. All I had was one fading photo, where all the colours were brushed by a thin brown haze.

I kept it in my bedside table drawer, but I had it memorised in my head. I couldn't help wondering if Olori looked like that now: a wide-open lilac sky, bright green wonky trees and a burnt orange sun.

I knew the woman in the photo was my mother. She was wearing a blue ankara headwrap with long fuzzy twists spilling out of it, and a beaded necklace that looped around at the end like an infinity sign. She had pale arms and dots of white under her eyes, but a deep complexion everywhere else.

Standing next to her was some madman with stripes of white paint bleeding into the cracks of his face. I knew he ain't my dad cause Uncle Tunji told me, which was bless in a way cause it meant I wouldn't end up looking like a low-budget Morgan Freeman in the next fifty years. But it was also peak cause I had no clue where my dad was, or who my dad was, and if he even knew about me.

Thinking about it got me down, cause he probably had a new family now, with normal, healthy kids.

The guy in the photo was wearing a long white robe and talking to my mum about something, and she was laughing with her mouth wide open. I wondered what her voice sounded like. I wondered who the man in the photo was and if I'd ever meet him. If I ever did, I was gonna ask what they were laughing about.

A loud, tinkling laugh filled my room as I touched the photo. It was the sound of my mum laughing, like coins dancing in the fountain in Trafalgar Square. I sank on my bed and held the photo close to my chest. *I'm actually hearing my mum's voice*, I thought, as her laugh rumbled against my body. It sent a warm buzz into my heart like I'd just drunk loads of Milo hot chocolate. My eyes got heavy as her laugh lulled me to sleep like a lullaby.

CHAPTER FOUR

Plane Ride of Hell

If Uncle Tunji thought it was weird that I was cuddling a photo when he woke me up, he didn't say nothing.

'Today you are going to Olori! You will spend the summer holidays there. Hurry up and pack your bags!' he ordered.

I couldn't believe he was actually going through with his threat. Just cause I broke a priceless sculpture that was stolen from my place of birth! It was so rude.

'Nah, there ain't no way I'm going there,' I huffed.

Even though I knew *nothing* can stop my uncle once he has made his mind up.

I got dressed, put on my Nikes and zipped up my Champion hoodie as slowly as possible. It's my favourite cause it's baggy around the wrists so it doesn't restrict my blood flow or nothing.

Once I was done, my uncle looped a lanyard around my neck. I have to wear it when I travel cause it baits me out as someone with an illness. So now anyone who saw me would know there was something wrong with me. Great.

'You will learn how to behave like a useful somebody in Olori. You hear?' Uncle Tunji declared, once we arrived at the airport. His voice bounced off the shiny silver walls.

'You're *seriously* sending me to Olori? That's out of order, man,' I complained, as we walked to Security.

My cheeks burned as I walked past Influencers with designer suitcases taking selfies, backpackers with drawling Australian accents and bankers in crisp suits.

They're probably wondering what's wrong with me. I tried to hide my tag so many times but my uncle was always on my case. Unless you had X-ray vision there was no way you would know about my shambolic sickle-shaped blood cells.

Once we got to the queue, Uncle Tunji tilted his egg-shaped head at me. 'Koku, you do not know where you are from. If you do not know where you are from, you do not know where you are going. If you don't know where you are going, you don't know who you will become. And if you don't know who you will become, how will you know who you really are. Eh?'

'Heh?' I blurted out, only half listening.

'That is why you are going to Olori. Please do not embarrass me, oh! You will be staying with Mama Oti and her granddaughter in the capital city. It is called Ile-Kiisan because it is the city that never sleeps. They will greet you outside the airport, so don't hang around inside.' He looked at me. 'You don't need to worry yourself – Olori has the best doctors in the world and Mama Oti uses her own herbal remedies with her patients. She used to look after you when you were living there. *Sha*, it was a long time ago now, eh? Don't you remember?'

'I don't remember nothing,' I said.

I only knew about Mama Oti from rumours. She was Uncle Tunji's ex-wife and a certified witch. When my uncle calls someone a witch, what he means is they violated somehow: Aunty Lola was the type of witch who didn't make Uncle Tunji's pounded yam soft enough; Aunty Bisi was the type of witch who left him for a guy with an American Green Card . . .

'Kokumo, are you hearing me?' Uncle Tunji yelled, making everyone in the queue's head swivel round, their eyes crawling all over the blue tag around my neck.

'Say no more, man.' I meant that, literally.

My uncle stayed with me while my bags got checked to explain about my condition and stuff. I hated holding up the queue. I wished I could just go through normally like everyone else.

My heart was beatboxing all over the place once we'd passed through Security. My Uncle Tunji is annoying, but he knew exactly what to do when I needed help. *What was going to happen to me in Olori?* I wouldn't have none of the doctors and nurses that knew me since I was a kid. There was no way Mama Oti would be able to care for me properly.

'Now, Koku, I have made sure you are having everything you are needing for your trip to Olori. You will arrive late at night, but the skies are always bright in Olori so you will easily find Mama Oti there waiting for you,' my uncle said, shoving some emergency meds in my pockets. The Olori government do not allow phones that are not made in the land. So I have taken away this useless iPhone of yours and replaced it with my very reliable Nokia. I don't want you to be distracted.'

'Rah, that's actually peak, you know!' I complained, searching my pockets for a smooth glass touchscreen and feeling knobbly buttons instead.

'I have borrowed you my Gucci sunglasses that Aunty Kemi gave me.' Uncle Tunji handed me a pair of crooked sunglasses that had *Fucci* on the sides in gold lettering. I pinched the frames and groaned internally. 'The sun in Olori is no joke oh!' my uncle continued blissfully. 'The light can cook your eyeballs so you better prepare yourself! And if you are feeling unwell on the plane make sure you raise the alarm.'

'Yeah, whatever,' I muttered, unzipping my bag and stuffing the sunglasses at the very bottom. Then my uncle pulled me into a tight embrace. The stench of crayfish and Supermalt hit the back of my eye sockets, momentarily blinding me. Once he was done, he had the audacity to wave me off like I was going on holiday or something.

I couldn't bring myself to turn back. My stomach was doing giant backflips.

I wouldn't miss my guy much cause he was a wasteman. But I already missed Jollof. And my iPhone.

When I finally boarded the plane it smelled like cheese and onion crisps. I should've known my uncle would've gotten me the cheapest seat.

Cold air whispered across my neck. It smelled musty and old. I almost jolted out my seat. I checked the buttons above me to stop the cold breeze, but the air con above my seat had already been switched off so it wouldn't trigger my condition. I buckled myself in to await take-off.

'KOKUMO, *E GBA MI O,*' someone mumbled in Yoruba. I looked around but didn't see no one there.

There was no time to question what was happening. Suddenly the plane churned into flight. My stomach lurched. This was it. If I made it, I was gonna end up on the other side of the world. I clung on to my armrest for dear life.

When I landed, the back of my throat felt like sandpaper. My eyes burned like mad as I walked through the airport. Sunbeams rained into my vision. I squinted and looked upwards – according to the giant clock on the wall, it was supposed to be 9 o'clock at night. The sun blazed outside, bathing everyone in warm orange light and the airport was surrounded by glass so it felt like you were getting slowly roasted alive. But there was no way it was 10 p.m. here. It was way too bright. I was actually done with the constant sunlight, it was giving me a mad headache. It was getting so bad, my uncle's *Fucci* sunglasses didn't seem so bad no more.

I decided against wearing them in the end. I had already gone through hell and back. Actually, hell would have been better than a six-hour flight with two Bollywood movies in Hindi, and plane food that looked like a pile of regurgitated worms.

'*E kaab o*. Welcome to Olori. You have arrived in Ile-Kiisan, the land where the sun never sets,' a robotic female voice echoed across the sleek, silver walls of the airport. 'Today we celebrate the god of Iron, Ògún.'

'Huh? What do you mean the sun *never* sets?' I thought out loud to myself. I got a couple raised eyebrows from women with colourful giant cotton headwraps styled over their eyes like flower petals, dragging kids with ankara-print baseball caps and sleek shades who looked just as miserable as I did. It was weird to see so many people who looked like me in one place. And pretty much everyone was wearing sunglasses. I could see men wearing knee-length *agbada* gowns and large square sunglasses shouting complicated instructions at their taxi drivers and old ladies in wrapper skirts and flowery sunglasses with wriggling toddlers strapped on their backs.

I had to admit, I had thought the plane was going to land next to a hut on sticks, but the airport was twice as big as Heathrow and it had everything: super-fast wifi, a McDonald's and a giant Apple store.

When I stepped outside, the heat hit me like a wave. It was ten times brighter outside. The sun was a streak of fire in the sky. I had to cover my eyes with my hand for a bit of shade just to see properly. It was so peak I had no choice but to pull out my cheapskate uncle's moist sunglasses. My cheeks burned with embarrassment as soon as I pulled them on, but my headache finally died down. *Was that airport announcement right about the sun never setting here?* My skin was melting, and suddenly my black and red Champion hoodie was a very, very bad idea. I was too hot for the first time ever. Man is usually *never* hot.

It was so weird to feel my baggy hoodie clinging to my skin, all warm and damp. The air forcing its way down my throat tasted like gasoline. It was still super bright even with my shades on, like the sky was broken here or something. The red earth that spread under my feet was dry and cracked and everywhere I turned there were palm tree skeletons with spindly bony branches and thin browning leaves. I saw the same lilac sky and burning sun from my photo, which was weird, considering it was already night-time. And it was then that it hit me: I was in a different country. A different continent. *This is Olori, where the sun apparently never sets*. A strange new world.

I pulled out the brick Nokia. It was tough trying to figure out how to work the giant rubbery buttons, but once I did I sent Mama Oti a message, and sent my uncle a quick text to let him know I was alive.

A couple centuries later, Mama Oti arrived. I checked the airport clock. It was 11.00 p.m. and the sky hadn't dimmed one bit. She was officially two hours late.

I heard her before I saw her.

'*Na wahala*-oh! Trouble has arrived!' She was dressed in green with a wrapper skirt and matching *buba* top, paired with a sash around her shoulders and sunglasses with giant frames that covered most of her face. Her name, Otipoju, means 'too much' in Yoruba. Anyone who had met her for at least five seconds could easily figure out why.

'Ah? *Se o le so* Yoruba? Do you speak Yoruba?' she demanded, pulling her sunglasses down to her nose.

I can't explain what it feels like to understand language, but not speak it at the same time. Uncle Tunji spoke a bit of Yoruba at home so I had been able to pick up on some words, but I always replied in English. So, I sort of get most things, but my tongue feels fat and heavy in my mouth whenever I'm supposed to reproduce sounds that vibrate so naturally in my head.

'Nah,' I replied.

'*Eh-ya!* You go learn sharp-sharp, eh? We have been waiting for you for a very long time now. You will not be leaving this place without knowing Yoruba. In fact, you go hear Yoruba small-small today when we carry you to the festival.'

I let out a fat yawn. I didn't want to go to no festival. I just wanted to get to Mama Oti's yard and chill with the curtains drawn so I could finally catch a break from the harsh sunlight.

Behind Mama Oti was a tall teenaged girl wearing baggy purple ankara-print trousers. She was watching me with her hand over her eyes to block out the sun, her full lips set in a straight, stubborn line. She had three white dots in the centre of her forehead, the rest of her skin spread out like the evening below. Her shoulder-length braids looked like furry tarantula legs, and not like the girls at school who wore theirs in high ponytails with slicked edges.

'Koku, this is Moremi, my sweet granddaughter and your age mate. You used to play together in my compound when you were a small boy,' Mama Oti said.

'I am two years older than he is! We are NOT age mates – please don't insult me, *abeg*,' the girl huffed, tugging at the strip of purple material she had tied around her arm.

I caught her eye cause she wasn't wearing no shades or nothing.

'Koku.' She said my name simply with a look in her brown eyes that I couldn't read. I tensed up expecting her to react badly to it, like Olori people always did when they knew the meaning, but then her eyes flickered to my shades and her lips tilted into a sideways smirk. Then the weirdest thing happened: one of her braids stretched out in front of her and made a fist – and it slowly lifted a hairy middle finger at me. Then, in the blink of an eye, it transformed back into a regular braid.

It must've been a trick of the light or something. Or

my jet lag was way worse than I thought.

'So, this is the one we are waiting for, eh? He is just an *oyinbo* baby.' Moremi was one of those people that spoke out of her nose. I could already tell we weren't going to get along.

'What does "*oyinbo*" even mean?' I asked. I always knew an insult when I heard one but I ain't never been called that before.

Moremi kissed her teeth for an impressively long time. 'It means you are a nobody from the land of outsiders.'

I hit the rude girl with my signature diss. 'Am I a chicken leg? Why are you roasting—'

'*Eh-ya*, don't kill me-oh! Today is a day of celebration,' Mama Oti warned, as she turned to lead us out of the airport.

As we walked into town it got a tiny bit cooler and easier to look around as we moved onwards. The streets of Ile-Kiisan opened up like a maze, as immensely high sun-baked red walls loomed over us, partially blocking the sunlight. Drums played steadily along with high-pitched flute sounds, and glossy-skinned people in colourful clothes and matching sunglasses kept singing and clapping as they walked by. 'Day of celebration?' I asked, staring at the silver sword-shaped lanterns dangling from drooping palm trees all around us. 'It's almost midnight, it's way too late to celebrate anything. Plus Uncle Tunji didn't mention nothing about that.'

'Well, of course.' Mama Oti's full cheeks creased into a generous grin. 'Your uncle was only permitted to tell you the basics of our way of life.'

That didn't make no sense: my uncle wasn't some guy you could *permit* to keep stuff to himself. He had a big mouth and no filter.

'Today is the most important day of the year in Olori,' Moremi supplied, with the eyeroll of the century. 'We give honour and praise to Ògún, the god of iron and war.'

'*Ehen!* This masquerade festival go teach you our culture so you will be knowing something about where you are coming from,' Mama Oti added, as we set off down the road. I never paid attention when Uncle Tunji was going on about Olori gods, so I had no clue about this Ògún guy or how important he was supposed to be, but celebrating the iron and war god didn't sound nice. I let out a long sigh. Not only was I being sent off to spend my summer in the middle of nowhere, while Atticus Sharp was going to *New York*, I was gonna die of boredom too.

'We must carry body before night comes.' Mama Oti stopped right in the middle of the road, rummaging in her large ankara-print tote bag. A man who looked like the wiry insides of an umbrella almost rammed his rusty cart into her side. 'Your grandmother is a goat!' he yelled, swerving from her and parking the cart right in the middle of where we were standing, 'So you go buy one yam, or three *sef*?' He pulled out one of his oblong yams with a toothy smile.

'Leave me alone, Mister man!' Mama Oti swatted him away with her handbag and then reached inside it once he hobbled away. She pulled out traditional clothes for me: a *buba* and *sokoto*, a long woven gown and matching loose trousers. They were of varying shades of bright green, the colour of cafeteria food you could expect at a nuclear power plant. 'This go do you well-well, oh,' she said, approvingly.

My uncle had tried to force traditional Olori clothes on me before, but I had always managed to find a way out of it.

'Why don't you lot go without me? I need to rest after that flight and stay indoors in the dark for a bit so I can get some shut-eye. I don't mind, all I need is your wifi password,' I offered.

'You cannot miss it, oh! Not when there is only one

hour of night remaining in Olori,' Mama Oti said.

'Huh, what does that mean?' I blurted out, totally confused. 'It's not even midnight yet – we got loads more night-time left.'

'Olori is not like the place you are coming from. We only have one hour without sun and that is all. You will soon see for yourself.' Mama Oti let out a long sigh when she said that.

Next thing I knew, I was blinded by a flash of green as she strangled the scratchy outfit over me.

It came all the way down to my knees.

Moremi chuckled under her breath, a light airy sound that didn't suit her savage personality. I couldn't wait to tell Child Services about this when I got back to the UK. I was being next-level violated out here.

CHAPTER FIVE

The Masquerade Festival

We joined a crowd of colourful people walking to the festival. By now I had my own views to fill in the blanks: a sea of burnt trees and some scraggly brown bushes with dark folded leaves decorated with mini silver swords surrounded me; tall buildings made of sun-baked clay polished so hard they shone like mirrors. The buildings close by were engraved with detailed bronze drawings of hench-looking warriors with thick lips and bulging eyes, holding spears. Each one seemed to tell a different story.

Drums sounded in the distance. Olori wasn't like how I imagined it, or like how it looked on TV. It was just more . . . well . . . *more*.

By the time we got there it was 1 a.m. The sky finally darkened and slowly transitioned from the bright lilac colour to a darker purple. But it was still pretty light outside for a night sky; it wasn't pitch-black like it should've been. But there was still a full moon high up in the sky, just like back home.

Even though the sky was broken, I was pretty happy about it getting darker: the constant sunlight from before had been turning my eyeballs to mush.

'How come it took so long for the sky to get dark?' I asked Moremi, while Mama Oti walked ahead of us.

She answered me with her usual heavy eyeroll.

Eyes bugged out when I passed by. The traditional clothes Mama Oti had forced on me didn't exactly blend with my Nikes.

I briefly lost Mama Oti as we moved through a maze of red clay walls. The air was filled with delicious smells from food carts. The air was smoky and way too warm; every time I opened my mouth I felt it clogging my throat. My stomach growled when I smelled dishes I remembered Aunty Bola making: spicy, skewered *suya* meats, fried fish, sizzling *akara* bean cakes, jollof rice and puff-puff balls rolled in cinnamon and coconut.

We caught up with Mama Oti at the end of the

path. She handed me herbal remedies to keep my energy up. They looked and tasted like dirt, but they worked great.

The red walls disappeared and revealed a towering, basket-shaped building made of rows of brass plates. There was a huge courtyard out front with a raised stage lined with satin silk, and two thrones and eight seats placed on top of it.

'Koku, you see this big-big building here? This is the Oduduwa palace,' Mama Oti explained, fanning her face while we walked towards it. 'It belongs to the descendants of the god of iron and war. They are the ones with the most power in this land.'

Suddenly, the crowd went quiet. Dust curled in the trembling heat as armoured goons marched in. The men and women's heads were bald and tattooed. They were all heavily pierced, and wore silver rings all the way up their necks. Their stiff iron armour was in the shape of menacing animals, instead of the woven ankara cloth everyone else wore.

A trumpet blew before the festival began.

'Who are those lot supposed to be?' I whispered to Moremi.

'The tribe we go celebrate today, yam head. Descendants of Ògún, the god of iron and war.'

That explained why
they were wearing metal and
stomping all over the place, but Moremi
didn't have to be so rude about it.

'You got an attitude problem or something?' I
asked.

'Don't test my mouth, *mumu*!' she snapped.

I wasn't fluent in Yoruba or nothing, but I knew
most of the curse-words. 'Oi! I ain't no idiot, idiot!'
I snapped back.

Moremi's lip curved, like she was impressed I knew
that much. Mama Oti's head swiped round. 'Ah-ah!
Today is not a day of argument! Now we must make
our way to the Ògún shrine and prove our honour.'
Her eyes sparkled as a musician wearing red ankara
print played a rhythmic drum beat.

One by one, we had to follow the silk cloth to a large shrine. It was covered by strips of silver cloth so you couldn't see nothing except for a large machete sword poking out. People bowed before it and kissed the flat side of its iron blade.

I guessed that was how you proved your honour to the iron god.

That sort of thing would never happen back home. I was finding it hard to believe I was really from here. These Olori rituals were so *extra*.

I faked it cause I didn't want to accidentally lipse someone. I noticed that when Moremi bowed she took in a shaky gulp of air. She hovered over the blade, like it was gonna come to life and attack her or something.

When we were done at the shrine, we returned to the crowd. Everyone had taken their shades off to show respect and was waiting in silence. A bunch of serious-looking men, each wearing a brass leopard amulet with gold eyes pinned to the centre of their robes, walked up to the fancy seats in the centre of the courtyard.

'Who are those guys?' I tugged on Mama Oti's *buba* top.

'They are the *Oyomesi* chiefs,' Mama Oti whispered. 'They are the only ones who can advise the king, as they get divine knowledge from Rùnmí, the god of wisdom.'

The chiefs walked slowly so you could appreciate every inch of their white lace *agbada* gowns, which were weighed down by rows of beads.

They sat in the seats on the stage. '*A dupe lowo Ògún! We give thanks to the wisdom of ancestors!*' one of the seated chiefs announced, while thumbing a white beaded necklace decorated with curved symbols. His voice was loud and clear, but his lips didn't move. '*Today we celebrate the descendants of giants. To sweeten the road of our mighty king, we feast our eyes upon tales of old!*'

A white ring flashed around his eyes before fading to black. Glowing white symbols crawled out from under his *agbada* gown and covered his hands and neck, before sinking into his skin. They matched the symbols on his necklace.

The heat was clearly getting to me more than I'd realised. I was sweating loads – but at least there would be less chance of a crisis.

'*In the time before time, there was nothing but darkness and raw energy. This energy developed into eight life forms, powerful beings known as the Òrìṣà gods. Each god controlled an element of existence.*'

The declaration roared inside my skull, making my teeth dance.

'Every tribe is made up of the descendants of a god. But a few are Omo Òrìṣà, the chosen children of the gods.'

The drum beat quickened, and the crowd cheered as groups of people wearing matching ankara prints stepped forward and moved to the middle of the courtyard.

'The Chosen Ones are the pride of our nation. They have the strongest ancestral link to the gods. While connected to our soil they can perform powerful feats that Westerners call magic, but we know as a way of life.'

Everyone nodded like they were all deeping it. I thought Uncle Tunji was insanely superstitious, but it seemed like everyone here felt the same way about magic.

'Ògún, the god of iron and war, was the first god to conquer the darkness. He cleared the way with his divine sword. This is why today we honour his descendants!'

The group of bald-headed tattooed peeps we saw earlier stepped forward. They held up curved blades covered with swirling designs. Moremi drew a sharp breath as glowing silver patterns appeared on their arms. Then they threw their blades to the sky. Silver rings flashed in their eyes as their knives spun in the air. After chucking them around a few times they opened their mouths, reeled their heads back and swallowed the knives whole.

I'd always wondered how the performers in Oxford Street did that stuff. You gotta train for years to swallow swords without cutting up your insides. I watched a Netflix documentary on it once.

Once they'd finished snacking, their skin merged with their metal armour. Clinking metal noise pierced our eardrums as an iron leopard mask with a snarling mouth rose over each face.

'*Rùnmí, the god of wisdom and divination, revealed the secrets of time and the mind through the Oracle.*' The chief's eyes were glowing again as his voice resounded in my ears.

I *had* to know how the chief was doing that eye-glowing and mouth-moving thing. I poked Moremi in the shoulder and ignored her murderous look. 'Is it just me or can you hear his voice in your head and his lips ain't even moving? And how come his eyes keep flashing?'

Moremi let out a long sigh. '*Shebi*, you really don't know anything at all, eh. That is because he is one of the chosen children of Rùnmí, the god of wisdom and divination. So, he has the power to speak to our minds directly and know our thoughts.'

'Yeah, right,' I said. Now it was my turn to roll my eyes. That level of sarcasm was just unprovoked.

'*Ṣàngó, the god of fire and lightning, brought light to our dark world using his double-headed axe.*' The chief continued his announcements as a procession of bare-chested and muscular guys wearing red print moved into the centre of the space. They had locs, dip-dyed red at the ends, trailing down to their ankles.

The crowd waved palm leaves energetically in the air like hyped-up K-pop fans. They stomped their feet and swiped at the air in fierce strokes.

That's when I started bugging. The air started glowing bright red around them and transformed into a giant looping pattern. I gasped as their bodies started glowing too, as red rings appeared in their eyes and intricate designs spread over their torsos and arms.

'But . . . how is that happening?' I choked out. 'Magic ain't *real*!' I said out loud, without meaning to.

'You go see today,' Moremi snapped. 'This is not like England, this is the land of the origins, where the gods have blessed our people with power that outsiders cannot even imagine.' She smirked.

A whoosh of hot air grazed my forehead. I looked up and there was a raging fiery cloud above me. It was so close I could see the colours in it twisting furiously: bright oranges mixed with gold and deep indigo. The guys in red were beating their chests and breathing fire, surrounding us in a flaming circle. The air smelled like burnt sand. One of the guys was actually on fire and walked around in front of us like it was happy days.

And still no one was questioning the glowing air signs or tattoos. Maybe the magic stuff *was* real.

They retreated, and a group dressed in orange print decorated with dried leaves, wild flowers and feathers emerged.

'*Aganjù, the god of the wilderness, used his talisman to sculpt animals and make them obey his command.*' The chief's voice vibrated in my mind.

They bent down and drew a large arrow-shaped pattern in the sand. The pattern spread across the courtyard, bathing our feet in a warm orange glow.

'How come they are drawing the signs in the dirt instead of doing the air stuff the red tribe did? That was way cooler,' I whispered to Moremi.

'So you are not knowing *any*thing about our magic, *abi*?'

'Well, it's not like this was on YouTube or anything,' I retorted, thinking maybe I should have listened to Uncle Tunji once in a while.

Moremi side-eyed me and took a long breath before answering, like it was physically hurting her to explain stuff to me. 'Listen and listen *well*, yam head. There are three different classes of our magic. The basic level allows the Chosen Ones to draw magic by connecting to the earth, where the gods were buried. The advanced level allows them to use magic from the atmosphere, and the highest warrior level allows them to use magic from symbols written on certain objects.'

That explained the glowing symbols on the knives from the iron guys, I guess, but I still had more questions. It made me wanna know what god *I* had links with. What if there was a special power lurking inside me, a tiny speck of the gods?

What if there was a power that could cure my sickle cell?

Moremi stared at me like she knew what I was thinking. 'You don't need to worry yourself. Only the ones *chosen* by the gods need to concern themselves with magic.'

Just then a group of the most peng girls, wearing yellow with dazzling afros and skin so shiny you could smell the cocoa butter radiating off them, started dancing. The chief introduced them to the crowd: 'Òṣun, *the goddess of love, used her mirror's reflection to bring love and sweet waters to the world, allowing plants to grow.'*

Goddess of love – that sounded about right. People were reaching towards them, declaring their love. My future wifey with a heart-shaped afro bent to draw a swirling heart symbol in the earth. Her eyes flashed gold as yellow, flowery patterns spread across her radiant skin like vines. She opened her palms to the sky and a light shower of rain came down while the other girls danced around her.

'Oya, goddess of tornadoes and hurricanes, used her whip to bring the winds of change,' the chief announced as a group of lanky, cornrowed girls wearing purple ankara came forward.

I liked watching the graceful way they bent to the earth and the way they drew long, swiping patterns in the ground, making it glow purple.

Once the drawings were finished, the group of girls stood upright. Then they bent their knees into a pose where their legs were outstretched and their toes pointed delicately. They bounced on their tiptoes for a bit and then leaped into the air. Their bodies glided like paper planes.

As billowy, purple material swooshed over my head as they flipped in the air, I realised something: it was the same print Moremi was wearing.

I hoped Moremi wasn't chosen by the gods, cause making rude signs at me with her braids was one thing; flying while doing it would be diabolical. And now that I thought of it, I was wondering what was going on with her, cause I ain't never heard of no god of hair or nothing.

I turned to her to ask but she held a braided fist to my jawline, so I was good for the moment.

Once their performance was over, a group wearing green ankara stepped forward.

I stared down at my green *buba* and *sokoto*. I hadn't seen anyone perform in this colour yet. I wondered if I was connected to this god in some way.

'Eh, Koku, you see this?' Mama Oti yelled, her *gele* headwrap sagging with the sudden movement. 'My people are looking fine-oh, like sweet potato!'

'*Babalú, the god of disease, was hated by the other gods for bringing illness, but he also used his sacred pot to bring healing,*' the chief announced in my mind.

As soon as the Babalú tribe walked in front of the crowd, everyone started shifting about. The guys in green drew their pattern in the earth. Fluorescent patterns crawled over their bodies till they looked like someone had thrown a vat of radioactive liquid on them.

A jolt of pain made me glance at my hands – they were covered in swollen, itchy lumps. '*Babalú, lend us your power!*' the people in front of me yelled together.

As soon as the chant was uttered, the lumps were gone.

'Rah, that's actually out of order, man,' I complained.

It was so typical that I would be connected to a god of disease.

'From disease we also find healing, or they don't teach you that in your *oyinbo* land?' Moremi snapped. 'Mama Oti got be the best healer in this land! Don't disrespect Mama!'

'Calm down, man!' I said. 'I was just saying I don't want no more diseases, innit.'

'This is our Olori culture: we don't expect an *oyinbo* baby like you to understand,' Moremi retorted.

'This is Koku's culture too.' Mama Oti turned and looked at Moremi with fiery eyes. 'We are all Olori here.'

I grinned smugly at Moremi and turned back to the performances.

'*And, of course, Olókun, the goddess of darkness,*

used her own heart, the legendary Night Stone, to split the sky from the dark, creating the ocean,' the chief continued.

For some reason, as soon as that name was mentioned, a hush fell over the crowd.

'Her children could command the shadows, making the earth rise beneath your feet, or an ocean swallow you whole.'

Those powers sounded sick. I craned my neck to see but no one came forward. *'But the descendants of the goddess disgraced her name by trying to plunge our land into eternal night . . . and now they are no more.'* The chief looked around, fiercely. *'The chosen children of Olókun earned their deadly fate by playing friend-friend to hellish foes: evil Night Creatures who roamed in the darkness.'*

Suddenly everything went black.

'Ten years ago, the strong iron fist of the Ògún tribe united our country to scatter our enemies.' As soon as the chief made this announcement in our minds, the light returned and a silver mask materialised. It held a large, curved sword with a leopard etched into the handle. *'Among these demonic creatures are the Mami Wata, who appear as snakes and drown men for their own enjoyment,'* the chief said. At this, a

mask in the shape of a woman covered in snakes came into view. '*The despised one who delights in the flesh of human beings, known as Àgbákò.*' The chief introduced a twelve-foot-tall mask that looked like a scorpion, elephant and anaconda mashed together. A chill ran through me as it glided past with a mouth the size of a double-decker bus. '*And we must not forget the dark death shadows known as Àbíkú that walk among us. They feed on the souls of children and steal their place,*' the chief added.

Finally, something I *did* know about! I thought.

The chief's voice got louder as he said: '*The leader of these creatures was the guardian spirit of the dead.*' The chief's voice trembled for the first time. '*A name that must never be spoken. The demon who did not let the dead sleep.*'

An enormous mask appeared with a puff of smoke.

It was half black and half red, with two curved horns.

The mask tilted its head and its two pupilless yellow eyes looked right at me.

My stomach squeezed so hard the plane food released an unofficial remix with my intestines. It was the creature that had come out of the sculpture I broke in the museum.

'Man's jet lagged, and you got demons of the dead and that staring right at me,' I squeaked out, breathlessly.

Moremi laid a braid on my shoulder and gripped it tight. 'Eh?' She wrinkled her nose in my direction. 'That one na craze talk. They will never show that demon's face in this land. It is forbidden to even say its name.'

'Are you alright?' I looked at her. 'Cause it's *literally . . .*' I let the rest of my words die at the back of my throat and gawped at the row of masks.

Not a single one had yellow eyes or horns.

It was like it had never been there.

Was that another hallucination, or am I just going crazy? I didn't feel a crisis coming on, so the random hallucination didn't make no sense. My breaths came so fast it felt like my ribs were going to break out of my chest.

'*The god of iron and war led us to victory.*' The chief's voice was sure and steady again, and snapped me back into reality. '*We claimed back our land of light, defeating these demons and the children of the goddess, Olókun.*' He raised his arms into the air. '*But as our great Ògún king will remind us, as long as night exists, our fight against these spirits will never end. We must end night for ever! As long as there is darkness there will always be a way for these abominations to torment us – the Mami Wata, the Àbíkú, Àgbákò and the demon whose name must not enter our mouths – passing into our country from the most treacherous place in the world, a terrible jungle, a land of eternal night, a forest of a thousand demons, a bush of ghosts that the outsiders named'* – the chief's eyes flashed white as the last word slithered into our heads like a juicy maggot – *'Jujuland.'*

CHAPTER SIX

The Àbíkú

Mama Oti was talking facts when she told me there was only one hour of night in Olori. Blotches of white punctured the indigo sky. The sky was already turning pink at the edges, signalling a new dawn.

As the sun rose, a bell rang out. 'That's how we announce the arrival of the king,' Mama Oti whispered to me. 'Then we bend low.'

I nodded, but I was still thinking about the forbidden jungle the chief mentioned. A forest with a thousand demons sounded mad still. An electric chill ran through my bones when I rolled the word under my tongue. It didn't sound like any Yoruba word I'd ever heard before. *Jujuland*.

Everyone knelt down and bowed so their foreheads were in the dirt. I did the same but craned my neck so I could peep the king. He was wearing some intense headgear: it was cone-shaped and made of orange, yellow and blue beads, with elephant tusks. His face was covered by a veil of cowrie shells. I got an all-body shiver when I saw slimy eyes beneath it, like puddles of petrol.

He used an ostrich feather to pat the shoulders of each chief before making his way to a large silver throne with two giant swords etched with battle scenes forming the back of the seat.

An elegant woman dressed in yellow appeared beside him.

'That's the queen,' Moremi whispered. That made sense, cause she was looking all boujee – high cheekbones and a wide smooth forehead surrounded by a gold, perfectly round *gele* headwrap. She took her time to sashay towards the throne draped with dazzling yellow flowers beside the king, and then sat down.

The couple and their entourage were surrounded by iron warriors, but I spotted a teenager who didn't seem to fit the picture. I got a sense of déjà vu from looking at him. Unlike all the others, he wore strips of purple ankara cloth in between his armour, and a constipated expression on his face. He looked unimpressed by everything and anything – the sort of guy that girls love.

'Mo *dupe lowo* Ògún. We give thanks to the wisdom of ancestors,' the Ògún king began in a measured tone. The crowd rose from their knees when he spoke. His voice projected easily. His lips were moving normally, otherwise I would've thought he was using mind magic like the white-robed chief guy.

'Sebi *Oluwa lo se e o*, the gods shine their eyes on the nation of Olori. Since the Olókun tribe was defeated during the war, we have one hour of night remaining,' the king announced.

The constant sunlight thing was starting to make a bit more sense. I looked up at the sky; the moon was fading away and it was getting lighter with each passing moment. I didn't know how I'd survive without night-time; I've always been more at peace at night, even with Uncle Tunji's earth-shattering snores.

'But as long as Goddess Olókun's heart, the Night Stone, remains in Jujuland, there will always be one hour of night,' the Ògún king said. 'As we know, this hour is when the Night Creatures can pass over from the Jujuland jungle. Over the ages, many innocent Olori souls have been claimed by these evil creatures in the hour of darkness. The only way we can be safe is if we completely eradicate night.'

The crowd got restless. It was peak cause the people closest to me started whisper-arguing. There was so much commotion I had to ground my feet to avoid getting trampled.

'But without night our land suffers,' a woman in a green wrapper dress called out. My eyes widened, properly taking in all the withering trees and decaying plants that lined the edges of the courtyard. I guessed she was also from the Babalú tribe, like Mama Oti. 'We no get rest from the sun. Our land has become barren. Even if we don't like it, it is a necessary evil we need to survive.'

Mama Oti nodded in agreement.

'O-ho, is that so?' The guy next to her, wearing purple print like Moremi, argued back: 'What kind of nonsense talk is that! Night is an evil thing – we must get rid of it. It has been twenty years since my niece was carried away by Àbíkú spirits at night, leaving an evil creature in her place. The legend says that if the Àbíkú don't kill the stolen child, they swap them back when the child reaches their tenth year. I waited and waited but she did not return. We reported this to the Ògún police and they took the spirit carrying my niece's face away from us. I have not known sleep since.'

'Mama Oti, I get the whole Àbíkú spirit swapping with a kid thing cause my uncle used to tell me those stories, but why would the Ògún guys take the Àbíkú kid away? That don't make no sense to me,' I said.

Moremi's sharp shoulder blades suddenly jerked upwards, stabbing my side.

'Oi, do you mind?' I said, rubbing the sore spot.

'Quiet, Koku!' Mama Oti whispered fiercely.

'But—' I protested.

'The Ògún are the ones who control our land, it is dangerous to question them in public. *They* believe the Àbíkú are a threat to Olori. That is why it is forbidden to hide an Àbíkú in your family.' Mama Oti explained quickly, turning from side to side to check if someone was listening to us.

Moremi was way jumpier than usual, her braids were vibrating like she'd been electrocuted.

'But what do *you* believe, Mama Oti?' I asked. I wasn't dumb, I knew something was up from the way she said it. Mama Oti pursed her lips tight and held a finger to her mouth. She didn't say another word on the Ògún no matter how many times I asked and Moremi wouldn't even look at me. So I paid attention to what the crowd was saying instead. I bet one of them would reveal what was *really* going on around here.

'You are talking plenty rubbish for mouth!' one of the performers wearing an orange ankara wrapper decorated with feathers was saying. 'I am *Aganjù!*' he declared, slapping his bare chest, 'We are the ones who protect the creatures of Olori. Do you not know that the great black leopard, the symbol of Olori, will die without night?'

The king raised his hand and waited for the crowd to settle down. 'Some of you may say that night is needed for our survival. After all, don't we need rest from the sunlight to grow plants and raise strong animals?' he said, and the crowd murmured noises of agreement.

'The Rùnmí chiefs here have used their power from the god of wisdom and divination to look into our future.' The chiefs beside him nodded in unison; their white beads made delicate clinking noises that sounded like champagne glasses touched in a toast. Mama Oti scoffed, shaking her head at the announcement. 'They say that if even one hour of night remains there will be no future in Olori. The god of wisdom has told them that the Night Creatures are planning a war against us.

On the day of the winter solstice, when they are strongest, the Àbíkú will take all our children from us, the Mami Wata will drown our men and women, and the beast Àgbákò will roam free and feast on our bones.'

'Gods forbid!' people yelled in reply.

'Our people fear too much,' Mama Oti said, under her breath. 'They believe anything the Ògún go tell them for mouth. They should know that the only one who can look into the future is the most powerful man in the Rùnmí tribe, the Araba priest, not these big-for-nothing chiefs.'

'Now, my people, the Western man does not come from a land touched by the gods, but what does he have that allows him to become so great?' the king asked the crowd once they had all calmed down.

When no answer came, he provided it: 'Greed.' The king now spoke in a booming voice. 'And a greedy man is a very resourceful one.'

He waved his long ostrich feather at the iron-clad warriors. At their cue, they brought him a large box covered by a metallic cloth and laid it at his feet.

'Many moons ago, a group of European explorers found a way to obtain energy from the Night Creatures and produce an energy greater than our own Chosen Ones.'

My ears pricked up.

'The outsiders were the first to discover that Night Creatures do not sleep. When they breathe, their lungs convert air to dark magic. This dark magic produces energy that helps them survive in Jujuland.'

The king was taking his time with the explanation, like when Mr Matthews draws formulas on the whiteboard in maths.

'An English explorer found that you can create superhuman warriors that do not require sleep if you can capture the dark magic the Night Creatures naturally produce and insert it into human beings. Once this is done, the warrior would be able to use the magic taken from the Night Creature.' The king looked around at the crowd, his voice rising as he came to his big reveal. One of his French comrades called this dark magic "*juju*" and they named the jungle where the magic could be found Jujuland. *Juju* is powerful enough to remove any need for sleep, so once we take the Night Creatures' magic we will no longer need the night!' The whispers started again: some excited voices mixed with some grumbling about still needing the dark. The king ignored it all and continued: 'The Night Creatures will be at their weakest in two weeks' time, on the day of the summer solstice: the longest day and shortest night of the year. On that day we can destroy the Night Stone, remove the threat of darkness and no evil spirits will enter our land again.'

I didn't know what side I was on. I couldn't imagine a land without night. But if all that horrible stuff the night peeps were doing was true, then maybe Olori did need to get rid of night once and for all. Either way, I made a mental note to log into my uncle's British Airways account and change my flight to an earlier date. I already knew his password. It was Mama Oti's middle name, cause my uncle was totally not over their relationship.

'We give the glory to our god, Ògún, the master of invention! Feast your eyes on the power of *juju*!' With a grand flourish, the king removed the cloth draped over the box, revealing what looked like an empty glass coffin with some chunky metal bangles in it. The reveal was pretty dead, to be honest.

Then he rapped his jewelled knuckles against the glass.

A small dark purple kid appeared, like they had been shocked into existence. The kid looked kinda weird, cause they had a perfectly oval head, slits for ears, and holes where the eyes should be. They were covered from head to toe in painted white lines in the shape of a skeleton, naked apart from a skirt made out of burnt leaves.

'Behold the Àbíkú,' the king said, proudly. 'Our battle-brave warriors have taken our soul-stealing enemy by force. I remind you that those of you hiding Àbíkús in your families, hoping your children will return, are going against Olori law! Once they have become a Night Creature, they are a threat to our nation.'

No way. That kid was an Àbíkú? You had got to be kidding me.

I wasn't the only shook one. Children screamed, pointing at the Àbíkú in the glass box.

'Soul stealer! Thief!' a guy dressed in purple yelled with shining eyes, while the rest of the crowd scurried to the outer edges of the courtyard. It was the guy who was arguing earlier. Most of the people dressed in green like me remained, so I stayed with Moremi and Mama Oti. Moremi's face looked like all the juice had drained out of it. She suddenly looked about a thousand years old.

The Àbíkú struggled against metal cuffs, making pain-filled clicking noises that echoed in the box. A thin, inky cloud of smoke curled around its wrists where the cuffs dug into its skin, like they were burning.

I knew it had probably stolen someone's soul, but I couldn't help feeling sorry for it. It just looked like a kid wearing white body paint.

'And now,' continued the king, 'Taiwo, son of Ọya, will show you how we have developed this *juju* for our warriors' safe use.'

Bare teenaged Olori girls started swooning when the sulky teenager I spotted earlier walked up to the king. Well, all of them except Moremi – *her* screwface was at maximum XP levels.

Taiwo was maybe only a year or two older than me. He had a low fade at the sides of his head, with cornrows on the top, a pierced eyebrow and smooth skin like a swimming cap. He walked slowly, dragging his feet. I guess I would move slowly too if I had a massive sword strapped to my back. The blade was made of a shimmering metal that seemed to make the air around it vibrate.

It sent a shiver down my spine – it looked like it could cut your head off in one clean swipe.

'*Kabiyesi!*' The cold-eyed kid warrior greeted the king with the Yoruba equivalent of 'Your Majesty'. He gave the trapped Àbíkú a dirty look before pressing his chest to the floor next to it. The Àbíkú squirmed in its glass cage as Taiwo performed the *dobale* pose to the king – the ultimate sign of respect. It's basically the way you've got to acknowledge important elders, by folding your left arm behind your back and touching the floor with your right hand. Uncle Tunji gets pressed when I refuse to do it for random uncles.

The king patted his shoulders with the ostrich feather, then he reached into his multicoloured robes and pressed a small metallic object into Taiwo's palm.

'*Kabiyesi!* I salute you, Owner of the Land,' Taiwo said, clenching his fist so we couldn't peep the new present he'd got from the king. Then he slowly rose to his feet.

It was weird, he didn't have no accent or nothing. He spoke in a flat, robotic voice – he didn't sound like no Olori person I'd ever heard before.

'Our scientists have created a device to extract the *juju* magic from the Night Creatures so we can use their power,' the king explained, as Taiwo clicked a button on the side of the glass cage with the Àbíkú in it.

A small flap slowly opened with a clunk. It opened in an ultra-smooth way, like Lamborghini doors.

The Àbíkú puffed its cheeks out like it was going to cry, or whatever evil, kid-spirit things do when they're having a bad day. It let out a whole bunch of clicking sounds, like it was desperately trying to say something.

I wasn't the only one who had no clue what was going on. The crowd's murmurs hissed like a pot of sizzling stew.

When Taiwo finally opened his palm, all we could see from where we were standing was a tiny blinking silver dot the size of a 5p coin.

EEEEEeeeeeEEEEEEEeeeeeeeEEEEEEEEEeeeeee EEEE! An ear-splitting noise erupted from the stage as soon as Taiwo opened his hand.

I knew it as soon as I heard it – the high-pitched shrill of a mosquito. Except the noise was sounding in a robotic way, like it had been autotuned or something.

People in clashing colours swiped at the air while the king continued. Man had to dodge some mad attacks to avoid getting slapped up.

Slowly, the crowd settled once they realised the noise was coming from the blinking dot on stage.

'The British explorer, Frobenius, was the first to

handle *juju* magic. He removed dark magic from an Àbíkú by capturing it using iron and keeping its life force inside a small wooden doll. But when he tried to release the dark magic it was too powerful for humans to use,' the king continued, calmly. 'We know that the best technology is inspired by nature. The mosquito is perfect for energy transferral as they extract the energy they need from human blood, removing any waste product.' Here, the king leaned forward in his throne, his eyes brightening. 'Now you may all watch this mosquito-bot take dark magic from the Night Creature and "donate" it to its human host.'

As the king spoke, Taiwo released the metallic bug into the Àbíkú's glass box and sealed the glass flap shut.

Before the Àbíkú's dark purple mouth could release another cry, the buzzing metal mosquito found its way to its neck. The buzzing stopped and the crowd fell silent as the Àbíkú fell like it had been shot. Bulging black veins spread across its neck. The Àbíkú shuddered like it was having a seizure.

Then the tiny silver dot buzzed over to Taiwo and latched on to his neck. He started to change too. The veins around his neck bulged and his eyes turned shiny black, as if a fat glossy black fly had burrowed into the whites of his eyes. He breathed heavily, and his eyes kept twitching.

The process looked worse than one of my sickle-cell crises: it made my stomach turn.

Why would Taiwo volunteer to do this?

'The scientists behind Ògún-tech have developed the mosquito-bot to work with our regulation armour. Now all Ògún armour has mosquito-bots installed inside it. The wearers cannot be too far away from the mosquito when it is released to find creatures with *juju* inside them,' the king said. 'Once we destroy night, we can use our technology to transfer the Night Creatures' *juju* magic to every person in Olori, so you will no longer need sleep. Even those who have not been chosen by the gods will be able to use this magic.' The king paused, then lifted his voice: 'We will be the most powerful nation on the planet, and never again shall spirits or outsiders steal from our land!'

As the king spoke, Taiwo started turning invisible in front of our eyes.

'As you can see, the Àbíkú's invisibility power is being transferred to Taiwo.' The king sounded like he was narrating a nature documentary.

'For a small amount of time, Taiwo can freely use the creature's magic,' he continued.

The Àbíkú looked done out there, and I was starting to feel extremely uncomfortable. I've always had a soft spot for strays. Abandoned things that don't belong nowhere. It reminded me of when I found Jollof.

Moremi had turned away like she couldn't bear to look. I could feel the Àbíkú's black eyes on me, like it was expecting me to do something.

Suddenly, cold, tingling voices rang in my ears like a death song. They got louder and louder until I felt like my head would burst. Then that static-y feeling I felt at the museum rushed over me in one surging wave, like I'd been electrocuted or something. I could barely breathe. But I knew it wasn't a sickle-cell crisis cause I didn't feel the usual ache in my bones.

Flickers sparked up my insides. I got the sudden urge to reach out towards the Àbíkú. I lifted my arm and the air rippled, forming a dark mist.

Then the mist transformed into a long, shadowy arm. It looked exactly like the hallucinations I'd been seeing back at home whenever my sickle cell flared, but this time I didn't feel sick or nothing.

I tried to ball my fist up but the shadow arm shot out of my palm before I closed my fingertips. It slithered on to the stage and swatted the metal mosquito away, knocking Taiwo aside in the process.

The mosquito-bot landed with a soft clunk on the stage.

'Rah!' I blurted, biting my bottom lip to stop myself from screaming out in shock. But Moremi was staring at me, scrunching her nose all funny.

I tried my best to not look guilty as Taiwo whooshed across the stage. He crashed into a line of armoured warriors as if a real, solid fist had pushed him into a bunch of metal bowling pins. Then the ghost arm used its scummy black fingernails to free the Àbíkú from its glass box and its shackles, with a loud click. The arm disintegrated into mist as soon as the Àbíkú was free, like it knew its work was done.

If the madness around me, or Taiwo's bitter screwface, was anything to go by, it wasn't a dream. *But there is absolutely no way I accidentally summoned a ghost arm to free one of the worst demons in Olori, is there?*

The Ògún army rushed forward and tried to get the cuffs back on it. The Àbíkú's mouth stretched into a wide, purple, gummy smile. Then it dissolved into thin air.

Taiwo got up and dusted himself off. His face wasn't as scary now that the bulging black veins were gone and the whites in his eyes had returned to normal. But he did unsheathe his giant sword, like he would quite like to shank someone with it.

And he was looking straight at me.

'My people, listen and listen well!' the king called. 'We have this under control. Our hunt for the evil spirits of Jujuland has only just begun.' He tried to keep the peace in the crowd, but everyone was too far gone.

If the crowd had been restless during the *juju*-mosquito demonstration, it was Armageddon now that they knew an Àbíkú was free, and that Taiwo had been merked by something they couldn't see. People ran this way and that, shoving anything and anyone out of the way. I was pulled further and further away from where I was standing, till a hand gripped my shoulder tight. It was Mama Oti pulling me into her side to stop me getting mashed up.

There was no way Taiwo could have singled me out so I was probably being paranoid, but I swear down Taiwo's eyes were on me again.

'*Eh-hen*, you see yourself, I told you that Koku is the boy we have been waiting for. The prophecy does not lie. He is our only chance for night-time to be restored in our land.'

Whispers pulled me away from Taiwo's awkward staring contest. It was Mama Oti and Moremi.

'You might be right about the boy, but this no be time for talk-talk! We must leave now.' Moremi gave me an odd look. 'Big, BIG trouble has arrived.'

CHAPTER
SEVEN

Lost in the Sauce

It had been a week since the masquerade festival. I was lying in bed at night, staring at all the dead plants Mama Oti had littering the place while white sunlight blazed through the blinds. Her home was a plant graveyard with empty terracotta pots filled with grey soil hanging from the ceiling and empty spider-like branches crawling over the walls. It still only got dark for a single hour in Olori, making a proper night's sleep impossible here. Even when it did get dark, aunties would bang tambourines, forcing everyone to keep watch for Night Creatures.

Every time someone mentioned the escaped Àbíkú I would get bare sweaty, even though I hadn't seen anything weird since.

Every time I tried to sleep, I was haunted by the shadowy arm slapping up Taiwo on stage. I had thought the ghost thing in the museum was a sickle-cell hallucination, but this time had been different: my illness hadn't flared up, and I was *still* seeing mad stuff.

Did I really unleash a ghost arm and free an Àbíkú spirit?

Clunky metallic-sounding steps suddenly echoed outside Mama Oti's house. The *clank, clank, clank*ing interrupted my thoughts, and suddenly Mama Oti was in my room, moving mad. She gave me a look that made me shook as she pulled me out of my bedroom and led me to the kitchen. Then she pointed to a gigantic pot, big enough to fit two of me, or a quarter of Uncle Tunji.

'Get in, carry yourself quick-quick, *e jo*!' Mama Oti said, lifting the heavy lid with her surprisingly hench arms.

The smell of *okro* soup wafted out, making my eyes burn.

'Are you . . . alright?' I asked, fighting back a yawn.

Mama Oti didn't answer my question. Next thing I know, I'm knee-deep in gooey *okro* soup.

I was lost in the sauce. Literally.

The footsteps got louder and entered the kitchen. I lifted the lid of the pot so I could peep what I was hiding from.

Lamplight fell against the stranger's face as he seated himself opposite Mama Oti. His eyes slid over the room like a dead fish. He had huge eyebags like he hadn't slept in a month.

It was the kid warrior, Taiwo, from the festival – the one I had maybe chucked across stage.

'Let us break the kola nut together, like the days of old, Taiwo,' Mama Oti said, moving a one-leaf jade plant aside and sliding a black nut towards him.

Mama Oti told me on my first day that in Olori culture, you offer visitors a kola nut when they visit your yard. The visitor accepts it and says a prayer to the god of the host tribe as a sign of respect.

The nut had been broken into four equal lobes. Mama Oti took half of them, and offered the rest to Taiwo. 'The Babalú *oriki* prayer is yours,' Mama Oti said, raising both parts to her lips.

'We give thanks to the one who clears the road,' Taiwo replied, sliding the kola nut across the table without eating it.

Mama Oti gasped. 'Taiwo, this is not how I raised

you! How dare you come into Babalú territory with praises for Ògún?'

'Our great king has waged war against night to protect our nation from the evil spirits of Jujuland. How dare you hide the last descendant of the Olókun tribe and protect the Àbíkú spirit?'

Taiwo spoke flatly, but when he mentioned the Àbíkú, his forehead veins popped out like he'd been screaming.

I had no idea what Taiwo meant by the 'last descendant', but I was stressing about the Àbíkú part.

'Which useless somebody told you? They must come from a family of goats. May thunder enter their nose and scatter their throat,' Mama Oti said, clapping her hands like he was telling a funny joke. 'I am telling you there is no "last descendant". That is just empty talk. Everyone from the Olókun tribe was put to sleep by Ògún swords years ago during the war. So, look for him well-well, *abeg*. Where would I be hiding him, eh? On my head? In my nose?'

Taiwo dusted down his shining armour and got up from the table. He still had the massive sword strapped to his back. The handle poked out from behind his shoulders – it had a roaring leopard design with ruby eyes.

'Taiwo, stop this nonsense and listen!' Mama Oti pulled the jade plant back to the centre of the table. 'What the Ògún are doing is not right. You know that night is needed for our crops' survival. Our plants are dying, and my people are suffering.'

'Once the Night Stone is destroyed, night will be gone, along with all its creatures,' Taiwo said, plainly. His eyes roamed over the wilting plant in front of them. 'If you obey the king, no harm will come to the Babalú tribe, or your crops,' he added, as he started to walk around the room, a bit like a panther stalking its prey.

Suddenly every breath I took seemed to echo loudly in my hiding place.

Taiwo turned on his heel and stopped in front of the pot I was crouching in. I bit the insides of my cheeks to stop myself from making another sound.

'You used to believe in night. Now your belly is full with the hate of another man's beliefs,' Mama Oti said, her shoulders drooping low.

'I am not full, I am empty. Now she's gone, there's nothing left of me. But you should know that.'

I wondered who he was talking about, that made him look human for once.

'*E pele o*, I am sorry, *biko*,' Mama Oti said, tears

gathering in her eyes. 'You must understand that—'

'Soon those cursed Night Creatures will *all* be sorry,' he snarled quickly. A smirk lifted his lips as he unsheathed his sword, fluorescent lines spreading across the curved metal like veins.

I didn't fancy being decapitated, so I desperately channelled the weird energy I felt at the masquerade festival. I flexed my palms, trying to feel that strange static sensation. But I didn't feel nothing.

I held my breath and shut my eyes tight, expecting to hear the hiss of metal slicing through the air.

'*O daaro*,' Taiwo said finally, walking stiffly towards the door. He closed it with a loud thud behind him.

Mama Oti sighed out. Relief flooded my bones, but only for a second. I had no clue why Taiwo said goodbye, cause I could tell he meant the opposite.

'What did that Taiwo guy want with me?' I demanded, after I'd washed and changed.

'*E pele o*. I am sorry, Koku. You should not have found out this way,' Mama Oti said.

I knew it had to be pretty deep cause Mama Oti's headwrap was all lopsided.

'When you were a small boy, you were hidden in London with your uncle, Tunji, until your return, because the Ògún wanted to get rid of you. If anyone found out who you really were, you would be in soup!'

'Well that didn't work out so well. I *was* in soup. Gallons of it.' I said, my throat squeezed as I puffed out a throaty fake laugh. 'But what do you mean who I *really* am?' My chest fluttered when I realised I was going to find out why my uncle had been secretive this whole time: I had low-key been curious about it for the longest time, the stories of my mum dying in the war and my dad being nowhere to be found had never been enough for me.

'Ever since the Olókun war, when the goddess of darkness was defeated, night started disappearing from the sky,' Mama Oti said.

Yeah, I get that bit, I thought. *These lot are obsessed with the night. But what does that have to do with me?*

'The Ògún king has made everyone fear night, even though he knows that our crops are not growing because the sun is too much.' Mama Oti waved at all the brown, disintegrating plants that cluttered her kitchen. 'And the poorer tribes, including the Babalú, rely on what we can grow for our chop.'

'What about the creatures attacking at night?' I asked.

'The spirits only attack when they are threatened

by human beings,' Mama Oti said, with a firm nod. 'The Ògún king was speaking nonsense – *juju* magic is too dangerous to replace night. But as long as the Ògún destroy night and increase their own power, they do not care if this land turns into bones and dust.'

'Huh?' I spluttered. I had so many questions. But I wanted to know about my parents most of all. 'But what about *who I really am*?'

'You think what happened in the museum go be accident, eh?' Mama Oti interrupted my racing thoughts.

'H-how did you—?' I stuttered.

'It was prophesied by the highest priest before he went into hiding in Jujuland! The one who goes by the title of Araba. When you broke the doll, you were bound to your destiny. We have all been waiting for you. The ones who still believe in the power of darkness were told that the last descendant would return to us to restore the night.'

'Nah, that can't be right.' I shook my head so hard my twists escaped out of their horns and flapped across my face.

'The Ògún king wants to destroy night for ever. The only way to do that is to destroy the Night Stone. He is terrified that the last descendant will find the stone first and unite with the Night Creatures of Jujuland to seek revenge.'

'Wait, why do you keep mentioning the "last descendant"?' I asked, my stomach churning nastily. 'What has that gotta do with me?' I asked.

'The king knows that a powerful Olókun woman had a secret child that survived the war. This child is the last descendant of Olókun. This child has more power than any person in Olori chosen by the gods.' Mama Oti's eyes darkened to coal. 'Koku, that woman was your mother, and the child is you, *omo iyanu*. You are our only hope of survival.'

All the new info whizzed around in my head. It was all totally insane. There was no way I had more power than the Chosen Ones. They could walk into flames, summon the rain to fall, or munch a bunch of knives and turn into Iron Man. I couldn't even join in on sports day at school.

'You no go believe me? You think I talk rubbish for mouth?' Mama Oti insisted, tightening her headwrap with trembling fingers. 'Then answer me one time – why did you free the Àbíkú, eh?'

'How do you know that was me?' I protested, repressing the memories of my tingling palms and the dark ghostly threads shooting out of them.

'The Araba taught me ways of telling . . . but there is no time to explain this thing now! Whether you like, or you no like, as a child of Olókun, the goddess of darkness, you have responsibility to all spirits of the night,' she said. 'Those spirits are needing your help, and so do we.'

She was right, something deep inside me *had* pulled me towards that Àbíkú. I clenched my fists so Mama Oti wouldn't see my hands shaking. 'What is this power, then?' I asked, turning my hands over and inspecting them carefully. They looked fairly normal to me: pale palms with dark lines intersecting them – nothing weird about that. And yet I had seen crazy stuff coming out of them.

'Only the Araba can explain this your magic. But I know that the universe would not have given you this power if it was not something you could manage,' Mama Oti said.

'And why does this power activate when I'm going through a crisis? I can't even manage my condition, let alone this weird stuff,' I asked. My insides were doing somersaults as I tried to make sense of it all.

Mama Oti's eyes drifted like she was somewhere far away. 'I thought we would have more time together so I can explain. But the one who knows all is the

Araba. He is from the Rùnmí tribe, and he is the most powerful priest of the god of wisdom and divination. He can use the Oracle, a magic device that helps him look into the future. Ten years ago, the king asked to know the future of Olori, and the Araba told him that a child from the land of outsiders will return to save night when there is a single hour of darkness remaining in Olori. That is why the king sees you as a threat, Koku.' Her full lips pressed into a single, solid line. 'The Ògún plan to destroy the Night Stone in six days, at the end of the summer solstice. It is the day in the year with the shortest night, and that is the only time the Night Stone will weaken enough to break it. You are the only one who can return night to Olori by finding the stone before the king's warriors get to it. The prophecy says that once the last descendant reunites with the Night Stone in Jujuland, balance will return to Olori and we shall have night and day once more.'

She must've thought I'm a mug, or something. There was *no way* I was going to Jujuland. That was where all the evil spirits lived.

I ain't risking my life for no magic stone.

'Whether you like or you no like, that is why they have sent Taiwo after you,' Mama Oti said, as she frantically began swiping some herbal potions and some roasted yams into my backpack.

As Mama Oti pushed me out of the door, her warm, spicy scent tickling my nose, I winced at the harsh sunlight and stumbled trying to get my bearings.

Mama Oti's house was the only one with a bit of privacy: it was more tucked away from the rest of the Babalú compound, cause she had a tangled web of dying plants out front.

'Taiwo knows I am protecting you. It is no longer safe for you to be here. Big-big *wahala* has arrived!' Mama Oti warned.

'Where am I supposed to go in the middle of the night?' I said, cause it was true even though it was super bright outside.

'You can either go to Jujuland and save night, or you can return to your uncle. There is no time to waste. Taiwo will finish you if he finds you! You must go to Jujuland to find the Araba, a miraculous, healing, fortune-telling priest. He has guided the greatest warriors of the land and used Jujuland remedies to bring back the sick from the brink of death. He will train you and help you find the Night Stone. He is the one who prophesied that your powers would awaken in the museum.' Mama Oti looked at me expectantly.

'But if you no like, I can send you back to your England. Either way today-today, you must be leaving this place.'

'Uhh . . .' I squirmed under her fiery gaze, shuffling my feet in the sand. The words 'miraculous healing priest' stood out in my mind.

What if he can cure *me?*

That would change everything.

'And one more thing.' Mama Oti's eyes glared right at me while I turned the decision over in my mind. 'Keep this power secret until you find the Araba, you hear? The Olókun tribe was wiped out because people in Olori were fearful of their power. The ones that will help you on your journey will do so because you are the only one who can return night to our land. If they knew you had power you cannot control they would—'

An obnoxious screeching sound interrupted her.

'*Oyinbo* baby!' someone yelled as they climbed off the back of the rusty motorbike. So much purple smoke spewed out I couldn't see who it was until a braid reached out in a wave. Oh, it was the rude Moremi girl I was stuck with.

I still had no clue how she did that.

The driver had a white T-shirt with sweat patches

under his armpits, paired with loose purple trousers. '*E kaale ma*!' He bowed his head towards Mama Oti.

'*E kuule*, Femi!' Mama Oti returned the greeting and paid him with thick *kobo* coins. Femi looked constantly shook cause his tight cornrows pulled his eyebrows up to his hairline. *He would make a great meme*, I thought.

'Where you wan make I carry you go, eh?' Femi said, nodding towards me as he fiddled with a chunky stud in his ear. It was the same design as the pendant Mama Oti wore around her neck.

It should've been a no-brainer – some madman with a shank thicker than Uncle Tunji's forehead was tryna kill me. But if I met that Araba priest guy maybe, just maybe, I wouldn't have to deal with being sick no more.

I'd waited my whole life for an opportunity like this. There would be no more meds, no more hospital visits, no more lying awake with a shuddery feeling that bleeds ice into my bones.

I took a deep breath and made my voice sound steady. 'I ain't going to no airport.'

Mama Oti's face lit up as soon as I said that. She pulled Moremi aside and they had a whole convo in shouty whispers that I only heard snippets of.

'. . . only one I can trust to protect him.'

'. . . annoying insect . . . I don't want to . . .'

'. . . find the Araba . . . the amulet.'

I coughed loudly to get their attention. They were being proper rude.

'*Ehen!* That is good-oh. It is agreed,' Mama Oti said, sharing a secret look with Moremi. 'Remember, you only have six days. First you and Moremi will go to Ekundudu in Aganjù territory to find the girl with the nose,' Mama Oti said, patting Moremi's shoulder softly.

'Girl with the nose? We all got noses. What is that supposed to mean?' I asked, wondering how Mama Oti made English more confusing than Yoruba sometimes.

'She is called the "girl with the nose" as she is a tracker who can follow any smell. The Aganjù girl and Moremi will protect you on this journey,' Mama Oti explained.

'No offence, but I don't really see how some girls are gonna do that, you get me?' I said.

Mama Oti grinned like she knew something I didn't.

'Fight me now-now. Today we must fight,' Moremi demanded, every one of her braids bunched up into tiny fists.

'No way, are you dizzy?'

'The goddess is my witness—'

'You're speaking out of your nose, fam—'

Before I could utter my next word, I found myself hanging upside down like a chicken wing. Mama Oti cackled as Moremi used a bunch of her braids to dangle me up in the air.

Moremi's braids drew me to her as she curled her top lip in a snarl. 'Girls are very, very dangerous, you hear?'

CHAPTER EIGHT

The Girl with the Nose

'Remember that your ancestors are with you. They will guide you to your destiny. And you will make your people proud.' Mama Oti's eyes welled up as she handed me my Champion hoodie. I zipped it up and then flung my legs over Femi's motorbike.

'I'll try my best,' I said, swallowing a lump in my throat. I didn't know how much use I would be cause my illness always held me back, but it felt like the right thing to say.

Mama Oti's lips curled as I leaned into the driver's knobbly spine. An earthy, cinnamon scent surrounded me as Moremi hopped on behind me. Her elbows were sharp and pointy, but her skin was soft.

The driver bent down and drew a symbol in the earth. When he straightened, his eyes flashed purple. Bright patterns spread across his bare arms. A spluttering purple cloud charged up the rusty Okada motorbike. And then we were off.

We hovered straight and then curved up so suddenly my skin almost peeled off my skull. I felt sick to my stomach, but lighter than ever. My sickle cell usually made my limbs feel heavy, but now I was as light as bubble wrap.

Femi flew over Ile-Kiisan and whooshed into the neighbouring Babalù territory. There were loads of tightly packed shacks with corrugated metal walls and shrivelled palm leaf roofs. Then Femi kept powering the bike higher and higher. We were so high Olori turned into a whirlwind of colours. We were hovering over houses, market stalls and sandy plains.

'Calm down, Femi!' I shouted, but Moremi just gripped on tighter with her legs, whooping, and swinging her arms around like she was at a rodeo.

We arrived at Ekundudu at dawn. A painfully bright white sky greeted us, reflecting up off stretches of sand so dry it splintered. The large cracks made the ground difficult for Femi to land on.

I threw up as soon as the bike screeched to a halt.

'You must get strength for stomach!' Femi laughed, patting his bony ribs to emphasise the point. I returned the smile as he drove away – quite a lot of my sick had splashed on his bike without him noticing. Happy days.

Moremi stretched her lanky arms and yawned. I doubled over again: my organs needed a bit of time to rearrange themselves. I inhaled deeply and held a hand over my eyes so I could take in the view in front of us.

A dusty harmattan wind blew, forcing me to squint as I looked and saw sun-beaten cliffs in the distance, huge boulders and steamy clouds. And there were animals – antelopes, giraffes, zebras with yellow droopy eyes and balding fur dragging their feet.

I opened my bag and guzzled down my sickle-cell meds with a large swig of water. I caught Moremi watching but when I stared back, her gaze flickered away.

There were no houses, just huge boulders among tall grass. Moremi walked over and stopped in front of a gigantic rock. It was surrounded by four towering identical totem poles shaped like a hippo, elephant and monkey all stacked on top of each other with a roaring leopard. The poles leered over us with snarling lips and red eyes.

'So . . .' I cleared my throat. 'How is the girl with the nose going to help us get away from that Taiwo creep?'

'We are about to meet the Aganjù chief, Inaki. You better show him some respect, yam head.' Moremi scowled at me. 'If you come and embarrass me in this place, I go make your backside chew pepper.' She turned away with a dismissive shrug and knocked on a door carved into the boulder. The knocker was a huge lion paw.

We could hear the high-pitched screech of some wild animal inside, and the scampering of sharp claws against the floor.

The stone door creaked open. A large man with a white afro, puffy eyebags and a fluffy beard stepped out and squinted down at us. He looked like a gorilla dressed as a scarecrow with dried palm leaves sticking out of his shoulders.

I stuck my head out, trying to see past the guy to figure out where that animal we heard was – I was hoping it wasn't the rest of that lion they used as a door knocker.

'*E kuule*. Good evening, sah.' Moremi bowed her head and chooked my side with one of her dumb braids to get me to do the same.

'*E kaab o*. You are welcome. How far, Kehinde? It has been too long-oh. How is Mama?' The chief bellowed. His voice was so deep it made the earth dance around us.

Moremi looked murderous, but smiled tightly at him. 'I go by Moremi now, sah, not Kehinde. Mama Oti is very well-oh. She asks us to send her greetings.'

I made a mental note to ask Moremi about her name change later.

'Moremi?' Chief Inaki twirled his long beard around his thick fingers. 'Moremi, the Ọya leader who sacrificed herself to protect her tribe from an army of outsiders? This name is very sweet-oh. We give thanks to the wisdom of ancestors.'

Then Chief Inaki grabbed my chin in his huge paw hands and studied my face closely, breathing hotly on my eyeballs. 'Ah-ah, so this small boy with stature like that of an insect, is the one the Araba promised will restore the Aganjù tribe to its former glory?'

I gritted my teeth at the insult about my size. My guy was lucky he was a chief, otherwise I would've cussed him differently for that.

The only thing that calmed me was remembering that once I patterned it with the Araba, I would be cured from my illness. Then I'd finally experience puberty and grow properly. It would be bless.

'The Araba does not lie, sah,' Moremi said, side-eyeing me like she couldn't quite believe it herself. I guess that made two of us.

'And what are you calling yourself?' The chief demanded.

'Koku,' I said, waiting for the usual cringe Olori people did when they heard my name.

'Your name is Kokumo, meaning "Don't Die Any More",' he corrected me. 'Say it with pride.'

Before I could reply, Chief Inaki turned to roar loudly at someone inside. 'Osoosi! Come and break the kola nut with our guests-oh,' he yelled, taking a few giant strides into the living room. We followed and watched as he took a seat on a wooden stool in the shape of an elephant head. He let out a huge sigh as he draped his hairy legs over two tusks. It had to be the least comfortable chair I'd ever seen. 'Osoosi!' The chief bellowed again, making the ground shudder.

The scratching sound came again, and got louder until we saw a large, spotted hyena with a huge hump,

black wonky ears
and flashing orange
eyes enter the
room.

Now the
weird scampering
sounds from earlier
made sense.

Chief Inaki beckoned
it closer, patting
it fondly. Its lips
stretched into a
toothy smile as it
dropped a dark nut into his lap.
It looked totally clapped. It made
me feel itchy just looking at it.

I couldn't wait for the girl-with-the-nose to come out
so I could leave and scratch that monstrosity out of
my eyeballs for ever.

'So, where is the girl, then?' I asked, finally.

Moremi jerked her head at the crazy hyena.

'Good one.' I laughed nervously – she had a dead
sense of humour. 'But for real, where is she?'

'You no get sense for head at all, at all,' Moremi
said.

And the hyena shrank before our eyes. Its ratty fur sank into smooth skin and gangly limbs, and an afro puff emerged from the top of its head. Then we were looking at a girl my age with a crazy grin on her face.

My jaw dropped to my chest.

'I am Osoosi, the girl with the nose.'

'And I am a cat person,' I said, my eyes bugged out of my skull. I thought *I* looked weird, but she really took the biscuit. She had three afro puffs with two beaded braids dangling around her ears, orange paint under her eyes in two upside-down triangles and a larger than normal button nose that didn't look like it had any magical properties whatsoever.

'*Baga!* How far, Moremi?' Osoosi grinned so wide you'd think it would break her face. '*Sha*, it is too long since I have been seeing you at Gidigbo training. And is this the boy of legends? The one that carries himself like cricket?' she asked excitedly, bouncing around on her toes.

Moremi nodded.

'Are you talking about me, fam?' I said, with an annoyed huff.

'Ehh?' Osoosi tilted her head to the side, playing deaf.

'Kokumo, Moremi, Osoosi,' Chief Inaki interrupted,

giving each of us a deep nod. 'We do not have much time, so let us break the kola nut and have small chop together.'

He broke the nut into four equal lobes. 'Today you are blood of my blood. Moremi, the *oriki* prayer is yours,' Chief Inaki said, handing us a piece each.

'*A fi iyin fun Ekun nla*. We give praise to the great leopard,' Moremi said, in between careful bites.

The nut looked like a piece of night between my fingers. Everyone stared while I put the kola in my mouth, so I couldn't be sliding it under my T-shirt or nothing. It was unbelievably bitter. I wanted to bleach my tongue after I'd chewed it.

Moremi snickered under her breath as she watched me choke it down.

'To sweeten the path of the kola, we must chop small, eh? Osoosi, go and fetch my sweet potato, your brothers and my strongest men. Tell them to bring food for our guests.'

Osoosi dashed into another room on her hands and feet. She was way too hyped, always bouncing around places. I hated people like that: they reminded me how slow my condition made me.

'So, the time has finally come, eh?' The Aganjù chief knotted his bushy white eyebrows at me. 'I go be the chief of a barren land if night does not return. The endless days are causing drought. The wealthy Òṣun tribe that owns gold and the Ògún who hoard all the other valuable metals can trade with outsider countries and collect what they need from overseas. But we serve Aganjù, the god of the wilderness. Just like the Babalú, we depend on the land for our chop.'

Their situation sounded terrible, but I was low-key jealous of their cool animal transforming powers. Moremi kept nudging me with her braids to keep me in check, but that didn't stop me from looping the maddest knots into my hoodie strings while the chief spoke.

'Many people from Olori, and even your England, have been waiting for your return, Kokumo.'

I cringed when the chief called me by my full name. I hated being 'Don't die any more'. I didn't want to be reminded of each time I almost died of my illness every time someone wanted to chat to me.

Chief Inaki rolled up his sleeve and showed off a tiny fish tattoo, its tail looped around like the infinity sign. 'The mudfish go be the symbol of Olókun. When you see this, know that you are protected by the dark guardians.'

Their posse sounded like a bad Marvel film. Still,

I realised I was gonna let a lot of people down when they found out I was only going along with the plan to get healed by the Araba.

'The Ògún king created a senseless lie that the Olókun were trying to create eternal night in Olori so spirits could invade whenever they wanted. *Babanla* and nonsense!' The chief pounded his fist on the table, jolting me upright. 'The ruling Ògún tribe has always hated the Olókun tribe. They know that if the Olókun joined forces with the Night Creatures, a great power would be born. We all know they lied because they were afraid of the Olókun's power. That is why the Aganjù and Babalú fought to protect them during the war. As a friend of the Olókun, after they were wiped out, I vowed that when the last member of their tribe returned, one of our own would help them.' He looked at me from under his eyebrows. 'I would be helping you myself, but the chief must remain to rule his people. My eldest son, Sebe, also has the power of Aganjù, but he must manage our household while I rule the people. But don't worry yourself-oh.' The Aganjù chief let out a long chuckle. 'Osoosi has inherited the great *Ashagidibi* tracking nose, just like my eldest. Look at this thing!' The chief flared his giant hairy nostrils that were so big you could get two thumbs inside and gave Osoosi a pat on the back.

I squirmed at the sickly sweet father–daughter moment. If I had a nose like theirs, I would want it sawn off.

'But *abeg* carry this for your head,' Chief Inaki said in a grave voice. 'If you allow any Night Creature to harm one hair on my daughter's head, I go cook you and chew you!'

Luckily, a bunch of bare-chested guys wearing orange ankara skirts chose that moment to bring plates of food to our table.

'*Eh-hen!* Breakfast has arrived,' the chief announced.

Mango juice splashed in my eyes as a teenager with a large afro with two beaded twists at the front slammed a coconut cup in front of me. I was about to say something, until he went around and did the same to Osoosi.

Moremi smirked smugly at us as he gently placed her cup in front of her. She took a long sip.

Chief Inaki grinned as the moody teen brought over a large keg of palm wine. 'This is Sebe! My eldest.' He gargled the words, chugging his drink immediately. Sebe's bottom lip curled as he gave me a look dirty enough to compete with Moremi's. I had no clue why this guy was trying to beef me.

The guys waited around with spears crossed over their chests like they were bodyguards or something. Sebe stood right behind me, holding a three-foot-long shank over my head. He was bad vibes. All the other guys had their weapons attached to their side, but his was so close to me if I leaned back I'd end up with a hole in my neck. Even though the meal looked delicious, knowing he was behind me sent shivers down my spine.

'Ako, my cherry *koko*, sit with us now,' Chief Inaki said to a thin hairy guy as he yanked my cushion out from underneath me and placed it next to himself. 'This is my fourth husband,' Chief Inaki said. I glared as I tried to get comfy on the stony floor.

Ten sons, one daughter and four husbands, I thought. *This family is insane!*

'Now, Koku, the *oriki* is yours.'

I swallowed. 'Er, we give thanks to the great . . . erm, lion, I think?'

'Leopard.' Ako corrected me with a gentle smile. 'When our god, Aganjù, roamed the earth he used the form of a black leopard. This leopard is not only important to our tribe; it is also the symbol of Olori.'

'Cool,' I said, cause it actually was. My eyes roamed over all the tiger, zebra and lion skins draped over the walls. Then I stared down at the plate of sweet beans and pushed them around, checking for wild animal flesh.

'We are vegetarians,' the chief announced, through a mouthful of food.

'Oh,' I said, my eyes flicking back to the animal skins on the walls.

'We are a people of peace. Any decoration you see was taken from an animal that died peacefully. We do not kill for enjoyment. We are not Ògún,' Ako explained.

Chief Inaki's eyes turned fiery as soon as the Ògún were mentioned. '*Eh-hen*, it is the Ògún man that wants every creature to taste their sword so they can make *juju* power for themselves. I rebuke this *juju* thing-oh!' Chief Inaki yelled, in between aggressive bites of his meal. 'We are from the land of origins – it go be our pride to be the only nation in the world that is still connected to the gods who created them. We do not need to steal magic. Stealing magic, even if it is from a creature of night, is an act with no honour. That is why outsiders are the ones who invented the process of how to steal dark magic from inside a Night Creature and named this thing *juju*. Now the Ògún want to use *juju* to kill them all and replace night so we will not experience normal night and day ever again. Don't you see that this *juju* thing is killing our very way of life?'

Chief Inaki polished his plate with one final angry lick and then turned to me. 'But this small-small *pikin* will save us!' He raised his palm-wine-filled gourd in my honour.

Sebe cleared his throat and shifted behind me, his knuckles grazing the back of my neck.

I gripped my mango juice tightly. Osoosi's brother was creeping me out and the chief wouldn't stop hyping me up. Like I wasn't feeling bad enough already about letting them down.

'We have waited many moons, but now we will suffer no more. Our enemies may have armies, plenty money, and a soul-swallowing sword, but we have the last descendant of Olókun.'

I almost passed out when the chief said that. 'Did you just say *a soul-swallowing* sword?' I asked.

'Of course now, that is the Ògún god's divine sword that he used to clear the road when the earth was created. 'What are they are teaching you in this En-gee-land, eh?' Inaki's bushy brows raised impossibly high. 'Don't you know of the divine Òrìṣà objects?'

I shook my head while Moremi gave me a heavy side-eye.

Babanla and nonsense!' Inaki let out a loud burp as he took another swig of his wine.

'Divine objects are the items the Òrìṣà gods go used when they created the earth. The Ògún king enjoys lying that his own god was the first to arrive in our universe, but we elders are knowing that Olókun, the goddess of darkness, was the first god. She go use her own heart, the Night Stone, to split the sky from the darkness, creating the night and day.

'And of course then there was the soul-swallowing sword of the Ògún.' Inaki paused, knitting his brows in a heavy frown. 'The sword of Ògún swallows the soul of any person that touches it. As long as you are holding the Ògún sword you may show no fear. If the metal senses any feeling inside you, the thing go swallow you whole. One must *feel nothing* to use the sword.' His huge hand slapped the table, making me jump. 'The sword contains the souls of thousands of men who have tried, and failed, to control it!' Then Inaki shook his head, as his eyes glazed over. 'It is strange that the only person to hold the sword is a boy of few moons, one that is not even a member of the Ògún tribe, the most dangerous warrior in Olori—'

The chief's eldest son suddenly leaned over me to interrupt. He scrunched his nose at me like we were beefing before turning to address his father: 'It seems the Ògún want to greet our honoured guest.' His spear hovered dangerously close to my horns. I ducked to save my hairstyle as bone-rattling steps approached.

'You are right, my son,' Inaki agreed, as he looked over my shoulder, to the outside. My heartbeat quickened. 'You must go to Jujuland now-now if you wish to survive. There is no time to waste,' he growled as the heavy steps grew louder. 'The portal to Jujuland lies within Ile-Kayefi. Osoosi will show you the way out of the back of the compound.'

'But, Baba—' Osoosi's ears drooped, like she was still in hyena form.

'Don't question Baba, you must leave now-now and do your duty!' her brother snapped. Osoosi flinched.

'Sebe is right,' Inaki said more gently, 'There is no time, my daughter,' Inaki said, gently. 'You have less than six days to find the Night Stone and save night before the Ògún destroy it for ever.' As he spoke, his fingers traced a sign in the air.

The chief's white hair began to cover the rest of his body until it formed a sleek wolf coat. A few other guys, along with Osoosi's older brother, transformed too. My eyes reeled back but I shut my mouth and tried to act like I was used to people turning into giant wolves.

The ground began shaking, making our teeth dance in our mouths. Outside, a massive slab of stone wall collapsed with an impact that would've landed on the Richter scale.

We all turned to make sure what we were seeing was real. I shook so hard I almost chewed my tongue off.

My man was at least ten feet tall and covered in iron from head to toe. He had destroyed the stone wall with his bare hands. And there were others behind him; I peeped their iron masks in the shape of different menacing animals – leopards, panthers and tigers.

Inaki's head snapped back. 'You must leave now! The boy is the only one who can restore night; you must protect him at all costs! If the Ògún take him, night is lost for ever!' The chief's lips peeled back to reveal a set of wolf teeth so sharp they looked like they could have chewed concrete.

But compared to the iron giant, the chief looked small.

As I looked closer, I realised the giant wasn't wearing armour at all. It was his *skin*. He was covered in glistening swirls that tattooed his entire body. It had even seeped into his eyes, silvering them into bullets.

My feet were glued to the spot.

'You want to live, or you want to die?' Moremi hissed, her braids whooshing out and wrapping around me to yank me away. Osoosi let out a quiet whimper, and then scurried after us on all fours.

As we made our escape, I felt ice-cold eyes boring into my back.

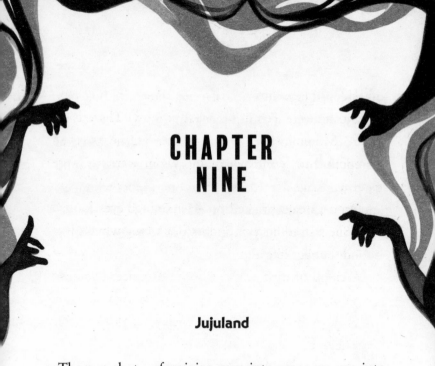

CHAPTER NINE

Jujuland

The sun shot unforgiving rays into us as we ran into the bush for cover. We stared as that iron warrior smashed the stone Aganjù compound like it was nothing. We were gonna get cheffed once he spotted our bait hiding place in the grass.

'I beg you, tell me Femi's number?' I reached for my Nokia in my backpack. If I had to choose between getting shanked by a giant metal man or getting yeeted off a flying Okada, my guy Femi would win every time. 'Well?' I shook my phone in their faces.

The ground trembled, making my heart rate quadruple. Osoosi used a stick to draw a wobbly sign in the cracked soil. Orange marks crawled up the sides of her arms.

'No time for Femi! We must go now! There is *no time*!' Moremi stole a few glances at the wrecked compound to see if any of the Ògún warriors were after us.

Osoosi's ears pricked up. Her orange eyes looked wet. She pursed her lips and let out a long whistle in a sound that cut like a knife.

A cloud of dust erupted in the distance. It moved closer until I was getting eyed up by two scrawny panthers with razor-sharp canines who looked like they hadn't eaten in a hot minute.

Moremi seemed chill, but I gulped. It was mad how close I was to animals I'd only ever seen on TV.

'Moin-Moin! Gizdodo!' Osoosi stroked their balding fur, making them purr like kittens.

'Are you alright?' I said, trying not to move a single muscle. 'I watched a show on panthers. I swear down they will rip your face off if you get any closer!' I warned.

Osoosi laughed. 'They go carry us to Jujuland quick-quick.'

Just as I was about to tell them more panther facts, I spotted the giant metal guy leaving the same way we had done. He had a trembling lump of white fur draped over his shoulder, and a smaller figure wearing a purple cloth in between their armour moving about next to him.

I nudged Moremi and she pulled Osoosi down so we were low to the ground. Suddenly, chilling with wild panthers didn't seem so crazy any more.

I squinted hard at the guy wearing purple print with a sword bigger than all of the others. *Taiwo*.

I poked out a hole in the bush I was hiding in to look at the iron giant. I craned my neck to inspect the new fur scarf he was wearing. It was a fallen wolf.

Big mistake: Taiwo's lifeless eyes caught me. His lips pursed and said the word, '*Oyinbo*'. Outsider.

The wolf scarf was still moving, but there was a darkened spot in the dust from where a thin stream of liquid dripped down and pooled. Blood.

Moremi had her arm around Osoosi to shield her. The wolf he was carrying could be one of the guards we saw transform, or worse, her dad or brother.

'Koku, grab one of the panthers and I will grab the other one,' Moremi instructed.

'But—!' I protested.

'We must move *now*-now,' she snapped. 'Osoosi go follow us.' Moremi patted Osoosi's shoulder and lifted her chin.

Osoosi gave a shaky thumbs-up.

It was a bumpy ride at first, as Moin-Moin limped before she ran. The panthers were all skin and bone so they weren't exactly comfy. I could feel Moin-Moin's muscles clenching and releasing underneath me.

Moremi rode the panther like a natural, her braids whipping the air behind her.

Osoosi transformed into a hyena and ran alongside us.

I had to lock my arms round Moin-Moin's velvety neck and hope for the best. It was proper mad. Somehow she knew how I wanted her to move. If I leaned to one side she would swerve that way, and if I relaxed she would slow down.

Despite the goons being after us, I felt *free*.

Back home, my uncle didn't want me doing anything interesting cause of my illness. Here, it was kinda mad how I was mucking around in a desert riding wild panthers.

Uncle Tunji will probably have a heart attack when I get back and tell him all about it.

If I make it back alive.

And then tall trees were creating a canopy of leaves above us. We lost the warriors as we rode deep into the tangled forest web.

The panthers shrugged us off when we arrived. Moin-Moin looked pretty interested in my knee, which I'd cut on a branch. I thought she was going to munch me up, but she just gave it a prickly lick. It kinda reminded me of Jollof when I got home from school. I hoped he'd still be there when I got back.

I scratched Moin-Moin behind the ear, and was rewarded with a headbutt. Jollof did that too when he got excited – the only difference was my guy didn't send me flying backwards.

'You see how Moin-Moin go 'gree with you!' Osoosi remarked with a half-smile, as she transformed back into her human self.

'Yeah,' I said, admiring Moin-Moin's jet-black fur. I liked running my fingers through it, even though it

118

was patchy in places.

'You no go find animals like this one in your *oyinbo* place. In fact, you no go look am anywhere in this world, except Aganjù,' Osoosi explained, puffing her chest out just like her dad did when he talked about their tribe. 'They are *needing* darkness to survive. That is why they look rough like this. And if we do not find the Night Stone before the Ògún and return night to Olori, these animals will not be here to greet another dawn.' Osoosi let out a quiet sniff.

At her words, all the feeling in my fingers felt like it had been zapped away.

'That is why we must keep moving forward. We must go,' Moremi added.

'Moin-Moin, Gizdodo, you have done very well to carry us here.' Osoosi pulled the panthers to her. They pressed their giant noses into her cheek. 'I know your legs are paining you because you no get rest. I swear on the spirits of my ancestors that I go return night to you!' Osoosi said fiercely as she gave the panthers one final pat.

'Thanks for bringing us here, guys. I'll try not to let you down,' I whispered, watching them hobble off into the distance. Once the Araba fixed me up and got rid of my illness I would be able to help find

119

the Night Stone and bring night back so they could rest up.

The black spot in the sand from earlier haunted me. Someone from Osoosi's tribe had gotten hurt tryna save me. I've had loads of blood transfusions cause of my illness, so I know blood when I see it.

'This very moment my people are risking their lives so we can protect this boy and carry ourselves here.' Osoosi clenched her fist tight.

'Your father is the chief of Aganjù. The king's warriors cannot seriously harm him – it is against Olori law,' Moremi reassured her.

'You are right, oga-boss,' Osoosi said. 'And my brother go be the next in line. So my father and brother will receive protection. But I still worry for my people.' Osoosi sighed, but then her lips curved into a small smile. 'This day go be the day we enter Jujuland. We will be greeted with rejoicing when we return night to Olori! Na big adventure-oh!'

'Yes now come and carry your leg into this place,' Moremi said, turning on her heel and marching ahead of us.

Osoosi and I had to jog a bit to keep up with Moremi's insanely fast pace.

'Well, yeah, it's not like we have a choice,' I

grumbled, slowing down to a walk once we kept up with Moremi.

'Eh?' Osoosi said, leaning in close like she always did when I spoke, like she was trying to see the words come out of my mouth. 'I get small problem for ear,' Osoosi explained now, pulling on her left ear. 'I no hear anything in this one at all, at all.'

I dunno why, but I'd always assumed people with hearing issues would be quiet, but Osoosi asked a billion questions about what it was like living in the UK. I spent ages explaining that I lived in a tiny flat on top of a Chicken and Chips shop, and *not* inside Big Ben.

Once she got her head around that, she told me about her dream of beating her oldest brother and becoming the chief of Aganjù. But whenever she mentioned the chief her voice would get all choked up and whispery. I didn't know what it was like to have a father who actually cared about you. I'd never even met mine before.

I guess she was proper worried about her dad, but she tried to play it down by transforming into any animal I wanted just for banter.

And Moremi *really* didn't appreciate it when Osoosi drew a sign in the ground, shrunk into a furry, orange-eyed rodent and lifted up a black and white tail to skunk-fart right in her face.

I didn't think I'd get on with Osoosi, but she was kinda jokes still.

As we walked further, the trees thinned out, revealing an abandoned town filled with painted sculptures and crumbling clay buildings painted deep blue, like water trapped in stone. The houses had curved window panes shaped like fish scales.

I stretched my arms. I normally have a billion thoughts slamming in my mind, but this place made it easy to relax.

'Where are we?' I asked, admiring a curved wall shaped like a lizard. My eyes burned tryna take it all in, I wished I had something to draw it with.

'This is Ile-Kayefi. *Abi*, you should be knowing this place—?' Osoosi saw my blank face and answered her own question. 'This is one of the most important towns in the Olókun district, the home of your people,' she explained. 'The chief says the entrance to Jujuland go be somewhere inside this town.'

Osoosi kept rambling, but I couldn't concentrate. This was supposed to be where my people where from, but it was like walking through an abandoned museum.

I got distracted by sculptures of armless women with long, twisted hair. This was supposed to be where my people were from, but it was like walking through an abandoned museum.

The sculptures looked like the stuff of dreams, or something a kid would draw, but in a way that filled you with wonder. The abstract ones were painted in clashing colours; they had tiny bodies and drooping eyes melting into one another. Now I could see where my guy Picasso got his ideas from.

I learned about abstract art one time when I was in detention with Miss Adebayo. She showed me Picasso paintings on the Internet cause she knows art is one of my favourite subjects.

'I go use my nose to lead us to Jujuland!' Osoosi announced, as she bent low into the earth. She stuck her nose right in and took a deep sniff, like she didn't care about the bugs crawling up her nose.

Then, without hesitating, she led us along a dried-up river bed and stopped next to the weirdest tree I ever saw in my life.

It was enormous, practically twenty feet tall. It was smooth and shiny, and had a pinkish grey colour but it looked wrong. It reminded me of one time when Atticus Sharp came back from holiday in Barbados, skin peeling left right and centre, burnt to a crisp like he'd been cooked inside out or something.

'This it-oh!
The entrance to
Jujuland!' Osoosi
announced.

'Rah! It's massive!' I
said. I almost bent over
backwards craning my neck
towards the tree. It had no
leaves, and its dried
branches seemed to be
desperately crawling
away from the
sun.

124

'What's in that hole?' I asked, peering into the total blackness in the centre of the tree trunk. It looked big enough to fit about forty people – even Uncle Tunji could get through easy-peasy, without being squeezed or nothing.

'This is strange. There should be Ògún warriors guarding the entrance to Jujuland,' Moremi said, circling the tree to inspect the hole.

Osoosi leaned over her shoulders. I stood still. What if it was a trap and there were Ògún guards waiting to shank us as soon as we made it through the other side? Then I remembered that purple Àbíkú with its disappearing powers and shiny black button eyes. There would be hundreds just like it on the other side. Plus the other mad tings: Mami Wata who would drown us if we stepped in their yard and that man-eating Àgbákò thing with the scorpion mouth, elephant body and anaconda tail.

There was no way I would survive in a place like that. *Why am I doing this again?* I thought to myself. *Oh, yeah, the miraculous healing priest guy.* When I was all healed and he taught me about my powers that I apparently got from being the last of the Olókun tribe, I would be able to sort out the night stuff for the Olori mandem – maybe.

Most importantly, I would make sure my guy cured me once and for all.

'There is no sign of Ògún. They must have left their post to attack Ekundudu.' Moremi nodded firmly. 'This is our only chance. Koku, are you ready?' she asked, squeezing my shoulder with one of her braids.

'Koku, this one nah delicious adventure-oh!' Osoosi grinned. '*Oga*-boss, let me go first!'

'As the eldest, I will be going first.' Moremi took a deep breath and crawled on to one of the knobbly roots at the base of the tree. She swung her legs over into the hole and they totally disappeared. 'I go see you on the other side, yam heads!' Moremi's voice echoed as she pushed herself into the blackness. Her braids trailed behind her.

The tree ate her up until nothing was left.

Osoosi scrambled up on to the rim of the hole and looked down into it. As she hopped from one foot then to the other, it was getting jarring. Like how waiting for a rollercoaster ride only makes you more anxious. I gave her a very slight nudge that sent her kicking and screaming until I couldn't hear her no more. It was bless.

Then it was my turn. I looked right inside the hole. There was nothing there. Just black. Blacker than black. I went around the tree a couple more times, but there were no sliding doors, no step ladder, no nothing.

I shut my eyes tight and imagined life without being ill – signing up to football, making friends in my year, growing taller and finally being able to chirpse the leng sixth-form girls. After thinking it all over, I crawled through and got swallowed into the—

CHAPTER
TEN

Magic Braids and Man-Eating Monsters

It felt like falling a thousand feet with nothing below, like trying to scream when you're drowning underwater, like being buried alive. Dirt was ripping my eyelids to shreds, scratching my eyeballs and shoving its way down my throat. I travelled through that hole for forever, until there was something solid underneath me.

I found myself at the base of the tree, looking up. My eyes opened properly for the first time in ages. The sky was pitch-black. But weirdly I could see perfectly cause the moon was ultra-bright here, way larger than I ever remembered it being. It shone a pale yellow light on everything, making my skin super glowy. I took a deep breath and smiled.

I didn't have to squint no more. The dark sky was a huge relief. It felt like I'd taken a long sip of ice-cold water. Slowly, I began to look around me, my jaw on my chest. All the plants and animals were neon coloured like they'd swallowed a bunch of disco balls. Hanging from the tree's branches were one-eyed bats with glowing wings and three-legged baboons with fluorescent fur. The jungle was mad. Not mad like on TV, or the books I read in school, or the anime I watch online, but *mad*. Glittering fish with wings flew about as I looked, glow-in-the-dark creatures with bright green insides slithered over my feet, as slimy as Mama Oti's *okro* soup. The sweet scent of tropical flowers mingled with wet soil and damp wood. The air was so hot and sticky I was sweating in places I didn't know I could.

I couldn't believe it. This was Jujuland.

It was mad, cause I was literally on the run for my life, but I ain't never felt free like that before.

Osoosi's eyes were wide, like saucers. 'The sky is so dark here. I have never seen this before. So this is the thing they are calling night. It is very beautiful-oh,' Osoosi said, quietly staring up at the sky. It must've been a long time since she'd experienced a proper night. I looked around for Moremi but all I could see was the jungle stretching its long leafy arms out in front of me.

Osoosi bent to draw a pattern in the earth. 'I go use my Aganjù power to become one of these Jujuland animals,' she explained, as the earth brightened, turning our toes orange. The cool patterns crawled up Osoosi's arms like before and soon the ring of orange flashed in her eyes.

I held my breath, waiting for some neon-coloured fluff to appear behind her ears.

Osoosi turned towards me with her flashing eyes. She looked the same as before, just with glowing patterns on her neck and arms.

'Nothing happened, fam.' I shrugged.

'I guess you can't turn into Jujuland animals,' I said. 'Your power is still sick, though – I can't lie.'

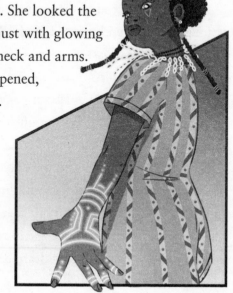

Osoosi drew in the soil quickly and disappeared with a puff of orange smoke. Before I knew it, a very squeaky, orange-eyed bat was flying way above me over my head, and further into the jungle.

'Koku, see wetin I go do!' Osoosi giggled, doing figure eights in the air.

It was jokes, but as I dragged my exhausted legs into the jungle after her, a part of me was low-key jealous that I didn't have any cool powers. Uncontrollable ghost arms that flew out of your palms at random did not count. *What am I even doing on an adventure like this?* I thought, stopping to catch my breath.

I walked back to the big, ugly tree we had climbed through to get here just so I could lean on it. Then I unzipped my backpack and took a long sip from the water bottle inside it.

As I gulped the water down I noticed that on this side, the tree was different. For one thing, it had leaves curved like little moons.

Then I saw a loopy braid sticking out behind one of the moon-shaped leaves. I followed it to Moremi who had been kneeling in front of the tree on the other side all along. She was lit up by the glowing birds in the branch nearest her. Then she started to sing.

'*I am an old iroko tree;*
Mo dagba iroko.
I will not die;
Mi o ni ku.
I am a thousand hills;
Mo digba oke.
I cannot be moved;
Mo duro gbon-in.'

Her voice flowed through the whole jungle. Osoosi transformed back into a human at the sound of her voice, her ears rolling up like a carpet, like she was trying to catch every word.

Even though I hated to admit it, Moremi had a nice voice; it had a grainy quality that was impossible to ignore. When she sang, a hush fell over everything, as all the creatures stopped to listen. She moved slowly to her own music, kicking the orange dirt up in the air like a whirlwind. Fireflies danced around her like fairy lights in the inky dark, and white furry flowers sprouted from the tree.

Moremi reached up to pull one down. As she did, a thick golden sap dripped on to her braids. She massaged it in slowly and kept singing all the while. As soon as she stopped, the flowers shrivelled and disappeared. And Moremi's braids stretched out into all sorts of shapes I'd never seen before, almost as tall as the tree itself.

'What kind of magic is this?' Osoosi gasped, stepping back from Moremi. 'Is this *juju* magic?'

Moremi gave Osoosi a look so dirty *I* felt filthy from it. I was glad Osoosi had asked instead of me.

'No! I do not steal energy from the Night Creatures to create nonsense *juju* magic! Goddess Qya is my witness!' Moremi licked the tip of her finger and held it in the air, making the Olori promise sign that my uncle used with his friends.

'Mama Oti's tribe are herbalists. She taught me many secret things. The Babalú have *iroko* trees in Ile-ewe that I use, but every plant and creature in Jujuland has stronger magic. That is all.' Moremi pursed her lips as she squeezed the last bit of sap into a small vial. It shimmered like liquid gold when it caught the moonlight.

That got me thinking. I wouldn't have minded having a bit of magic in my twists, if I was being honest. Not cutting my hair wouldn't be a big deal – as long as I could get a shape-up and a fade at the sides now and then, it would be calm.

Moremi narrowed her eyes at me when she caught

me staring. 'Don't jealous me-oh. You don't chop this thing for free. If this thing give it also take.'

'What did it take from *you*, then?' I asked, beating Osoosi to it. I tried to keep it low key, but Osoosi leaned in so close to Moremi's face she was practically headbutting her.

'We don't have time for this foolishness. The Ògún will be on their way.' Moremi tried to dodge the question, weighing some flower petals in her palm. Then she sighed deeply. '*Iroko* tree no go tell you which thing it go take from you.'

She still aired my question, but I didn't press it. I knew what it was like being asked why you're different.

Then we walked through the jungle. We didn't speak much, as we were all mesmerised by our surroundings. We kept glancing upwards expecting the sky to get light but it never did, it was always pitch-black with a bright shining moon. Osoosi kept saying, '*E kaasan*. Good afternoon,' to every creature she came across while we walked, even the gross-looking ones.

Snakes with zebra stripes slithered through the lush grass, dogs with slitted cat-eyes moved alongside us, and red winged lizards howled at the moon.

Even though I liked looking at all the crazy stuff, like polka dot ants collecting a bunch of glowing leaves and flying rainbow fish that chirped above us, it was pretty tough going. I had to take a breath every minute.

'*Ki lo se e?* What's wrong with you?' Moremi asked, watching me trying to catch my breath.

'Man's good out here, trust,' I lied.

'Should we stop here and rest?' she asked. But her dark eyes darted sneaking glances behind us and her feet tapped a nervous rhythm in the earth.

I shook my head. 'The Ògún guys on their way, aren't they?'

'I go tell you the truth. Everyone knows how to get to Jujuland, but it is usually guarded by the Ògún warriors. They are the only tribe allowed in this place. But even they do not know where the Araba is hiding himself. The only ones who can track the Araba's scent are the Aganjù tribe. The Aganjù won't help the Ògún because they want to save night. And the Araba is the only one who knows where the Night Stone is. As long as we find the Araba before they find us, we are safe. If they find us before then . . .'

'Say no more,' I gulped and stood upright, ignoring the ache in my ribcage.

Moremi ripped my backpack off my shoulders and zipped it open.

'Oi, what are you doing?' I asked, as she pulled out a

small vial with a brown liquid inside. It was one of Mama Oti's remedies. She threw it to me and marched on ahead.

My fingers closed around the glass vial.

'Thanks, man,' I said, as I shut my eyes and downed it, remembering how it gave me a burst of energy during the masquerade. As soon as the sour liquid ran over my tongue, the pain around my ribs subsided.

Soon I had enough energy to walk through the jungle again.

Eventually, Moremi stopped walking and tapped the ground with a pointed stick. 'We sleep here tonight,' she announced.

All I saw was dirt. 'Sleep? Here?' I asked.

Moremi turned her back on me. Her braids started pulling mud out of the ground and pulled vines from the trees, which she started crafting into a little shelter.

'Rah, I ain't sleeping in that,' I complained – even though I was so tired from walking I could've passed out where I was standing.

'If you want Ògún warriors to find you and finish you, go sleep outside like donkey,' Moremi said, as she crawled inside.

I got a flashback of Taiwo's soulless eyes staring me down. Suddenly sleeping in the shelter didn't seem like a bad idea no more. It was pitch-black under there cause once Moremi plucked the vines from the bush they didn't glow any more. So Moremi made a small fire – her braids got busy rubbing two sticks together. Once it was done, she yanked my backpack out of my hands, pulled a yam out and slowly warmed it over the fire.

'*Eh-hen!* Dis my hunger dey chook me,' Osoosi said, practically dribbling as Moremi split the yam. Osoosi inhaled hers as soon as she got it.

Moremi threw my piece into my lap without warning; it was pure evil. I didn't order a side of roasted nuts with my yam.

'What no sauce, or nothing?' I complained.

Moremi grunted and threw my bag back at me.

'Ah! Dis food sweet well-well. Koku, I go help you chop that one!' Osoosi offered with shining eyes.

'Are you mad?' I said, choking it down.

I looked into the backpack. There wasn't any more food, but Mama Oti had stuffed my backpack with a few extra things alongside my sickle-cell meds: my precious photo of my mum and that random guy, a leopard amulet, bug spray and a bunch of healing herbal potions. The leopard amulet caught my attention: it looked expensive, like, way outta Mama Oti's price range.

Moremi picked the amulet up. I was admiring its shining gold eyes when she threw it to Osoosi.

Osoosi caught it with her teeth. Her flat nose wrinkled as she sniffed the bronze metal. 'Ah, this is belonging to a priest that worships the god of wisdom. A divine healing master!'

'This is why you are the girl with the nose!' Moremi said, giving Osoosi a pat on the back with one of her braids. 'Mama Oti told me that this thing is belonging to the Araba. You must help us locate him.'

'The Araba! Yes, *oga*-boss, I go find this man,' Osoosi said, with big round eyes. Then she looked at the rest of the contents of the backpack. Her eyes settled on my photo.

I yanked it away before she said anything and tucked it carefully into the safe inner pocket of my bag.

'This go be the last of Mama's potions.' Moremi laid out all the bottles Mama Oti had filled up, so we could all see. 'She go give everything to help the last descendant fulfil the Araba's prophecy. She is hoping that when night returns these plants go grow again and she will make more remedies and heal the sick in Olori.'

I swallowed my pills with a huge swig of water. Moremi watched silently but Osoosi's eyes bulged out her head. 'Ah-ah, which kind sickness be this?'

'I don't wanna talk about it, you get me?' I retorted. No wonder she was the girl-with-the-nose – she was the *nosiest* person I ever met.

'Leave him, Osoosi. Not everyone wants to talk themselves finish like you.' Moremi kissed her teeth at her.

I blinked, making sure I was hearing that right. Moremi had actually *backed* me.

Osoosi's ears drooped a little, just like they did when she was in hyena form. '*E ma binu o*. I am sorry-oh! Me I don't mean to cause offence.'

'Yeah, it's . . . whatever.' I shrugged.

'You are the one who go help us restore night to my tribe. I ask because I am wanting to understand you small-small,' Osoosi said, earnestly.

I'm not gonna lie, I felt bad at how hopeful she looked.

I took a deep breath. 'Well basically yeah, it's got to do with my red blood cells innit. Basically blood cells are meant to work as a team but mine are just buffoons. They get stuck together, and sometimes they even attack each other. The pain caused by the blood cells clashing is called a crisis. It's different for everyone who has it. I've got to take meds to manage it but nothing can really stop the pain.'

Somehow the words flooded my lips like a waterfall. When I finished, I waited for the fake pity, but Osoosi and Moremi just listened quietly.

'It gets me proper tired. Not sleepy or nothing, just tired,' I continued, watching them hang on to every word. 'Recently, I've been seeing things when I have a crisis – creepy, shadowy things . . . Actually, I don't think it's sickle cell related any more, but I mainly see it when the crisis starts—' I started to say, before I caught myself. I wanted to open up more, but Mama Oti's warning before I started this crazy journey rang in my head: *keep this power secret.*

'You really are a tough somebody,' Osoosi said, finally.

'Huh?' I blurted out, proper confused.

'She means that you are strong to be dealing with this thing on your own,' Moremi explained simply. 'She is not wrong-oh. I hope you are knowing that, Koku.'

I turned away, blinking really fast. I hoped that once this was all over, my new friends would understand why I had no choice but to choose myself over saving night.

The sky was totally dark but the Jujuland moon was full and round. It looked close, almost like you could reach up and touch it. I stared at it through the vines that Moremi had hung over the hut to keep the bugs out. I kept twisting and turning because of the constant sounds, and, worst of all, the ache of an oncoming crisis.

Since I had just taken my meds, it wouldn't get too bad. But at that moment a sharp pain shot into my eyes, making me lightheaded. My hands felt all tingly. I gripped the earth beneath me. Hideous transparent shapes rose out of the ground I'd just touched, staring at me with no eyes. Their broken voices called out to me.

I looked around desperately for a distraction.

Osoosi was snoring next to me with her tongue hanging out.

I felt bad when I nudged her awake. 'Oi, Osoosi!' When she didn't move, I whispered it into her good ear.

'Have the Ògún arrived? I go show them today what a daughter of Aganjù can do!' Osoosi said groggily, crouching into a fighting pose, the two braids at the front of her hair sticking up in opposite directions.

I shook my head. 'Nah, I can't sleep. I was

wondering if you could tell me more about Jujuland stuff,' I said, picking a topic that would keep her chatting for ages.

Osoosi let out a relieved sigh and nodded eagerly.

For some reason, Osoosi had a family-related tale for every single Jujuland spirit. 'Did you know my dad's second husband was possessed by an Àbíkú as a young boy?' Osoosi said with a wide grin.

'You're so unserious bro.' I shifted closer to her so I could say the words directly in her good ear. I knew she'd struggle to lip-read in the dark.

'Oho, so they did not tell you what an Àbíkú is in your Eng-ee-land?'

I shook my head even though I *did* know, cause my ribs were aching pretty badly and it was easier to just let Osoosi drone on. 'If foolish children go into the night and enter Jujuland, then the Àbíkú go come and steal their souls from inside their body! The spirit go chop their brains and thief their body.' Osoosi looked at me. 'When they return they go fool everybody because they look the same but inside they are the evil spirit. They make big *wahala* for the child's family. Their favourite meal go be parents' tears. They drink this like palm wine! And—'

'You better reset your brain and let us catch small

sleep,' Moremi interrupted; she was turned so her back was facing us. Even though her back was turned, I could *feel* Moremi rolling her eyes.

'So . . .' I encouraged Osoosi once Moremi fell back asleep, lowering my voice but still speaking loudly enough so Osoosi could hear me. 'Tell me about the other monsters then.'

'The man-eating monster Àgbákò was once a man, called Osanyin Ashagidibi. Na him be the father of my father's grandfather!' Osoosi explained.

This had to be the most ridiculous one yet, but the distraction was working.

'Your great-great grandfather *ate* people?' I asked.

'Yes-oh!' Osoosi clapped delightedly. 'You see my big grandfather was one of the strongest and most respected warriors in Aganjù. He was the only one to control the Aganjù talisman.'

'The-what-now?'

'The god of our tribe is Aganjù, the ruler of the wilderness,' Osoosi explained. 'When earth was created, Aganjù used the divine talisman to create animals. That is why the person who wears the talisman gets the power to control all animals.'

'Woah,' I said, cause I'm not gonna lie – that power sounded sick.

'*Ehen*, so you see my big grandfather was a talisman wearer; he was even the first of Aganjù to join the highest chiefs of Olori,' Osoosi boasted. 'My big grandfather teach the Ògún king to respect nature, and explain the importance of all animals, including the leopard, which is our god's favourite animal.'

I shuffled about to get comfy, while Osoosi kept going.

'When my big grandfather was chief, the king decorated the Ògún palace using the leopard to celebrate their friendship.'

Now all the leopard symbols I saw around Olori, from the airport to the Ògún palace, started to make sense.

Osoosi sighed. 'No one is knowing what devilish thing enter my big grandfather's head. Him get power and plenty money, so he should be happy, but instead him get greedy. The legend say him use *juju* magic with the Aganjù talisman and lost control and died. Then his ghost became twenty animals in one. They call him Àgbákò. Now he go be part elephant, part scorpion and part snake with sixteen terrible eyes.'

My knees knocked against each other crazily whenever the monster was mentioned.

'Àgbákò eat many people and almost destroyed Olori until the Ògún king ordered his army to exile him to Jujuland.'

'Jujuland!' I exclaimed, my eyes darting around our makeshift shelter. 'So this mad ting could find us at any moment?'

'If you don't close your mouth, yam head . . .' Moremi warned, turning around to look at me, her eyes half open and droopy braids flopping over her small, pointed ears.

'Àgbákò is why the Ògún say the Aganjù tribe are not to be trusted. They go say we are all animals in human skin,' Osoosi continued.

'Yeah, that's peak,' I said, once Osoosi's Ted Talk was over. 'But that's ancient history, man! It only matters if that thing finds us in Jujuland, and we're obviously gonna stay out of its way, right?' I said.

Osoosi looked at me, her hazel eyes brightened by the moonlight coming through gaps in the shelter. 'It is only right that Osanyin Ashagidibi's great-great-great granddaughter fixes his mistake. That monster is still wearing Aganjù's talisman around its neck. I go defeat the monster Àgbákò, and bring dignity to Aganjù when I return the talisman. That is one of the reasons I am in this jungle,' Osoosi said.

A tiny flutter danced over my ribcage – maybe I wasn't the only one in Jujuland for selfish reasons.

'I swear your dad said you were supposed to return night to Olori—?' I said.

'One day I go be the chief of Aganjù. My father has grown soft in his old age. He has taken the Ògún insults for too long. And my brother Sebe does not want Aganjù to make *wahala* with Ògún because they are the rulers of Olori. But I believe we should not let the Ògún disgrace us! Koku, you saw with your own two eyes how they dishonoured my people in Aganjù before we escaped here!' Osoosi said. I winced as she punched the ground next to her. 'When I control the talisman, Aganjù will become a powerful nation once again and the Ògún will have to respect us!'

Osoosi nodded when she spoke, like what she was saying was super important.

Then her voice calmed down to a whisper. 'You see, Koku, if we do not protect our own, no one else will. That is the meaning of tribe.'

I tried to deep it. But when I thought of the Olókun tribe, I couldn't think of anything except abandoned blue buildings.

'Taking the Aganjù talisman back and defeating Àgbákò go be my dream!' Osoosi said.

'Personally, I don't think trying to kill a twelve-foot man-beast was exactly what Martin Luther King Jr had in mind when he talked about dreams and all that,' I said, raising my eyebrow.

Moremi snickered but didn't turn over.

'Yes-oh! If him rips my arms, I carry my legs to finish him. If he scatter my legs I go use my teeth to chop him and chew him!' Osoosi exclaimed, jumping up and kicking her leg in the air.

'I thought you were a vegetarian?' I said.

Osoosi raised her own eyebrow at me. 'I am saying Àgbákò can try me anyhow, he can even fry me like plantain, but I no go give up.'

Osoosi had a messed-up way of putting things, but I respected her confidence.

'Ah-ah, Osoosi, it is enough! Stop this senseless talk now.' Moremi's eyes pierced into ours without warning. 'That is not what you promised your father, Osoosi! We are here to protect Koku and locate the Night Stone, not provide meat for that monster's soup. Now, both of you better stop this talk before I make war with you!' Moremi's braids hovered over us.

Osoosi held her hands up in surrender.

'Alright, calm down, man,' I said.

'Tomorrow, we go find the Araba. Now we catch

147

small sleep.' Moremi's eyes twinkled menacingly as she lowered her braids back down to her shoulders.

Osoosi didn't need any more encouragement – she was fast asleep in seconds, curled up in a little ball with half a braid in her mouth. When she released an obnoxiously loud snore, Moremi caught my eye and we laughed.

I lay down on the soft moss Moremi had gathered. Jujuland was so *noisy*. There were hooting owl noises, chirping crickets, and a whiny bug that sounded like chair-legs-on-a-floor screeching. It was getting louder and louder. I wasn't cut out for this jungle stuff. I rummaged around for my mum's photo and hid it under my makeshift leaf pillow. Bubbling laughter sounds burst inside my eardrums as my head hovered over the photo; my eyelids felt warm and heavy as soon as I heard my mum's laughter.

'O *daaro*, Koku,' Moremi blurted out softly as I was about to drift to sleep. I just nodded and, when she was asleep, I whispered, 'Good night to you too,' to the sharp edges of her back.

CHAPTER ELEVEN

Mami Wata Lagoon

'Rise up!' Moremi yelled, dismantling the canopy of vines above us.

'*E kaaaro*!' Osoosi said 'good morning' with a toothy grin, though the night spread as far as we could see.

'The Ògún are on their way and we only have five days until they destroy night for ever.' Moremi said, kicking our mossy mattresses about so we couldn't sleep no more.

Once I was up, I tucked my precious photo into my backpack. Enough time had passed for it to be morning, but the pitch-black sky was still as dark as ever. I squinted first, then my eyes relaxed when

149

I got used to the neon animals that skittered about, lighting up the darkness like fairy lights.

Osoosi pulled me to one side. '*Ehen*, this thing I want tell you now is a secret-oh. Don't tell Moremi about this, *abeg*!' she pleaded, sneaking glances at Moremi to make sure she wasn't listening.

'We're good, fam,' I said. Moremi was stomping out the last bits of smoke from our fire to make it harder for the iron warriors to track us.

'You see, I go help you find the Night Stone. But you must do something for me also,' Osoosi said.

'Ayy, what is it?' I asked, hoping it was a normal request like making a banging Spotify playlist.

'You see, Moremi will not let me search for Àgbákò. But that beast still wears the talisman around his neck. I need you to distract *oga*-boss while I destroy Àgbákò and return the talisman to my people.' Osoosi's words came out so fast I had to lip-read, like we'd switched places.

'Without the talisman to protect us we will always be beaten by the Ògún warriors,' Osoosi continued. 'You saw with your own two eyes how they defeated us back in my compound!' She paused, took a deep breath, and then: 'Koku?' Osoosi asked, her voice wobbling on the 'oou' part of my name.

I flinched, haunted by the memory. 'I saw an injured wolf that might have been—' I started to say.

Osoosi put her hands on my shoulders. 'I cannot allow the Ògún to harm my people anyhow. Koku, will you help me?' she asked. Her eyes watered up and got so big I saw she had the same eyes as her father, the chief of Aganjù.

'Sure,' I said. 'But I'll only help once you find the Araba. He's gonna help with the night stuff, you get me?' I made sure to enunciate my words cause I mumble a lot, according to my teachers. 'Then I'll help distract Moremi while you fight that monster, I swear down,' I promised.

At least that part wasn't a lie: once I was healed, distracting Moremi while Osoosi fought some monster wouldn't be a big deal.

I held out my pinky finger to her. 'It's like the Olori promise sign, but more hygienic cause you ain't gotta lick your fingers or nothing. It's what we do in England when you're making a promise.' I demonstrated, linking my pinky fingers together. I held my finger out to her again and she linked her sweaty finger in mine and squeezed way too tight, like she was tryna wrestle or something.

'Can you stop that rubbish and pay attention?'

Moremi fiercely whispered at us, from over her shoulder.

Osoosi and I stopped immediately. It must've looked moist.

'I can explain . . .' I stuttered, my cheeks burning up.

Moremi held up a braid to my lips. 'Do you hear that, Koku?' She crouched down, squinting into the dark, while her braids spread out like giant feelers.

'What noise *be* that?' Osoosi asked, as she turned around in circles trying to place her good ear towards the sound.

I listened. I could hear something now. 'That high-pitched whine . . . like a mosquito, but worse than a regular one . . . the mosquito-bot we saw at the festival!' I gasped at the realisation. 'The Ògún are already here!'

Moremi's forehead creased.

I let out a slow breath and tuned into my surroundings. Things moved in and out of visibility, you could only see if something was directly under a moonbeam or if a neon animal happened to be nearby, like passing shadows. I'm good at paying attention to details like that: it's the only thing that helps me stay grounded during a crisis.

I traced the noise to a small blinking dot in the dark

hovering just above a clump of glowing leaves in a nearby bush. 'There!' I pointed.

Moremi's braids knotted together, forming a massive insect swatter. *Whoosh!* Her braids swung down with a gust of wind. The metal dot fell to the ground with a soft *kerplunk*.

The contraption was mashup once Moremi was done with it. We crowded around it. Its cracked wings buzzed violently. It had long needle pincers that would do some damage if they ever got near you, spidery legs, a streamlined body and a slim set of glass wings. It had a small sack underneath that looked like it was filled with a black shining liquid. Staring at it made my stomach turn.

'I no understand this one, *oga*-boss,' Osoosi said.

'The Ògún are not far behind us,' Moremi declared, her thin brows knotting together. 'The mosquitos are connected to the iron suits, so the Ògún warriors cannot be too far away.' When she looked at Osoosi's confused face, she huffed a little. 'It go be like wireless headphones connected to your phone,' Moremi explained. Osoosi nodded. I got what she was talking about – it reminded me that Uncle Tunji hadn't got me the AirPods on my online wish list.

Moremi dug into my backpack and chucked the leopard amulet at Osoosi. 'Use your nose to find the Araba quick-quick, Osoosi!'

Osoosi caught the amulet and gave it a deep whiff, then stuck her nose in the air, sniffing like a dog. She then pinched a bit of dirt, threw it in the air, and pointed. 'Make we go this way and find the Araba, no *wahala*.'

'That is good-oh.' Moremi's almond eyes narrowed. 'The fate of Olori is depending on it. Gods help us all.'

I grinned in spite of Moremi's emotionally constipated pep talk and the iron mandem chasing after us. Today we were going to find the healing priest guy. That meant no more sickle cell. I was gonna be normal.

All I had to do was survive until then.

My ear vibrated with the low humming of dragonflies as Osoosi brought us to a lagoon. The moonlight was the brightest here and the water was so clear you could see all the way down to the bottom where giant, people-sized snakes coiled around jagged rocks, their dazzling rainbow scales glittering.

Abandoned boats were piled up around the edge of the shore. Some of them had flags attached to them; I clocked Portuguese, Spanish, French . . . But before I could get a closer look, Moremi yanked us both down with a braided grip.

'I no fit die for nothing,' Moremi said, aiming her braided fist towards Osoosi. 'Osoosi, why you go bring us here? The Mami Wata are waiting to drown any person that enters their sacred place!'

'Mami Wata are here?' I gulped. I remembered all that stuff the chief was saying in the festival – how their favourite hobby was drowning people. I couldn't even swim.

'The Araba's smell go lead me to this place,' Osoosi explained. 'God of Aganjù strike me down if I dey lie to you!' She pointed to the near distance, where a thin moonbeam shone on a lone hut on a small bed of tangerine sand surrounded by water. 'That must be where the Araba lives!'

'And how do we enter this place, eh?' Moremi whispered, her eyes narrowed, but her braids fell flat against her shoulders again. 'You think Mami Wata will let us pass?'

'She has a point,' I agreed. 'The Araba's yard is on

an island. And I can't swim, not with my condition. I don't have the energy, and the cold water can trigger a crisis.'

Osoosi nodded, then dragged us over to some reeds. My feet sank into the mulchy wet soil as we hid behind them. Just then a dozen Mami Wata emerged from the water, slithering over the rocks with a dancing rhythm. Their glittering scales turned luminous as they bathed in the bright moonlight, and when they unhinged their large mouths, pearly fangs and black forked tongues stretched out as long as Moremi's braids.

My heart was beating so fast I tasted metal at the back of my throat. 'What if we distracted them somehow and got to those boats. Do you think we'd make it across?' I whispered, expecting the eyeroll that went with anything I suggested.

'I see you have small sense,' Moremi nodded. 'Your forehead is not big for nothing-oh.'

'*O dun*! This plan is very sweet-oh,' Osoosi grinned.

'Obviously I already patterned the ting,' I said, smugly.

'But who go provide distraction for us?' Osoosi asked.

Moremi and I looked at each other, and then back at Osoosi. She was done out here. 'If you can shapeshift into any creature using your magic, simply transform into a snake and distract them,' Moremi explained. 'Then we will collect one of the boats. Wait for us to call for you before you make it over to the boat. You hear?'

'Eh . . . there is one thing—' Osoosi nibbled on the end of her braid.

'The matter is settled!' Moremi said firmly.

'I am only a beginner of this Aganjù magic thing, I can only . . .'

'There is no need for talk-talk,' Moremi interrupted. 'You turn into a snake that looks like a Mami Wata and tell them you see plenty people from overseas coming into the lagoon so they go to find them.'

I was transfixed watching Osoosi. 'How does it feel when you're using magic?' I asked, as she drew a triangular pattern in the earth. The shape was the symbol of a palm leaf made out of two opposite triangles crossed over each other.

Osoosi paused and stared up at me with wide eyes. I noticed her pupils were three times the size they were before we got to Jujuland, like they'd adjusted to the constant dark. I asked again slowly so she could lip-read.

'When I connect to my Aganjù power I hear his voice calling my name. Then I smell fresh earth.' Osoosi's eyes went all dreamy. 'I get excited like I finish running my race but I can still do more and more. My heart is beating fast and my belly dey hot! I feel the moment the caterpillar is changing and when a bird is taking its first flight. When I open my eye again after I draw this symbol, everything I see is covered in orange light and then I transform.'

I nodded. 'That sounds pretty cool.'

It was hard not to feel a tiny bit jealous. I had powers I never wanted. I couldn't even talk about it with my friends cause Mama Oti said everyone would hate me. I kept seeing dark shadows that looked like broken fingers and, worst of all, that giant creature that came out of the doll in the museum.

What even was *that?*

My power was kind of like my sickle cell: it was awful, and there was no way of controlling it.

I tried to focus on Osoosi's transformation instead. The orange flashing ring had appeared around her eyes and patterns were crawling up her arms. She squirmed around on the ground as her powers activated. As she writhed in the dirt, a few colourful rainbow scales started to appear like polka dots on her legs. The scales spread quickly until she was totally covered.

We kept ourselves hidden behind the reeds as Osoosi finished transforming into a snake. Then she slithered towards the Mami Wata lagoon.

The Mami Wata were daintily dipping the ends of their tails in the pool, bathing themselves with perfect arcs of water. Osoosi tried to do the same and ended up spluttering all over the place. We could hear laughter and light splashing noises as the other snakes danced around her.

Osoosi pointed the end of her tail at the opposite side of the coast and hissed. The Mami Wata bent their sinuous necks and followed her lead, then slithered out towards the lagoon.

Moremi gave me the sign, and we crept along to the boats, keeping low in case the mosquito-bots were still around, even if the Mami Wata weren't.

Then Osoosi's afro puffs started poofing out of her scaly skin, and her snake tail shrank and disappeared into her body. Hissing in outrage the Mami Wata stood up on their tails and encircled her.

Their tails shimmered and slowly shifted into long, glittery dresses.

'*Yepa*, I am finished-oh!' Osoosi screamed as she changed back into her human form again.

Long, lean arms with manicured razor-sharp nails appeared out of the Mami Wata's scales. Their scales dissolved into soft shiny skin. Their terrifying snake faces transformed into human faces with glossy smirking lips and wet, coiled hair.

'Help me! *E gba mi o!*' Osoosi pleaded, shouting in our direction as the Mami Wata dragged her away.

So that's what that e gba mi *word I keep hearing when I'm seeing things means*, I thought randomly, ducking even lower in the reeds as one of the Mami Wata suddenly pulled a golden comb from their coils and threw it in our direction.

It landed right in Moremi's neck, its vicious prongs sticking in hard.

Her eyes fluttered closed, and she fell to the ground.

The Mami Wata squad stalked towards Moremi's totally still body. I crouched right down so the reeds would hide me from sight.

I needed time to figure out how to rescue Osoosi and Moremi.

I heard them moving away again, and waited a little. When I next looked up, a Mami Wata was hovering over me, twirling a three-toothed comb between her fingertips. She had loose wet curls framing her face and peacock feathers wrapped around her torso. The really crazy part was her lower half – it was all snake. I wish I was lying.

She hummed a really nice tune as she stuck the comb into the side of my neck. It made my eyelids super heavy. I tried hard to keep them open, but I couldn't stop it: I felt warm and cosy, my muscles relaxed and honey filled the air. Then everything went black.

I woke shivering. The tide lapped at my feet on the edge of the shore. My bones ached from the cold. I knew that if I didn't get up soon, a crisis would send waves of pain crashing through me, but my body felt like a dead weight.

I could only move my eyes. At first it didn't feel like

I'd woken up cause all I saw was the pitch-black Jujuland sky. Then my eyes adjusted to my surroundings. If I hadn't been trapped, it was a decent view: the moonlight rained on glossy pebbles so shiny they were like mirrors scattered across the deep orange sand of the shore, and the crystal blue water that rippled over our bodies was so clear I peeped starfish floating around us.

I looked around, and I saw Osoosi and Moremi lying on either side of me. The Mami Wata had really done a number on us.

'What . . . happened?' I asked, in a cracked voice. I looked over at Moremi. 'Can't you use your braids to get us out of here?'

Moremi rolled her eyes. 'This *mumu* has allowed the Mami Wata to capture us. They put a spell that make us no fit to move again.'

'*Oga*-boss! I cannot move my leg! *Yepa!*' Osoosi squirmed, her eyes darting frantically from side to side.

'We wouldn't even be in this mess if it wasn't for you,' I hissed. My head was already aching. I felt a crisis coming on.

'*Ehh?* Wetin I go do? It has only been one moon since I have been using the Aganjù power. I am trying to tell you true talk but you no go listen.' Osoosi said, defensively.

'You are supposed to transform for longer and instead you are doing rubbish. How can great chief Inaki born someone like you?' Moremi seethed.

'Rah, that's a bit harsh,' I said.

'They go drown us because of her foolishness,' Moremi retorted.

'Hold on a second, *drown* us?' My heart started a beatboxing match with my ribcage.

'No go blame me, *oga*-boss!' Osoosi said. 'You no listen! I try tell you I am not knowing how to hold my animal form for long.'

Our bickering was interrupted by Mami Wata voices raised in harmony.

Guardian of di dead,
mi worship yuh as lang as there wata inna di sea.
Keeper of di Crossroads,
mi gi respect tuh di immortal one dat neva ages.

The voices didn't sound like no Olori person I'd ever heard. They made me feel warm, even though I was cold and wet. The more they sang, the more the tide lapped at my feet, but I was smiling so hard it hurt. I turned to look at Osoosi and Moremi and they were smiling too.

Was this a magic spell?

The Mami Wata stood in a circle formation, their eyes rolled back to the whites. Then one of them broke formation, revealing the beautiful snake woman I saw before I passed out.

She was sitting on a throne of cowrie shells, fireflies all around her. When she stood up, the other Mami Wata bent low to the ground.

'Yemaya, di humans awake,' one of the Mami Wata said.

Yemaya winked at us with lilac eyes. 'Yuh may start di ting. Let di ocean tek dem, ocean drown dem.' She had a syrupy voice, like a jazz singer.

The cold waves left me breathless. The pain in my temples meant the crisis was coming soon and there would be no way to stop it.

'We mean you no harm. Don't drown us, *abeg*!' Moremi pleaded. As our limbs were still under the Mami Wata's magic, I mentally crossed my fingers that Moremi's plea would work. 'We are on an important mission to find the Araba—'

'Save yuh begging fi Lègbá, di guardian of di crossroads, who knows all di unknown tings,' Yemaya interrupted.

For some reason, I jerked internally when I heard that Lègbá name. I wasn't the only one.

Osoosi gasped, swallowing a whole bunch of water. The tide was coming in fast. '*Yepa!* We are finished-oh!' she yelped, spluttering and wheezing as the water went into her nose. 'I rebuke any evil from the demon of the dead!' she managed to choke out, in between coughs.

'Lègbá is wi protector!' Yemaya clapped her hands defensively. 'Humans always harm. Humans cyaan be trust,' she added with a full lipped smile as black ink swallowed up her misty lilac eyes.

Then she started to sing.

As the spell left her lips, a bright moon mark appeared on her forehead.

By now, the water was lapping my chin, and every breath I took meant swallowing water till my lungs were drowned.

'Yuh finished yuhself,' Yemaya said, calmly.

'We didn't even do nothing! Just let us go!' I gurgled.

'Mi kno dat voice.' Yemaya frowned, tapping her luminous tail against the shell throne. 'It ave been lang since a *oyinbo* come pon mi shore. Yuh outsider people dem ave dun plenty. Yih nuh satisfied wid wah yuh given, so yuh tek what not fi yuh an tun it tuh filth.'

'I ain't no *oyinbo*!' I coughed as my mouth filled up with salt water.

'*Oyinbo* in na Olori skin. A beast of no nation. A pitiful ting.'

I tried to argue but I had to focus on holding my breath. I was almost submerged. I couldn't even hear Osoosi yelling no more.

'Osoosi!' Moremi yelled. She screamed until her voice was hoarse, but it was too late – Osoosi had already gone under, and I knew I was next.

Moremi's lanky neck was giving her more time than the rest of us – the water had only risen up to her shoulders. Osoosi's afro puffs poked out of the water. Her face rippled beneath the clear water, her mouth stretched in a scream no one could hear.

It was mad cause I always thought my death would be sickle cell related. I watched as Osoosi's tight fist loosened as she lost consciousness and her fingers spread, letting go of something metallic that flashed beneath the water's surface. I took in a last gulp of air as the water rushed over my head.

CHAPTER TWELVE

Beast of No Nation

The water filled with ghostly, bony forms wearing loose khaki shirts and cargo shorts. One reached out towards me. Clammy fingers slid in between my palms whispering '*E gba mi o*' at me.

I finally knew what it meant cause Osoosi had yelled it earlier.

It was a cry for help.

Then the crisp sound of metal hitting ground cut through the water. The phantoms disappeared instantly, releasing only a low raspy moan.

The spell must've broken, cause I could move again. As soon as I could feel my toes, I kicked my legs like crazy.

Muggy air burned in my throat as my head broke the surface, and my eyes popped open, blinking out salt water. I pulled myself up to the rocky shoreline. I was half-drowned, the dull ache of a sickle-cell migraine that was near the end of the crisis irritated my eardrums, but I was alive.

Moremi panted as she pulled Osoosi out of the water. I helped her lay out Osoosi over the rocks. Osoosi had finally shut up, but it didn't feel right at all.

I counted the seconds.

One.

Moremi thumped her braids against Osoosi's chest, trying to pump the water out.

Two.

Moremi shook her by the shoulders.

Three.

I peeled Osoosi's eyelids back and saw blank eyes staring up at me.

Four.

Moremi and I pressed our ears to her chest.

Five.

We could hear a small, steady heartbeat.

'*Baga!*' Osoosi spluttered out seaweedy water on Moremi's face. I waited for the savagery, but Moremi wiped it off with a smile. '*Oga*-boss! Koku! You see that a daughter of Aganjù cannot die like this-oh,' Osoosi gasped.

Suddenly, a tall figure loomed over us with misty lilac eyes. 'Mi stop di spell when I look pon dis ting. Dis amulet belongs tuh di Araba. How yuh know im?' Yemaya interrupted our reunion, twirling the amulet in one hand. The dark drained out of her eyes and the misty lilac colour returned.

'Check the photo. It is in the backpack. See for yourself,' Moremi said, as her braids twisted around themselves, wringing the water out.

My jaw dropped to my chest. How did she know more about my photo than I did? Suddenly, the mystery of the random guy in the photo made sense. My mum was laughing in it with the Araba?

The Mami Wata stared at us with shining eyes. Yemaya ordered one of them to bring my backpack to her. She rummaged around in it with her pointy red nails and eyed my medicine suspiciously, before pulling out the photo.

'An who dis?' Yemaya asked, tapping my photo.

'My mother,' I said, getting to my feet.

'An Olókun sista born ya?'

'Yeah, I swear down.'

'Yuh nah kno descendants of Olókun and friends

of di Araba always welcome pon mi shore?' Yemaya laughed, like trying to kill us a few moments ago was just jokes. She slithered up to me and stroked my chin. 'But yuh blood fi mixed wid sumpin strange.'

'This boy is the one the Oracle has chosen to return night to Olori!' Osoosi blurted out.

'It's true,' Moremi said. 'This boy is the last surviving member of the Olókun tribe, and the Night Stone is his birthright. But the Ògún are in Jujuland trying to thief and destroy the stone. If they find it, night will be gone at the end of the summer solstice and all of you spirits will die.'

Yemaya's lilac eyes had turned to black as soon as the Ògún were mentioned. The Mami Wata held each other's hands tight, shaking like they were the ones that'd just been nearly drowned.

'We only get five days to find it,' Moremi said. 'If they find it before us there go be no such thing as night again. Your own people are in danger. We need to take this boy to the Araba to protect night.'

'Honoured chile of Olókun,' Yemaya said, stepping forward. 'Wi duh anyting wi cyaan tuh help yuh pon yuh journey.'

I wish we'd just started like that in the first place, cause the whole drowning thing was long.

The Mami Wata turned one of the old, abandoned boats the right way up. I noticed the boat we were given had a British flag.

We climbed in and the Mami Wata pushed the boat out into the shallow water, where it just about floated.

'Di Night Stone di source of fi wi powa, and it's not just di Ògún searching for it. Many explorers from all ova di world ave try tuh find it. Wi only protect di Araba who is keeping it safe. And wi drown any outsider who comes pon wi shore because wi cyaan trust that they won't steal from us, kill us – or use wi energy for dem wicked *juju* ways.' Yemaya explained. 'Yuh an exception, of course.' She gave me a mischievous wink, then clapped her hands. 'Get these pickneys a likkle sumpin fi eat!' Yemaya ordered.

The Mami Wata disappeared under the water and rose to the surface to pile our boat with seaweed dumplings. A spicy aroma filled the air.

Osoosi wolfed hers down immediately, while Moremi and I waited to see if anything dodgy would happen to her first.

'No poison inna dis one, *pikin*,' Yemaya reassured us, running her golden comb through her coils.

Once I started eating, the Mami Wata fussed over me, rubbing cocoa butter into my skin and rebraiding my twists with coconut oil. My hair shrinks when it's wet, so my horns ended up shorter than usual, but I didn't mind. I felt way more like myself now that my signature look was back and we had less enemies than we had thought.

The Mami Wata kept calling me 'Honoured *Omo* Olókun' and reminding me how important I was supposed to be. Moremi rolled her eyes every time they did that. Even I found it kinda jarring. I didn't know nothing about honour, I wasn't someone special, just a sick kid.

The VIP treatment was nice, but I couldn't properly relax, which was hella peak cause I had sweet ones giving man back rubs and that.

Just then, I heard a high-pitched whining noise. At the same time, Yemaya's eyes bled to black. My heart pounded – it was another mosquito-bot.

'The Ògún are here!' Yemaya hissed. 'Ocean tek dem!' she commanded, as a giant wave roared under our boat. We held on for dear life as her spell sent us spiralling out to sea. 'Don't worry, pickneys. Wi can protect ourselves,' Yemaya called out after us as a forked tongue whipped out of her mouth. 'Make sure yuh find di Araba n save night!' Yemaya screamed, as a swarm of silver hovered over the lagoon.

I watched as the high-pitched robot whining got louder and an army of silver dots merged into an angry cloud. But the combs that were thrown towards the mosquitos fell to the ground instantly, like they'd been chewed up. Soon the Mami Wata started clutching their necks and falling one by one.

'*Yepa!* The mosquito *wahala* will finish the Mami Wata-oh. *Oga*-boss, turn the boat back!' Osoosi yelled.

'Are you normal?' Moremi shouted back. 'We are minutes away from the Araba; we cannot enter this problem on. Use your big-for-nothing head – we are too far away, my braids cannot reach them. And the Mami Wata are stronger than our own power, don't worry for them.'

'But they go help us find the Araba!' Osoosi protested.

Moremi kissed her teeth at her and turned to me for backup. I didn't say nothing, but I nodded in agreement.

'Even Koku has small sense!' Moremi said, poking a finger into Osoosi's forehead.

It was peak, but Moremi was right. The Mami Wata had drowning powers and snake abilities. My sickle cell made me the weakest out of everyone. But a strange energy boiled inside me as the boat ebbed towards the Araba's little island. It didn't feel like a crisis, so man high-key thought it was the seaweed dumplings, until my palms tingled and I suddenly felt wide awake and hyper aware of everything around me: the salty breeze that licked my cheeks, the dark Jujuland sky lit by stars so bright it felt like the whites of a thousand eyes were staring down on me.

I felt the same way I felt at the festival as I raised my hands towards the Mami Wata's lagoon.

A ginormous, decaying, zombielike arm shot out of my palm and reached the Mami Wata. I made a few swatting motions and it shot up into the dark sky and decked the mosquito-bots. Silver dots rained out of the sky and the Mami Wata cheered as they crash-landed.

The ghost arm dissolved into the dark sky like it knew its work was done. I slumped on to the deck and breathed out shakily.

'*Chai! Oga*-boss, you were very right-oh! They go beat the mosquitos using their own power! Koku, did you see that?' Osoosi nudged me with her elbow.

'Mhmm. Yeah, I saw it.' I nodded, staring down at my tingling palms. *What was that?* It was like when I rescued the trapped Àbíkú during the festival. But I didn't feel ill or nothing like I normally did when the ghosts appeared. It was making me think my power wasn't connected to the illness at all. It had to be something else.

I decided to move into the lower deck of the boat to collect my thoughts. Going carefully down the steps into the pitch-black interior, I almost choked to death on the smell of rotting wood. It was super dark. I pulled the Nokia phone out of my backpack so I could use its torchlight.

The light revealed a table covered with fallen-apart books. There was no manga or nothing, just bloated copies of old-timey adventure books – *Treasure Island* and *Robinson Crusoe*.

I was curious about the people who'd sat on this boat, ever since I clocked the British flag. Fuzzy cobwebs coated my fingertips as I walked around. I found a rusty telescope, a brown leather jacket and a fedora hat.

I picked up the hat to see if it would go over my twists, but as soon as I touched it I heard whispering.

'These people talk of hundreds of demons and twice as many gods. I can hardly keep up with the names. A load of rubbish, obviously.'

'Well, Monsieur, the Olori are a superstitious bunch. They've hidden that priceless dark jewel – what is it they call it? The Night Stone? – for centuries, claiming that . . . hold on, what's that racket?'

'It sounds like . . . singing.'

'Why are you smiling like that, Vic?'

'Something strange has come over me.'

'Well, it's not funny at all.'

'The water's rising! Sacré Bleu! Good Lord – look out . . .'

The boat shuddered to a final halt. I dropped the hat and the voices stopped. My neck was wet with cold sweat. The awful realisation dawned on me – there was no way the men I'd heard had made it out of this place alive.

Bile rose in my throat. This was a mad ting. First I had zombie arms shooting out of my body, and now I was hearing dead people when I touched their stuff. It had started with my mum's singing and now I heard some random dead man's conversation after touching some mouldy hat. Ever since I got to Olori, I had been unable to control myself. *Is this the power that's supposed to help me save night?*

'Yam head! We have arrived.' Moremi's announcement interrupted my muddled thoughts.

'Yeah, alright, I'm coming!' I yelled back, steadying my breath, and pushing all the insane stuff to the back of my mind.

CHAPTER THIRTEEN

The Araba

When I got back to the top deck, Moremi had found a rusty anchor attached to a rope and was swinging it overboard so our boat was docked.

The Araba's hut was right in front of us, surrounded by an orange cloud of luminous fireflies. It was a prism shape made out of pale strips of wood that were all perfectly slotted together, like puzzle pieces. The hut was the only thing on the tiny island. I wondered how the Araba managed to live all by himself – where did he get his food from?

Moremi found a ladder on the boat and threw it down. Then she and Osoosi climbed down and waded through the water.

I followed them, clenching my teeth, expecting the water to trigger a crisis, but it wasn't too bad and we were so close to land I was only submerged up to my knees.

My Nike Airs sank deep into a brownish-red earth as I stepped on to the island. I had a massive knot in my stomach, but I acted like it was calm. This was it. The moment I'd been waiting for my whole life for. The chance to never have sickle cell again.

All I had to do was convince this priest guy. *No long ting.*

Moremi led us all the way up the beach and to the hut. Once we were there we saw it didn't have no door or nothing. We knocked on different sides of the prism, but no one came out.

Moremi spread her long fingers over the wood and turned to Osoosi. 'You better be sure this is the place-oh. We no get time to waste!' she warned.

Osoosi nodded, her damp afro puffs dancing as she spoke. 'The Araba's scent go lead me to this place!' She insisted.

'Yeah, she ain't lying bro. The Mami Wata said the Araba was here too, remember?' I added.

Moremi kept pressing her fingers against the wooden panels until one of them shifted aside.

'*Baga!* Look! A secret opening!' Osoosi said, taking the first step inside.

Moremi and I followed after her. Once we were through, the panel slid back into place. I looked up: thin slats of wood were hanging down like stalactites. The thin gaps between the slats allowed moonlight to rain down in threads of light.

I was still admiring the pixels of light dancing on my skin when a gruff voice called out to us. 'Kehinde, *e kaab o*. And you are bringing . . . the girl with the nose . . . and the boy of two worlds.'

Moremi's eye twitched like someone had rubbed a scotch bonnet pepper in it or something. *That Kehinde name is clearly a big deal.* I could tell she really wanted to bust him right there and then, but she bowed her head and said, '*E kuule o*, Baba.'

My photo had been brought to life. And he was still just as mad looking. The Araba's head kinda looked like a hexagon and it was too big for his lanky body. He had white lines painted sloppily across his forehead and tribal marks carved into his cheeks. A fancy necklace with patterned white glassy beads hung from his neck.

It made me even more desperate to know exactly what he and my mum had been talking about when the photo was taken. Why *had* she looked so happy?

Maybe if I know the answer I will feel closer to her, I thought.

'*Ah-ah*. Nawa-oh! *Kehinde, have you truly arrived? Or are the gods deceiving me?*' He stared *over* Moremi instead of at her as he spoke – without moving his lips.

Moremi couldn't resist rolling her eyes. 'I don't know this Kehinde-oh. I am Moremi.' The Araba threw his head back and laughed. It was the first time his lips had parted; he had a gap tooth so wide you could have put a whole finger through it.

'*Chai!*' Osoosi yelled, interrupting. 'Priest of priests! Big-big *Oga*! I salute you!'

'*I am knowing this energy anywhere. Daughter of Aganjù, eh?*' the Araba remarked.

'You are very correct, sah! I go be Osoosi,' Osoosi said, bouncing on her toes.

'*Your name is a royal one, your father must be the chief. Inaki Ashagidibi is one of the greatest warriors this land has known. Help me greet your baba, you hear?*'

'Yes, sah.' Osoosi's grin wavered a bit at the mention of her father. I bet she was still worried about whether or not he was okay. She rummaged around in her pockets and pulled out the leopard amulet. 'We have returned what is yours.'

Osoosi placed the amulet in the Araba's palm.

'*So-so is that so?*' The Araba's milky white eyes filled with good humour. He rubbed the metal in his weathered hands. And suddenly the meaning of his actions became painfully obvious: he was totally blind.

When he had figured out what it was he let out a long, gravelly laugh. '*Thank you-oh. Mo dupe pupo.*' He carefully laid the amulet on a cushion next to him. Then he slowly turned in my direction.

'*Hnn!*' The Araba flapped his nostrils at me, his pupils disappeared from sight and his eyes seemed to glow brightly till they were toothpaste white. It made me kinda nervous. '*Now, tell me, Kokumo Akanbi, last of the Olókun, are you ready to disturb the universe?*' He laughed with his lips sealed shut, rolling his eyes wildly in his head like they were dice.

My ears rang painfully with the force of it.

'*You see, the* Ku *connects our destinies. You are Kokumo.*' He projected with shining white eyes. I tried not to squirm at my name being said aloud. '*I am Anikulapo. My own means "the one that holds death in their pocket"*'. He spoke like someone who knew the world's deepest secrets. '*Some say the "Ku" means die, but it is not so. It is a new beginning, a possibility to be born again.*'

My stomach twisted like I was on one of those loopy rollercoaster rides. *That's exactly what I want – a chance to start a new, healthy life without always worrying about my illness.*

'*I know we have plenty questions for each other*,' he said as his pupils slid back into his eyeballs. '*And answers that will decide the fate of Olori*,' he continued. '*But first you must all wash and chop small.*'

'*Ehen.* You are very right, *sah*!' Osoosi clapped at the mention of food, even though she had eaten loads of the Mami Wata's seaweed rolls.

'*Let me take you to wash, then you will all eat well-well!*' the Araba announced. He sauntered off into a corridor.

We followed, cause a shower was probably a good idea after all the stuff we got up to in the forest and the lagoon.

The hut was so much bigger on the inside – like an Underground station. I stared at the Araba's stuff as I walked. It reminded me of the museum: colourful rugs lined the floors; a matching pair of wooden figures decorated with tiny necklaces; voodoo dolls with pins in them; and shells, flowers, bones and giant teeth organised neatly with braille labels underneath.

I paused for a moment, letting the others go on without me. I was desperate to touch them all. I wondered what strange voices were trapped inside the objects . . .

'What do you think you are doing, yam head?' Moremi's eyes pierced into me without warning as I reached out to touch an orange pot with a bunch of dried-up leaves and tiny dolls sitting in it.

'*Ehh*, wetin you go do?' Osoosi piped up.

'Nothing! Allow it, man.' I shrugged.

'These things are what the Araba uses for his divine healing. That pot is older than your grandfather's father. If you touch, you go see double.' Moremi was still glaring at me.

'Whatever. Calm down, fam,' I said, forcing myself not to grin like a maniac. I was low-key gassed cause maybe the Araba would use some of that healing stuff to get rid of my condition.

'*To ba fe lo we, omi lo maa lo*,' the Araba sang out cheerfully, ahead of us. 'If you want to wash, na water you go use, eh?' He pointed at the bathrooms.

I took my sweet time. I still hadn't fully warmed up from almost drowning.

I stared down at my clothes. It was peak, cause my

Champion hoodie and my Nike Airs had been totally destroyed by the journey.

I set my backpack down in the corner and plugged in the Nokia phone so I could send my uncle a quick text while it charged. The Araba's bathroom set-up was pretty nice, I can't lie – a mini waterfall ran into a large stone bathtub. The water was just the right temperature, and there were lumps of black herbal-smelling soap so I could finally get rid of the Jujuland stink.

I sat in the tub, the warm water up to my chin. Looking down, I was able to stare at my reflection in the waters. The more I stared, the more my face started to change: I had smoky skin so see-through the white skull showed underneath. In the bony hollows, where my eyes had been, a yellow light slowly flickered. I shut my eyes tight. *I don't want whatever this is*, I thought, as ghostly voices once again whispered '*E gba mi oo*' over and over again.

When I opened my eyes, I looked normal again. I tried to distract myself by redoing my twists. But cause my hands kept shaking, my horns ended up more lopsided than usual.

I got out of the tub and examined the new clothes the Araba had brought for me. He had laid out a white *agbada* robe with some biblical-looking sandals. The robe was at least ten sizes too big for me, and it weighed about a hundred pounds. And you could tell the robe was expensive, not the cheap stuff Uncle Tunji wears to weddings: this was proper lace, feathery soft, with real gold lining the hems.

It made me wonder why the Araba wore those clapped *sokoto* trousers.

The robe had pockets so I could tuck my photo inside. I was planning to bring the photo out at dinner, when the time was right, and ask the Araba about my mum.

As I came out of the bathroom, Moremi was coming out of the room opposite. Her eyes widened when she saw my new outfit, and I'm sure I must've gawped when I noticed her new, white, billowing dress and matching white headwrap. She still had a strip of purple cloth tied over her arm, but it was the first time I had seen her without her hair in the way. The headwrap exposed her pixie ears and softened the edges of her face a little. It suited her.

There was a kind of awkward pause, and I said the first thing that came to my mind: 'The Araba's a proper weirdo, know what I mean?' I whispered. She lifted a single eyebrow at me. 'It's like he can get into your head. It's so creepy, man!' I said.

'He is the high priest of the god of wisdom so of course he has power over the mind,' Moremi revealed. 'Don't you remember the Rùnmí chiefs in white robes at the festival?'

I nodded – that explained the glowing white eyes thing. But the Araba didn't really fit in with the serious Rùnmí chiefs with their pristine white *agbada*s. This guy was so lanky all his clothes wore him instead of the other way around.

'The Araba is the greatest of the Rùnmí with this power,' Moremi deadpanned, but her eyes glittered at me. 'He go read your head like book.'

That meant the Araba already knew I didn't really care about saving night for Olori and the only reason I'd come to his place was to get cured by him. If Osoosi and Moremi caught on, there was no way they would still want to be mates.

'So, I'm basically doomed, yeah?' I said.

She nodded.

There was a short pause before I started laughing to stop the awkwardness, then Moremi joined in and then we both started laughing so hard our cheeks hurt. I crossed my fingers behind my back, hoping the Araba would keep my secret for a bit longer. We walked back to the main room, where the Araba and Osoosi were playing a game of *Ayo*. They were a happy pair of opposites: the chief projecting his low voice and Osoosi giggling loudly. She was wearing a matching dress to Moremi's and it almost drowned her, just like my robe swallowed me.

Moremi and I settled around the low table. *Ayo* is this dead board game my uncle forced me to play last Christmas, where you've got two rows of six holes each filled with four seeds. The aim is to place your one seed in the next hole while stealing someone else's from the previous one; the person with the highest number of seeds wins.

Osoosi was losing badly by the time we joined them, and the Araba was clearly enjoying it.

'*Don't you know I am a thousand hills? I cannot be moved.*' The Araba let out a rumbling chuckle and Osoosi let out a surprised '*Yepa!*' when she got merked for the fiftieth time.

'*Kehinde, So-so, Kokumo – let us break kola together*,' the Araba announced, laying the nut out before us and breaking it into four equal lobes.

'Baba . . . my name is Moremi,' Moremi said, through gritted teeth.

The Araba rapped his knuckles against his

protruding forehead. '*Oho! Is that so, eh?*' he remarked.

I guessed now wasn't a great time to mention that I hated being called Kokumo.

'Yes, it is so.' Moremi bit out the words like she had a chunky piece of *shaki* meat between her teeth.

'Can I say the *oriki* prayer and break the kola first?' Osoosi chirped.

'*So-so, what is mine is forever yours,*' the Araba said.

'The sky knows who will prosper. *Orun mo eni ti yi ola,*' Osoosi said, in between crunching bites.

I recited the words after Osoosi, surprising myself with how much my Yoruba had improved.

'*We must swallow food to sweeten the kola's path,*' the Araba remarked.

Osoosi's tongue wagged, like she was in hyena form.

I thought I wasn't hungry, but it turns out that almost being murdered and seeing ghosts everywhere really works up your appetite. So when the Araba laid out a colourful feast, including three banging stews, I ate like I hadn't yammed loads of seaweed dumplings. There was a peppery paprika one that made my eyes water just by looking at it, a spinach *efo riro* stew with orange palm oil swirls around the edges, and an *okro* soup with loads of juicy prawns. And there was a generous ball of pounded yam in the middle, wrapped in banana leaves. Plus there was dessert: oily strips of plantain with guava and mangoes.

'*I am sure the Mami Wata gave you all a warm welcome.*' The Araba smiled, rolling a yam ball between his wrinkled fingers.

'Something like that,' I muttered under my breath, as he continued: '*I know you have been sent here for the Night Stone, but if I am going to help you . . . you must first explain why you are* really *here.*'

There was a short silence, and then Moremi started: 'The Ògún warriors are in Jujuland trying to thief the Night Stone before the end of the summer solstice. If they find it before we do, they will destroy night for ever,' she explained.

I stared down at my plate.

Osoosi nodded, mopping up sauce from her plate with a slab of yam. 'Koku is the only one who can save the stone and restore night to Olori and the rest of the land. If they find the stone before us, night will be no more, all the animals in Olori go die, my tribe is finished.'

'*Ah, now you dey make me laugh!*' The Araba

slapped his knees. '*The three of* you *will stop the strongest Olori warriors from destroying night in five days, eh?*' The Araba wrinkled the skin where his eyebrows should have been.

Moremi crossed her arms over her chest. Osoosi stopped eating for a second, her hand hung mid air and a ball of yam splattered on her plate, throwing flecks of red stew on her cheeks.

I shifted uncomfortably and pushed my photo deeper into my pocket – there was no way I could ask about it now.

'*The Ògún warriors are powerful because they are united by one mind,*' the Araba continued. '*They are all trying to find the Night Stone. But you are three individuals pretending to be one. Not one of you is here for the stone. I know your true minds. One of you is running away from their true self, another one is afraid of their own power and the third wants to lead their tribe by fighting for something they do not need.*'

The Araba projected his voice so powerfully our brains turned to liquid mush. '*My Oracle showed me that you three were the Chosen Ones. And I am the one who is to train Kokumo to control the Night Stone. But this kind adventure no fit you at all, at all.*'

CHAPTER FOURTEEN

A Land without Night

Once he was done lecturing us, the Araba leaped from the dining table like he'd been electrocuted. His necklace rattled against his bony chest. Plates danced near the edge of the table. He cleared our half-eaten dishes away and disappeared into the kitchen.

'Baba, I was still chopping this one!' Osoosi grumbled through a mouthful of food.

I had only tried two of the stews and I had wanted to try them all.

The Araba ignored us as he re-entered and walked to the corner where his stuff was neatly arranged on shelves on the wall. He ran his wrinkled fingers over the many dotted labels there until he stopped at a circular wooden tray. He turned and gave us all a gap-toothed smile, then pulled a crusty-looking tray out.

It had a bunch of frowning faces with bulging eyes carved around the edge. As soon as he got it out, Moremi's eyes turned into fat black discs and Osoosi's were bugging so much they were practically on her chest.

'Now this is Rùnmí's divine Oracle that he used to create Time when the world began. Only an Araba, the most strongest of the Rùnmí tribe, can use this thing. Wetin I go show you is a secret-oh. Don't tell anybody outside.' He removed the beaded chain from his neck and moved it around the board in a slow circular motion.

We watched in amazement as white tribal marks crawled over his arms and neck. His eyes shone white and his pupils faded away as he chanted a spell. His lips were set in a firm line, but we could hear every single word:

> Atiwaye ojo,
> Atiwo oorun,
> Ma fi ire pe'bi,
> Ma fi ibi pe're.

> *From the dawn of day,*
> *To the setting of the sun,*
> *Never say it is evil when the message is good,*
> *Never say it is good when the message is evil.*

Once he finished chanting, the Oracle started to change. Its red wood turned black, and a silvery moving image appeared, looking a bit like a fuzzy TV screen. The Araba quickly covered it with a white cloth. '*It is dangerous to look into the seeds of time,*' he warned.

Then he instructed us to close our eyes and link hands so we could see what the Oracle had revealed to him. It was too bad that I was the closest to him. His hand felt leathery, like he hadn't used a decent lotion in a hot minute. But before I could make a couple helpful suggestions a burst of colour exploded behind my eyelids.

'*Who were we when we lived a thousand lives? Who do we become after we have had our time? I would like to know the secrets of our tribes.*' The Araba's croaky voice vibrated inside my bones.

We saw a painfully white sky, the ground underneath a grey slab. Craters in the soil formed a sprawling web. There were no plants, no flowers or nothing, just the burnt husks of palm trees. It was especially weird seeing the Olori people: there were no bright ankara colours, no lively music, festivals or bustling markets. Just tired people with grey skin and giant eyebags shut up in their houses, trying to avoid the never-ending day.

'*Without the lips, the teeth become grinding stone. Without ears, the head becomes a block of wood. Without night, Olori becomes a barren land,*' the Araba's voice echoed in my skull.

Osoosi gasped when we were next shown a scene with no animals except vultures perching over a stack of sun-bleached bones.

'*Without night, Olori will suffer . . .*' The Araba's voice rang in our heads as the images flickered. '*Every tribe, that is, except Ògún. They will use their* juju-*powered mosquito technology on all their citizens so that they will no longer need to sleep. The wealthy Ṣàngó and Òṣun tribes will pay to use it, too, but the poorer tribes suffer in endless sunlight,*' the Araba said.

We saw everyone in the Ògún territory including tiny kids stomping about in regulation armour making the ground tremble.

'*What you are seeing here will surely happen if you*

three continue as you are.' The Araba squeezed my hand, almost cutting off my blood circulation. '*Accept your destiny, Kokumo, if you don't want this to happen to Olori.*'

The Araba let go of my hand and before I knew what was happening, the vision faded and the room returned to normal.

My tongue felt fat and useless, like someone had ripped it out and shoved it back the wrong way around. Osoosi's jaw hung open, and Moremi's dark eyes were glossy and wet.

'What . . . what . . . does that mean?' I gulped.

'*Truth dey bitter, needing no salt,*' the Araba said, simply. He tucked the board away, and tapped a long rhythm out on the table. '*Kokumo, you are not here to save night. Instead, you are here because you think I will use my power to make you healthy and well,*' he said.

I shifted uneasily as the other two looked at me.

The Araba's lips crawled into an all-knowing smile. '*But you do not know the saying of our ancestors.*' His glowing white eyes settled on the bridge of my nose. '*Spirit won't give what head can't accept. That means it is not my place to change your destiny. Sickle cell is a genetic condition; it is not caused by a bacteria or virus; it is inherited from your parents. And your powers are also inherited from your parents. It is too dangerous to remove this from you, in case you lose your powers as well,'* the Araba said finally.

The feeling I got when he said this reminded me of when I was diagnosed as a kid. I couldn't think straight. I got this far-away feeling, like I was watching someone else go through these motions.

'My ancestors taught me that the things that make you weak in this life, make you strong in the spiritual world,' he continued. *'The strongest warriors normally have something they struggle with. My own tribe, the Rùnmí, can enter the mind but cannot see for eye. Osoosi's own, the Aganjù, sometimes have all animal senses except for hearing—'*

'But I don't care about this stupid power!' I choked out, not caring I was interrupting him. 'I want to be *normal!*' I shouted, blinking away the stinging behind my eyes.

'Your name is Kokumo. You are a child of miracles. A child with more power than any Ògún warrior in this land. The Night Stone contains Goddess Olókun's dark heart. The energy inside it is the same energy that was used to split the skies from the ocean when the earth was made. It is so mighty that anyone who does

not know how to control it is blown to dust and bone as soon as they touch it. Kokumo, once I train you, you will be able to use your power to survive the Night Stone and return darkness to Olori,' the Araba said.

I was glad he could read minds cause I needed my guy to know that I didn't ask to be born this way. I didn't want to touch a magic stone that might discombobulate me.

Being sick was bad enough: I didn't need the entire weight of Olori in my hands.

I welcomed the anger rushing through my veins.

CHAPTER FIFTEEN

Haunting Shadow

Static energy surged through my body with terrifying speed. My arms stretched like an invisible puppeteer was yanking my strings. Transparent shapes wobbled in the air around my fingertips.

'Koku!' Osoosi called out, but it was too late.

Thinking about it made me so mad the air rippled. I had no *choice* but to go on the mission to save night.

It's not like I could escape Jujuland on my own, plus the Ògún were still trying to kill me.

And we had less than five days left.

Dark shadowy mounds morphed into the warped shape of a human who once was. Decaying bones creaked as they appeared from the ground. The phantoms wrapped their translucent fingers around the Araba's collection of voodoo dolls. I clenched my fists and the ghostly hands squeezed so tight the pins popped out of the dolls and bounced on the floor.

Everyone got up from the table at once – Osoosi was on all fours, in hyena form, trying to sense the invisible enemy only I could see.

Moremi had braided fists hovered in front of her like a shield.

I swung my arms back and forth and the ghosts copied my movements. Before I knew it, the Araba's room was mashed up like a tornado had hit it.

And then a massive explosion sounded in my ears. I dropped to my knees, my head ringing.

'*Enough!*' The Araba's voice pounded in my mind like a ten-tonne truck driving over the squidgy bits in my brain. His eyes flashed brightly at me. Blinding white light filled my vision. The electric feeling left my body in an instant. The ghosts let out a long, horrible wail and disintegrated into a sludgy black mist. All that was left was a whirl of smoky dust.

I caught my reflection on the shiny surface of the upturned dining table. I was so far gone I hadn't even remembered chucking it like that.

I almost fainted when I saw myself.

I had black holes where my eyes used to be and a skeleton face decorated with faint black and red lines. I looked like a beast, a terrible monster, a haunting demon shadow.

'What kind of magic is this?' Osoosi was the first to speak. She backed away, pressing her back against the wall. Her eyes flashed orange and her bushy spotted tail spiked up. Moremi's braids lifted and hovered over Osoosi's shoulder, like she was trying to protect her from me.

'This cannot be Olori magic! Is Koku using *juju magic*?' Osoosi asked, her furry ears flattening her afro puffs.

I didn't know how to answer her. Luckily, I didn't have to.

'*Listen, and listen well,*' the Araba's voice boomed.

Moremi and Osoosi's shoulders jerked, just like mine did whenever the Araba yelled in my head. '*Kokumo is the last surviving member of the Olókun tribe. But their people were so mysterious even I do not know the full extent of his powers . . .*'

Mama Oti had warned me that if anyone knew about my powers, they wouldn't want to help me no more. After this reaction, I totally understood why.

'*I gave instructions that Kokumo was not to be told about this power until he landed in Olori. This secret was for his safety.*' There was a long pause. '*And Kokumo is not the only one here being deceitful.*' The Araba hovered a wrinkled finger in Moremi's direction. '*I think the time has come for you to tell them about your own lies, Kehinde.*'

'That is *not* my name, Baba!' Moremi ground out.

'*I have known you since I lived in Olori. Back then you were smaller than a cockroach. It was I that taught you the secrets of the* iroko *tree, which gives your hair its strength,*' the Araba continued. '*As the oldest, you have led the group far, but you have not been honest about who you are, and why you are here.*'

It kinda stung that I wasn't the only one keeping secrets.

'*You must ask yourself, are you here to protect Koku, or to save Taiwo from destroying himself with stolen* juju *magic?*' the Araba said.

Why would Moremi save the guy who's been trying to end us? I thought, watching Moremi carefully.

She avoided my gaze and pulled at the purple cloth

she wore wrapped around her arm.

'Names are important,' the Araba added. '"Moremi" has an important meaning, but "Kehinde" is a twin name. You are one half of a whole. Taiwo was the first to touch the earth, but Kehinde is older. In our culture, the second-born twin becomes the elder.'

'So let me get this straight, yeah?' I said. 'The guy who has been trying to kill me . . . the guy who beat up Osoosi's family and wants to get rid of night . . . *that* guy . . . is your twin *brother*?'

'Ah, Koku, you see, it's not Moremi's fault,' Osoosi interjected, trying to dead the beef. 'The Ògún king took Taiwo from their home and made him join his army because he could control—'

She kept talking but I didn't hear nothing. It was too late, there was no way Moremi could explain her way out of this. I was getting so mad it was almost spiritual. Something powerful surged within me.

I should've seen it coming, to be honest. When I thought about it, like *properly* thought about it, Moremi (or Kehinde, or whatever) had the same screwface that Taiwo had. Plus, she was always trying to kill me, so I should've clocked from day one that she came from a family of assassins.

'You no go understand anything with this *oyinbo*

mentality of yours!' Moremi yelled.

I dunno why, but this time that word hit differently. 'The only thing I *understand* is that you're a snake,' I yelled. 'How do we know you weren't leading your brother to us the whole time?'

'*Ki lo de?* We no dey for the same category! You have no loyalty to Olori. You only care for yourself. Where you come from, people just do their own.' Moremi's braids whipped around her head, hissing.

Osoosi's eyes darted between both of us. 'Ah, Koku, *oga*-boss . . . we don't want *wahala*-oh!'

'You don't know nothing about where I'm from! Or what I have to deal with *every day* with my condition,' I said.

Moremi hovered her stupid braids over my face. 'You better respect yourself, *oyinbo* baby.'

That's when I lost it.

'I ain't no *oyinbo*, man,' I hissed. The air rippled around me as I visualised Taiwo and Moremi's face merging into one and saying that same awful word – *oyinbo*. The word reminded me how much I've never belonged anywhere.

The ripples transformed into a translucent arm only I could see. It shot out in front of me and reached towards a fuzzy braid. Moremi shivered at the ghostly touch. I clenched my fist and the ghost arm squeezed tight.

CHAPTER SIXTEEN

The Lesson of the Rock

'I didn't mean to—!' I stuttered, trying to explain how I'd almost ripped one of Moremi's braids out of her skull.

But the truth was, even though I didn't hurt her, I had *wanted* to. And the ghostly hand I had summoned had somehow picked up on that.

Moremi glared at me before storming out, like she knew it too. Her dark eyes looked like they had no pupils in them.

Osoosi stared at the ground.

The Araba shook his head, '*What is done cannot be undone. The unknown can become known, but the known cannot be unknown. If you do not learn to control your powers, you will harm the people closest to you. The choice is yours to make.'*

I stared at the ceiling in bed that night, I didn't mean to go psycho on Moremi. Things were normal before that museum trip. I wished I'd never broken that stupid figurine, cause then I wouldn't have ever unleashed my powers. I wished I'd never set foot in Jujuland, and, most of all, I wished I didn't have nothing to do with the stupid Night Stone. But the Araba was right: once you know something, you can't unknow it. Even if you really, really want to.

After twisting and turning for hours, my eyelids finally got heavy.

I woke with a start. The room was filled with a painfully bright light that was hitting me from all angles. I tried to move, but I was stuck. My nails were sharpening, my skin was withering and stiffening. My fingers crawled towards my face, but instead of skin beneath my fingertips, I felt oiled wood.

My eyes stung like mad. I was surrounded by glass. I could see my reflection everywhere, and it was horrifying. My body was covered in ashy white spots from head to toe and my face was a gigantic wooden mask sloppily painted red and black, with two curved horns sticking out of it.

People stared at me in my glass cage. I tried to scream, but my mouth was sealed shut.

It suddenly became clear: I was trapped in the museum.

I saw a fuzzy braid and a flash of orange. Moremi and Osoosi were there. No matter what went down, I knew they'd do anything to get me out.

They stared at me blankly. I was so lonely it hurt.

I woke up in a cold sweat. I pinched myself to make sure I was actually awake this time. It was strange, cause I never dream. If I was able to get a decent night's sleep, I was out cold.

I staggered to the bathroom.

When I bumped into Moremi, she stared daggers at me. But still I breathed a huge sigh of relief, even though she clearly hated my guts.

*

Moremi's eyes cut into me as I sat at the table the next morning. I pulled my stool as far from hers as possible. I was stuck in between being angry at her for lying and feeling guilty about the braid situation. Plus, I didn't want to accidentally unleash another ghost attack.

The Araba had left to check the Oracle.

Osoosi kept distracting us with hyena facts while she slurped her *garri* – a mushy cassava pudding. 'People no like hyena, but did you know hyena have plenty head for sense? They are very strong-oh, they can chew through anything, they have teeth stronger than lion!' She laughed extra loud to fill the silence. 'Me I have ten brothers. They born me last. My big brother Sebe always say I go be last in everything. But in hyena pack lady na master! This is why I always transform into hyena.'

'Yeah, well, who cares what people think, as long as you're real about who *you are* . . .' I flickered a glance at Moremi. 'That's the main thing, I guess.'

Moremi got up so fast I had to wipe *garri* out of my eyes for the next half hour. It was so rude. I didn't even *like garri*.

'*He who does not have antidote should not swallow*

cockroach!' The Araba's voice vibrated suddenly in my head. He had returned from checking the Oracle – and his face looked thinner and greyer than before.

I wondered if he peeped the *garri* landing on my head in the Oracle and if he did, I wanted to know why he didn't give me a heads-up *before* Moremi busted up my signature hairstyle.

'*Kokumo, are you ready to learn how to control yourself?*' the Araba asked. '*Once you learn how to control your powers, then you will be able to learn the secrets of the Night Stone.*'

I nodded, staring down at my hands.

I never meant to hurt anyone.

'*The Mami Wata are allowing us to use their lagoon for practice,*' the Araba said.

My stomach rumbled – I was craving one of those seaweed dumplings.

'You go teach us to become like you!' Osoosi said.

'*Yes-oh! Kokumo will be joining us, while Kehinde minds this place for me.*'

'It go be *him* that receives training from the great Araba, eh?' Moremi snarled, her eyes screwed menacingly at me while her braids flapped viciously around her. 'The boy that does not know his own tribe? The boy that does not know the language of his own ancestors?' She ended her delightful little speech by kissing her teeth loudly at me.

'*Whether you like or you no like, Kokumo and Osoosi are the ones with powers from the Gods. And Kokumo is the one chosen to save Olori.*' He pinched his nose and let out a long sigh '*It is the duty of the two of you to protect him, you hear?*' He projected in a drained voice.

'Yes, sah!' Osoosi gave me a reassuring grin.

Moremi looked like she'd quite like to shove my face into the rest of my *garri*.

I was on edge as we walked out of the Araba's hut. The sky was pitch-black as usual and the water sparkled, reflecting the moonlight. The Jujuland moon was still high in the sky, but it wasn't as bright as it was in the Mami Wata's lagoon. The shores were dimly lit by a cloud of fireflies that followed the Araba around. I tried to keep up with him so I could actually see. It was so dark every little thing made me jump. I immediately looked out for our boat that we had docked on the island yesterday as soon as the water's edge became visible, but it was missing. There was a deep hole where the anchor had been so I knew I wasn't making it up or nothing.

But it was surrounded by huge footsteps that had

pressed deep into the sand. They definitely didn't belong to us.

'How are we going to get across the water with no boat?' I asked.

Osoosi's nose wrinkled up and she squinted hard like she'd just noticed a new smell.

'Well?' I asked the Araba, while Osoosi was distracted.

He ignored me totally and kept singing, '*Yeye oo, Omi oo, Omi o l'ota o*,' while playing an off-key melody on a flute.

'Koku, are you hearing this smell?' Osoosi asked, suddenly bending down and grabbing a handful of sand.

'Nah, man. How can you hear a smell?' I asked, sneaking glances behind us. All I could see was a total blackness. 'Does it smell like the Ògún?' I continued as the thought occurred to me. 'Maybe Moremi gave her twin clues to lead that maniac to us.'

'I cannot smell any Ògún,' Osoosi said, getting up from her knees. 'But someone must be using the *ewuro* leaf to disguise their smell.' She sneezed. 'My brother show me how you use this thing to disguise your scent.' Her flat nose scrunched up as she sniffed the large footsteps by our feet. 'No *wahala*, Koku.

Don't you know that the Araba go tell us if there are enemies around us?'

I let out a sigh. That was a good point. I looked at the Araba, who had his face turned to the water. I guessed he already knew today's fate and would probably give me a heads-up if my assassins were nearby.

Fireflies hovered over the Araba's shoulders as he played his tune. It looked like he was surrounded by a small constellation of stars. The water rippled violently as the flute played, as if it was dancing to his music.

'You know, Koku, make I tell you one thing about *oga*-boss,' Osoosi said. 'Taiwo is the youngest warrior in Olori. He is the only one who can use the Ògún sword without getting swallowed by it. As soon as the king noticed his talent he asked him to join his army. So Taiwo left his tribe and joined the Ògún.'

'What has that got to do with Moremi being a snake?' I scowled.

Osoosi shook her head and clicked her tongue against her cheek. '*Chai!* Make you listen well-oh! When the twins' parents joined the side of the Olókun tribe against the king and lost, they were sent to Mama Oti's tribe, the Babalú. This is seen as a great dishonour. To be raised outside your own tribe.' Osoosi shivered like the thought made her physically uncomfortable.

'So you see, eh? Moremi's case is not too different from your own. Mama Oti is not her real Grandma, she only has her brother. Then her brother left to join the Ògún.'

'So?' I said, burning inside. It was *totally* different. Moremi had someone, a twin brother. I had no one.

'You don't know what it is to leave your tribe. Taiwo is not her family any more – he is now her enemy. He made that decision long ago. Moremi is our friend, so *abeg* oh, stop punishing her for it. You should be speaking to her,' Osoosi added, wiggling her pinky finger in my face. 'And remember I helped you find the Araba, so you must come and help me with *oga*-boss when the time comes for me to face my big-grandfather.'

I couldn't believe she was still planning to face that monster after everything that had happened. *And I thought I was stubborn.* But a deal was a deal.

'I can try and distract her, but that don't mean things are going back to how they were.' I sighed.

'One day, you go act the way you feel.' Osoosi waggled her eyebrows at me.

'You're literally crazy, man,' I replied.

She tilted her head at me. 'You say what? Wetin I go do?'

I grinned for the first time in a while at Osoosi's antics. I knew she had heard the last part, cause I always made sure to speak clearly so she could lip-read. I was glad things seemed to be normal between us.

'*Yeye oo, Omi oo. Omi o l'ota o.*' The Araba interrupted us with his annoying melody. He was in a great mood for someone totally stranded on an island with no way to get back to the forest.

'Do you know any Drake songs?' I asked him, hopefully.

His lips curled as he continued to play the same dead tune as before – until a huge wave crashed on the shore and a group of Mami Wata women emerged from the water in their human forms.

'Yuh nah kno yuh always welcome pon mi shore?'

I'd recognise that smooth voice anywhere. The half-snake Mami Wata leader slithered right up to us, her rainbow scales sparkling in the moonlight and illuminating the entire shore so we could finally see properly.

'Yemaya!' The Araba projected her name into everyone's skulls. He had the goofiest grin ever planted on to his face. '*Ife mi, my love, my sweet plantain,*

I call you no dey answer?' He laughed while she fluttered her eyelashes at him.

Osoosi and I shared a look while they exchanged sweet nothings. I guess that explained why Yemaya stopped drowning us when she saw the Araba's photo.

The Mami Wata dug their hands into the sand and chanted slowly, 'Ocean split inna two!'

Immediately, storm clouds rumbled above us, and a powerful wind suddenly split the sea open in front of us. Walls of turquoise reached up to twenty feet above us, revealing dry sand underneath.

Osoosi and I gaped in wonder.

'*We no get time to waste ee-o*,' the Araba warned us, as he started walking along the dry, sandy path.

We followed his lead.

There were Jujuland sea creatures revealed by the huge water walls that looked so crazy I had to push my eyeballs back into their sockets. There were alien-looking guys with eyes at the bottom of their face and green fires burning on their heads, zebra-striped turtles with dolphin eyes, and three-headed alligators with thick copper bangles around their necks.

'*It is time for the first lesson*,' the Araba announced, once we reached the empty Mami Wata lagoon.

216

The Mami Wata had gone for a swim, salty water spraying over us as they did backflips in the water. As I walked along the jagged rocks I spotted a tiny glass wing. A mosquito-bot! My fingers trembled with the memory of the zombie hands I summoned to whack them out of the sky.

'*It is safe to practise here, Kokumo. I have seen the fates using the Oracle and the Ògún will not trouble us for now.*' The Araba's voice rummaged through my thoughts. I shivered automatically, it was so creepy!

'So, which one you dey teach us first, eh Araba? How to draw air signs and use magic?' Osoosi hopped excitedly.

The Araba totally aired her and sat down, cross-legged on the stony ground. '*Ehen!*' He said, holding a single stone.

'You dragged us all the way here to learn about rocks?' I said, irritated at my guy for not getting rid of my illness and instead focusing on the dumb rock stuff.

'*True power comes from the head, which is where your soul lives. And the eyes are the ruler of the head. You must learn to focus your eyes before you can control your soul. When you control your soul, you can control your power,*' he said, cradling the rock between his palms.

'Baba, *abeg* oh, no dey joke with us. We want to learn the real thing.' Osoosi wrinkled her nose at the rock in the Araba's hands.

'Jokoo jeje! *Sit and be still!*'

For some reason, being told off in Yoruba always hits harder. We crashed to the ground. The Araba looked furious, his chain rattling over his chest.

'*The two of you are different but both powerful in your own ways. Kokumo, yesterday we saw that you have the power to summon the dead and manipulate darkness,*' he said, gravely. 'Osoosi, your connection to animals is from the god of the wilderness.'

He slammed the rock down hard, practically burying it. '*If you do not learn how to control yourselves, you will bring danger to yourselves and Olori. I have brought you both here as this is the very place where the Òrìṣà Gods bathed. Their essence is strongest in this water, this soil and these rocks. So, you will not move from this place until you become like this rock!*' He looked at us, clearly working to calm himself. When he spoke again, his voice was gentler. '*The rock is the highest form of consciousness. Do you know why?*' he asked, rapping his knuckles against his forehead. '*It knows that it is one part of a whole. It knows that it is not separate at all. It is connected to everything. So-so, if you want to learn to draw magic from the world around you, you too must learn that you are an expression of the divine, just like this rock is.'*

'*Be like the rock.*' The Araba's voice would sneak up behind us from time to time, and here he was again. '*Are you like the rock?*'

'Erm, no?' I replied, with a huff. It was so dead, man. We hadn't done nothing all day except stare at the rock. We didn't even eat nothing. I would've even slurped that *garri* if I'd had it in front of me.

I snuck a glance at Osoosi. She was still as stone, her eyes in a focused stare ahead. I hated that she was actually taking it seriously.

'*Seek total darkness! A cloud of unknowing! Once you have done that, Osoosi, you may lift your hand in the air and draw signs,*' the Araba instructed, breathing hotly over our shoulders.

Osoosi nodded and went right back to staring, while tracing patterns in the air over and over again.

The Araba came around to sit in front of me. '*Kokumo, since you are the one chosen to restore night, the Goddess Olókun has blessed you, so you do not need to draw patterns in the earth or the air to use your power. Your power is inside you. Even I must wear this for my powers'* – the Araba pulled out his necklace and showed me the patterns carved into the pale beads – *'to summon from Rùnmí, the god of wisdom.'*

I didn't feel blessed at all. *Why did Goddess Olókun give me powers I don't want instead of taking my illness away from me?*

'But you must learn to activate your powers on your own. Your powers are tied to your emotions at the moment, which makes you very dangerous. That is the reason your sickle-cell crisis can trigger your powers,' the Araba said.

Dangerous? Was I actually *dangerous?* My ears burned, remembering the way I had accidentally unleashed the ghosts to attack Moremi yesterday. I clenched my fists tight – I never wanted to lose control like that again.

'*I will not teach you the secrets of the Night Stone if you cannot control yourself.*' The Araba furrowed the leathery skin on his forehead. '*I was once foolish enough to teach those who hungered for power without giving them the sense to go with it. I knew that Taiwo had the potential to be one of Olori's most talented warriors. That is why I taught him the secret of the Ògún sword, even though he is not from the Ògún tribe.'*

'*You* taught Taiwo to use that sword?' I shivered. I remembered the ginormous shining blade at Mama Oti's while I hid in the pot of stew. Taiwo's twisted smirk flashed in my mind. *Moremi's brother.* Thinking of him that way was still weird. Sure, she had the same screwface but there was warmth behind her dark eyes no matter how much she tried to hide it.

'*To gain control over this thing inside you requires you to unknow everything you think you know and empty your mind . . .*' the Araba continued.

'But why would you . . . ?' I started to say, until I got blinded by a flash of orange light.

I turned to look. Osoosi's fingers hovered in the air. Each time she traced a pattern it exploded with bright orange sparks. Glowing tribal patterns crawled over her arms, matching the ones she was drawing with her fingers.

It had actually worked.

She had learned how to use air signs to activate her powers just by staring at the rock.

'Ehen! *Well done-oh.*' The Araba gave Osoosi a victory pat so hard you could hear it echo.

Osoosi beamed so bright her eyes turned into crescent moons.

'Yeah, good job, man,' I said, totally not jealous at all. It was easy for Osoosi to empty her thoughts and think about nothing – it's not like she had to worry about being constantly ill, or having the fate of Olori in her hands, or having powers that could unleash the undead at any moment.

CHAPTER SEVENTEEN

Gidigbo Fight!

For the next two days the Araba dragged me to the Mami Wata lagoon and made me sit and stare at the dumb rock.

It was dark as usual, but the moonlight cast shimmering light on the rocks so they looked like someone had greased them up.

'I can't do it!' I yelled for the billionth time. 'I can't do nothing. Don't you get it? I ain't special! I ain't no "Chosen One". You got it all wrong. I ain't nothing except a sick kid!'

'*So, you think I should pity you because you are sick?*'

I nodded. To be honest, yeah, I did. The poor-me-

I've-got-an-incurable-disease thing had always worked before, even with Uncle Tunji.

The Araba threw his head back and laughed. My cheeks sizzled as my man really went for it: his mouth was wide open and his chest was shaking as he slapped my back so hard I almost coughed my teeth out. I had only seen someone laugh like that once before – in my photo.

'*Your mother was a very stubborn somebody with a big basket mouth, just like you, Kokumo,*' the Araba revealed, his cloudy eyes twinkling.

'My mother?' I asked, eagerly. I wanted to know what she smelled like and what foods she enjoyed and if she was left-handed like me. I sat up straight even though the rocks were digging into my backside like crazy. 'So, you were, like, her teacher?' I said, figuring that was a good place to start.

The Araba nodded, stretching his cheeks wide. '*Many dawns ago, I had the honour of training the last protector of the Night Stone. Tolani.*' His voice broke when he said the name. '*Tolani Akanbi,*' he repeated.

Something inside me just clicked – like sliding the right puzzle pieces together. As soon as the Araba mentioned my mum's name I heard her laughter echoing around me.

'*Your* iya, *your mother. When she was a small* pikin *like you, I taught her the secret to activating her Olókun power.*' The Araba tilted his head to the sky like his sightless eyes were looking at something I couldn't see. '*At first, she did not understand how to summon her power at all. But she kept trying*' – he tapped my knee – '*and then she became a master of Olori magic. She learned how to manipulate the darkness around her to move objects. And she grew to be one of the greatest warriors of Olori and one of the strongest protectors of night.*'

A warm, giddy feeling rushed into my belly like I'd eaten some spicy pepper stew.

'*Kokumo, you have the potential to become even more powerful than your mother since you do not need to draw patterns to activate your magic. This is your mother's gift to you. She would want you to learn how to respect your power and control it so you can use it for good,*' the Araba finished.

I stared down at my hands. I wondered how my mum felt when she activated her power. *Did the weird ghostly voices creep her out too? Or did she experience a burst of energy and light like Osoosi?*

I always thought I had never gotten anything from my parents except sickle cell.

But maybe I was wrong.

'*Kokumo, do you know how many people in Olori are counting on you to save night?*' the Araba asked.

I felt a lump in my throat, remembering Mama Oti parcelling up the last of her herbs and bundling them in my backpack.

'*You must learn how to control your power. Your deepest fear is not that you are weak or sick,*' the Araba said. '*It is that you are powerful beyond your own understanding.*'

I'd never been called 'powerful' before. My whole life I'd been treated like something people expected to break – like those fake AirPods you could get at the Pound Shop near my flat.

For the first time, I wanted to properly give it a try. I'm good at focusing when I put my mind to it. I reached over to the rock and picked it up, placing it directly under a bright moonbeam. I stared until I knew every single crack in it; I knew when it curved, dipped, slanted and sloped. I knew all the colours: the greys, the blacks, the purples, and the slight smattering of red earth that tainted the edges.

I stared for hours until it came to me – a calm feeling of being part of everything: the rock, the earth, the moon and the night's sky. Silvery voices caressed my ears. The staticy feeling washed over me. My heart was beating in a crazy rhythm. I had never felt so alive. My breaths came in hot pants. I was shaking. Time seemed to slow down, lights flashed and everything got very, very quiet.

I knew before I saw my reflection in the water. I instinctively wanted to shut my eyes as soon as I saw it, but I forced myself to keep looking.

It wasn't nothing like Osoosi's power. She had glowing patterns that covered her skin and blazing eyes that shone like they had fireflies inside them. I had hollow, black, empty eyes in a skeleton face decorated with faint black and red lines.

But, for the first time, I didn't see a monster staring back at me when my powers activated. I saw something ancient and powerful inside me that was worthy of respect.

'*Kokumo.*' The Araba said my name like a prayer. '*You have arrived. Are you ready for the next part of your training?*' The Araba's white eyes hovered over me. I nodded shakily, adrenaline surging through my arms all the way down to my tingling palms. Dark shadows rose from my hands and curled around my fingers. I stared in wonder as I closed my palms and the shadows disappeared completely.

The Araba led me back through the lagoon and called the Mami Wata to split the ocean for us so we could return to his hut.

He wanted to teach all of us inner balance. Moremi refused to come out of the hut; she was still mad at me and she'd apparently already done it ages ago and didn't want to be stuck with us. It was bless being without her complaining anyway, even if we did have to carry baskets on our heads all day long. If Osoosi and I didn't walk in a perfectly straight line the Araba would nudge us and we'd collapse in a heap in the sand. It was dead until I realised I was actually pretty good at it. I had spent so many nights with Jollof lying on my head in a fluffy ball, I never knew that would actually come in handy one day. Once we'd got the hang of the basket balancing, the Araba announced that it was time to teach us how to protect ourselves from the Ògún, and anyone else coming after the Night Stone.

'So, you go teach us how to fight in the Gidigbo martial arts style?' Osoosi asked, bouncing on her toes.

The Araba shook his head with a wry smile. '*I* no go teach you.'

Osoosi's shoulders slumped, until we heard stomping

footsteps and the outer wooden doors slide open. Moremi finally appeared, her eyes sharp and deadly.

Just great.

Luckily, Moremi totally aired me and walked towards Osoosi. Once she was right in front of her, she crouched low, moving her hands in slow circles across her chest.

You could tell she was gonna enjoy this.

'Maintain your balance. You should become grounded like rock, yet flexible like rubber,' Moremi instructed Osoosi as she swayed from side to side. There was a rhythm to it.

'Me I have balance-oh!' Osoosi boasted, bending over into a handstand. Her mouth split into a wide smile as she dangled her legs in the air.

Moremi nodded but, just when Osoosi landed, Moremi suddenly swept her foot across the floor, striking Osoosi's ankle hard.

Osoosi let out a sharp hiss as she fell to the floor. I thought she was done for, but she used the momentum to flip herself over and return to a crouching stance.

'With a poor stance you are unbalanced and anyone go knock you,' Moremi said.

'*Yepa!* I no dey find your trouble-oh. This your leg want chook me, but I no go gree,' Osoosi said, delivering a swift kick to Moremi's side.

Moremi side-stepped it like it was nothing, and catapulted her body backwards like some sort of crazy acrobat. It was no contest.

'I sorry for your *yansh*-oh,' Moremi said, with a smile.

'Why you dey worry for me?' Osoosi narrowly dodged a few well-aimed jabs.

'Because I go make your backside chew pepper!' Moremi promised. Her braids flew behind her as she rushed towards Osoosi.

A whirlwind of red dirt spewed over us as Moremi dragged her foot across the ground: she had rubbed out the pattern Osoosi was trying to draw to activate her powers. She chased Osoosi away with a few helicopter kicks, forcing her back on her feet. '*Ehen*, keep your heels grounded in the earth,' Moremi instructed, her words disguising her lethal striking leg.

Thwack! Moremi's leg snapped like a rubber band and struck Osoosi's ankle again. This time Osoosi did end up kissing dirt, landing with a heavy thud.

'In Gidigbo one leg is always heavy and one leg is light,' Moremi explained. 'I no give my all to one attack. This is why I am standing here and you are lying there.'

Osoosi looked up and grinned, her eyes bright orange. Her fingers had dug into the earth and the pattern was finished. She stood up on her hind legs, her spotted fur spiking up like razor blades as she transformed.

Moremi didn't even look bothered. She dug her heels into the earth and pushed forward, her arms locked at the elbows. Osoosi flew across the ground, the shock startling her back into human form.

'This magic power no matter in fight. With a poor stance you are unbalanced.'

Moremi still had a smug look on her face even as she kissed dirt – the Araba had snuck up behind her, sweeping his foot across her ankles in a perfect arc. Her eyes widened as she toppled over and ended up kissing dirt, just like Osoosi had.

'*Yepa! Oga*-boss, the Araba go finish you!' Osoosi yelled.

I laughed so hard my teeth almost fell out.

'*You see, my dear student, with a poor stance you are unbalanced and anybody go fit knock you.*' The Araba chuckled.

Moremi jumped up and returned to the crouching stance. 'I challenge you to a Gidigbo fight!' she shouted to him.

'*I see . . .*' he growled, crouching low. '*Don't you know that the sparrow that dines at the banquet of eagles shall be eaten with the food?*'

Osoosi had the good sense to scramble away quickly from the battlefield.

We watched the madness unfold. Moremi was the first to strike. The Araba was calm as she flew around him, launching powerful kicks, lethal uppercuts and deadly jabs. But she didn't land a single hit on him – he seemed to know everything she was going to do before she did it. And his eyes weren't glowing white so he wasn't even using his mind-reading powers or nothing.

Every time she hit him with a jab or kick, the Araba would let it connect with him and then strike exactly at the moment of contact, making Moremi fall back on herself. He barely moved, like he wasn't even trying.

Meanwhile, Moremi looked like she had dunked her face in a vat of jojoba oil.

She used all her braids against him, but the Araba's arms moved so fast, it was like he had a dozen of them. He blocked every braid in a flurry of movement.

Finally, the Araba put her out of her misery and tied her up with her own hair. As Moremi struggled in her braided prison, he bent down to her level: '*Wind can shout from now till tomorrow, Mountain will never kneel for him.*'

CHAPTER EIGHTEEN

Real Power

'*So, Kokumo, you think I have forgotten your own, eh?*' The Araba crept into my thoughts without warning. '*Wa nbi! Moremi, come here!*' he demanded.

Moremi grinned at being called the right name for once, and then scowled when she caught my eye.

'*You will be teaching this boy Gidigbo, you hear?*'

'I can't exactly fight cause of you-know-what, so I think I'll just pass on this one, yeah?' I said.

'*Don't let your sense miss road!*' the Araba roared. '*The Gidigbo fighting style has nothing to do with physical strength, you hear?*' He rapped his knuckles across his forehead like that would somehow help me get the message.

'That's calm still, but why can't I train with Osoosi?' I asked.

The Araba chuckled as he walked back into the hut. *'Because the two of you have plenty to learn from each other.'*

Annoyingly, Moremi was actually a decent teacher. She still huffed and puffed every five seconds, but by the end of the first lesson I had learned how to knock someone off balance while staying upright at all times.

And the more I trained, the more I actually understood why the Araba had made us carry those baskets on our heads. Balance was the key to learning how to defend myself, and it was too easy to trip over my own feet. And it was ten times harder not to fall when I was trying to stop a teenager with serious anger issues from busting my forehead wide open.

Once Moremi got bored of pounding me to a pulp – or 'helping with my training' as she liked to call it – she dismissed us to go and eat something.

I caught up with Osoosi on our way back to the Araba's hut.

'You are doing very well for somebody that has not tasted this Gidigbo fighting for long,' Osoosi remarked.

'Thanks, man,' I said, giving a limp smile. 'But I

don't think I'm ever gonna get the hang of it, you get me?'

'I use the spirit of the god of the wilderness to help me fight. Why don't you fight using your *real* power, eh?' But as she said this, her eyes twitched, like she was stuck between feeling terrified of my powers, and being super interested in them at the same time.

Osoosi's question twisted in my head that night. I couldn't stop thinking about it, even though I was having one of the worst crises I'd ever had.

Ever since the museum incident, whenever I had a crisis I felt a much more intense rush of power surge through me. The ghosts that appeared when I was really angry, or when I was in danger, were broken, half formed things. But when I was in pain, I would see those undead forms.

Now, I had an idea. It was a properly mad one, but I had to give it a shot.

This time, when the pain hit, I forced myself to concentrate on their shadowy forms.

I reached out for a glass of water across the room. The air began rippling around me, and I got flashbacks of when I'd gone ballistic on Moremi a couple of days ago. Tingly voices crept into my ears, coming from a dark fog that had a strange, shimmering quality to it.

And then a blackish shape shot out from my palm and wrapped its sludgy fingers around the glass.

A warm wetness coated my hands like I'd shoved my fingers into the hot guts of a living, breathing thing. The moment I felt that I wanted to dip, but I powered through. Then I felt the sense of cool glass beneath my fingertips, even though I wasn't anywhere near it.

'C'mon, man,' I whispered to myself, as shadowy fingers crawled around the edge of the glass. The glass wobbled violently as it gave a little hop, a little nudge to the edge of the table. Until I felt a sharp stab of pain in my side, and the phantom arm disintegrated into a dark mist.

I kept concentrating, though, cause the more I concentrated, the more I didn't notice the pain.

I spent the rest of the night seeing if I could pick up the glass. By the end of the night, I could bring the glass to my lips and take a sip without lifting a single finger.

It was just like Osoosi said. This was *real* power.

*

The air hummed around us. I focused on that feeling of being at peace with everything – the warm sand beneath my toes, and the cool spraying breeze from the lapping waves on the shore. I'd eaten my fair share of dirt by the time Moremi's lesson was over, but still I found myself asking: 'Can we do that again, but for real this time?' like I had a death wish or something.

Osoosi stared at me in surprise, but said nothing. Moremi just got back into the Gidigbo stance. 'You want to test my power, eh? *Nawa* for you-oh,' she warned, bouncing lightly on the balls of her feet. 'No be you I blame – I blame the world for rewarding stupidity.'

I didn't say nothing. I crouched low and focused hard so that I couldn't hear Moremi cussing me out any more.

Suddenly, Moremi lunged forward, but instead of reaching out to block her with my hands, I summoned an undead arm. A shadowy shape burst out from my outspread palm and pushed her square in the chest. She flew back so hard that a cloud of dust erupted behind her. She stared at me, open-mouthed.

The shadow disintegrated almost as soon as it had made contact with her. I couldn't believe it actually worked.

'This is a
big *wawu*! *Yepa*!
You have finished
oga-boss! Now you be the original
Gidigbo champion!' Osoosi clapped so hard I
thought her fingers would fall off.

'So, what is it you were saying about me being too
slow to fight properly?' Okay, maybe not properly,
cause I had some ghostly backup. But for the first time
ever I had a physical advantage, and I didn't care if it
was technically cheating.

'Goddess Qya is my witness, today I go give you a lesson you will never forget,' Moremi promised, as her braids began to whip around her shoulders. She crouched low into the usual stance. I did the same.

I knew how deadly Moremi was up close, so I kept her at arm's length by throwing a few ghostly jabs at her.

I was starting to get the hang of summoning the ghosts. I wasn't that strong physically, but when I focused really hard the ghosts could deliver attacks I would never be able to do myself.

The craziest part was it was actually working.

Although Moremi whirled her braids around her head like a lasso, and each time a braided fist came into contact with a ghostly hand it disintegrated, I was able to dodge every single one of her attacks. Moremi couldn't see the ghosts like I could, so I always had the element of surprise on my side.

Then Moremi delivered a swirling back kick that sprayed dust all over me, momentarily blinding me. I shut my eyes and focused on making the arms appear around me to protect me from her attacks. But it was too late – she'd figured it out. She'd sprayed dirt to outline the shape of the ghosts and avoid their attacks.

By the time I realised what she'd done, her foot was

already chilling at the back of my head. She tapped me lightly cause it was practice, but that didn't stop her retracting her leg with a smug smirk.

But her next words were a surprise. 'Koku,' Moremi called out. 'So this your brain is not just for decoration, eh? You have done well-oh. Sense has arrived.'

Something warm bubbled in my chest at her words. 'Well, I guess it might've had something to do with an alright teacher,' I said.

Moremi gave me a half-smile. 'Don't jealous me-oh.'

'About the other day—' I started to say, but there was no use. Her smile wobbled and dipped until her screwface made a comeback. 'I just wanna talk to you, man!' But I spoke to the edges of her back, watching her storm away.

CHAPTER NINETEEN

Secrets of the Night Stone

It was two days before the summer solstice when the Araba called the Mami Wata back so Osoosi and I could cross the waters again. For some reason Yemaya wasn't there this time.

'*Kokumo*.' The Araba's voice rang in my mind as he patted my shoulder gently. '*The time has come for you to learn how to use the Night Stone.*' His voice echoed as we walked beyond the lagoon and deeper into the jungle. '*Your mother would be so proud*,' he added.

My cheeks warmed at the mention of my mother. I clenched my fists tight. This is it, I thought, as I pushed onwards. I had to find the Night Stone, even if

I was never going to get rid of my illness. There was no way I was gonna let my mum down.

Osoosi walked ahead of me. The humid air stuffed its fingers down my throat, slowing me down. It took tons of effort to just breathe right. The more I walked, the more plants tangled into a spirally mess.

My bones were starting to ache – my condition makes it harder to walk long distances, but I forced myself to focus.

Misty outlines hovered in the air, their silvery, mystical voices pulling me along a single narrow path. Here the footprints were so deep you knew people had stepped in the same ones for decades until they had forced the earth to harden underneath. I was walking in someone else's shoes; someone bigger than me, stronger than me – someone who actually deserved to learn the secrets of the Night Stone.

'*Kokumo.*' The Araba shoved his voice into my brain once I reached the end of the path. I stopped walking, panting heavily. '*During this last part of the training, you will communicate with your Olókun ancestors and learn their secrets.*' His voice echoed as I sprawled on the ground to catch my breath.

'I'm going to meet my family?' I said, savouring the taste of the word *family* on my tongue. I was desperate to know more about my relatives, the people who had created the abstract sculptures in the Olókun district and the colourful paintings. Most of all, I wanted to know more about my mother.

'*So-so, you go be my eyes during this burial ritual,*' the Araba said as Osoosi materalised behind him.

'Hold on . . . did you just say *burial* ritual?' I protested, as Osoosi started piling heaps of soil on me.

'Yes-oh! You must become one with the earth,' Osoosi said, burying me up to my eyeballs until I could only wrinkle my nose the tiniest bit.

'Why can't my feet become one with the ground?' I asked, keeping my mouth closed as much as possible. I tried to wriggle in the soil but my body was stiff.

'My father go do this ritual for me already, so you don't worry yourself, eh?' Osoosi reassured me. 'They go do this *Iwapele* burial ritual to every person chosen by the gods when their power awakens, to see if they can use their tribe's divine object. This is how I know I can use the Aganjù talisman one day.'

The Araba's voice buzzed next to my eardrums. '*The use of the divine object is normally passed down within families, but the person connected to it spiritually is the only one who can actually use it. I have taught great Olori warriors to use the Oya* hurricane whip, the Òṣun mirror and Ògún's soul-swallowing sword.' He winced, like it hurt him to admit it.

'Ògún is fearless like iron,' the Araba continued. 'As long as you are holding the Ògún sword you may show no fear. If the metal senses any feeling inside you, the thing go swallow you whole,' the Araba revealed.

Something terrible must have happened to make Taiwo so emotionless he could handle that sword. The Araba continued: 'Today I will teach you how to connect to your Olókun ancestors. The last user of the Night Stone will teach you the secret to the Night Stone . . . Many Olori men have greeted an untimely end trying to hold this thing. Outsiders from all corners of the earth have tried and failed to control its power.

'The Night Stone is made of darkness. And the darkest thing we must face in this life is death.' His eyes flashed white as he projected his voice into our brains.

I had no clue how I was just supposed to get over being scared of dying. No matter how painful each crisis was, I kept fighting through it cause there was stuff I needed to do. There was no way I was dying without knowing anything about who I really was. What the Araba was asking was impossible.

'Iwapele *means "I come to greet the earth"*,' the Araba continued, while Osoosi patted me all over with dirt. '*We say this because we believe that our ancestors and the gods did not die, but became one with Olori.*' His eyes flashed over me.

It was proper mad, you know, thinking that what I'd been mashing up under my Nike Airs was once part of the gods. I hoped they didn't mind.

The Araba pulled out a gourd shaped like an hourglass and held it out to Osoosi. She grinned at me, forcing my mouth open and making me chug down the mysterious drink.

'Oi, what do you think you're—?' I gurgled as the drink hit the back of my throat.

'This one na *Agbalumo*,' Osoosi explained, before I got around to asking. I'd never heard of it before. '*Ag-ba-loo-moh.*' She stretched out the sounds so I would get it.

It wasn't half bad. It was tangy and sweet, with a creamy, custardy taste.

I suddenly felt very, very sleepy. But then my head started spinning around crazily, and I didn't know which way was up. 'Wh-what's happening to me?' I stuttered through a mouthful of dirt, watching everything grow hazy.

'This go help you well-well. When I take this I speak to all my ancestors that have passed and they teach me how to use the Aganjù talisman,' Osoosi reassured me.

'*Remember the key is in your blood,*' the Araba added, as dark circles spun in front of my eyes. '*To use the Night Stone you must understand that your ancestors have passed away from themselves and become an important part of you. You should see your mother, the last Olókun to use the Night Stone, waiting to help you,*' the Araba's voice resonated, while spots of colour rushed in front of my eyes, drowning everything else out. '*Let the ancestors show you the way.*'

Then the Araba's voice faded until I couldn't hear him no more. Everything seemed to just melt away.

CHAPTER TWENTY

Demon Dad

A chill filled the air. I was standing upright in some random cave. The cool air wouldn't be enough to cause a crisis, but it put me on edge.

Rows of teeth-shaped stones hung high above me, splashing water on my forehead. My breath stilled in my throat as floating skulls emerged from the darkness and then materialised into Àbíkús. They passed their painted bodies through the cave's walls like they were made of air.

I hadn't seen them since the festival. This was my chance to see them up close. I held out my hand and waited until one approached me. It looked like a six-year-old kid had been dyed purple then painted with glow-in-the-dark white skeleton paint. It only came up to my waist. When it closed long fingers around my hand, its solid touch slowly turned my hand invisible.

As soon as it let go, my hand was visible again.

'Where am I?' I said to it, my hands shaking. The Àbíkú tilted its head as it looked at me, and then it ran ahead of me, swiping its hands across ancient blue patterns carved into the walls. As soon as it touched them, they sparked to life. The dark blue glowing symbols splashed fluorescent colours on my skin.

It looked properly peng, like someone had trapped a sky full of stars in the rock for ever.

Then I recognised one of the symbols. It was looped around like an infinity sign: the symbol of Olókun. The Araba hadn't been kidding about me meeting my ancestors.

I looked up, and my heart started thumping like crazy when I saw a looming, person-shaped outline at the end of the cave.

My tongue felt like dead weight in my mouth as I moved closer, a gigantic figure surrounded by a glowing army of Àbíkú kids slowly materialising in the dark.

My heart plummeted. The figure was too large to be human.

Black phantoms hovered over its shoulders like a ghostly cape, as it sat on a throne made of bones too big to belong to any animals I knew.

Its head moved, and then a pair of familiar yellow eyes burned through my skull.

I was totally bugging as I examined his rectangular wooden head more closely. His wooden mask with its drooping mouth and hollow eyes kinda looked like the Grim Reaper – if he had a new drip with giant horns.

I'd hoped to never see this creature again.

'Kokumo, blood of my blood, *e kaáb o*. You are welcome.' The spirit from the museum spoke with a voice as deep as the earth's insides. Its croaky voice made the cave walls tremble.

I stood in stunned silence. A thousand eyes rained down on me.

'What is the matter with you?' the spirit asked, pointing a black fingernail my way. 'This is an *Iwapele* ritual to meet your ancestors. Did you not expect to see your father here?'

My mum was nowhere to be seen and this crazy demon spirit was calling itself my father. *Why didn't the Araba warn me about this?*

'Nah, you ain't my father,' I said, shaking my head hard.

The demon threw its coffin head back and laughed, clutching its ribs like they would break. 'I used my power to keep your true identity a secret, even from that priest they call the Araba.'

My stomach fizzed like the strawberry laces I always got after school from the corner shop.

'You don't have to believe what I tell you. See for yourself,' it said, shrugging its hefty shoulders.

My heart thumped crazily as its fingers crawled to the giant mask and removed it slowly. Underneath, it looked like a human man – if you ignored the towering horns sprouting out of his head. But the pale yellow eyes were gone, along with the dusty black and red of the mask. His real eyes were dark maroon, like mine. He had unnaturally sharp cheekbones set in an ageless face that shone with black and red paint.

It was insane. It's like the guy cloned himself to produce me or something. I hated to admit it, but the resemblance was crazy.

I ain't gonna lie, though – I didn't feel no blood connection.

He beckoned me closer with a single finger.

I half expected the guy to plunge his long nails through my chest and rip my guts out, so I didn't move a muscle.

The shadows surrounding him shot out in blackish strings. They got more fleshed out as they reached towards me. I saw grime beneath their grey fingertips, rotting sleeves that flapped about as they wrapped their cold, undead fingers around my shoulders. Before I could even blink they had yanked me across the cave and pulled me right in front of him.

He took a long, hard look at me like there was something missing. Then he dipped his black fingernail in the white paint of an Àbíkú that was close to him.

'We do not have long before you return to the human world, so there is something you must understand,' he said, poking the centre of my forehead with a wet finger. 'The universe began as a crossroad between darkness and death. I was the guardian of death, born along with the goddess of night, Olókun. Your world began with the goddess giving her heart of night to me. I accepted it and used it to mould creatures from the dark to keep me company. The goddess and I agreed to separate the night from day, the sky from the ocean and the dead from the living.'

The demon fingers still roamed over my face. A cool sensation spread across my skin as his fingers travelled to my eyelids.

'This is why the ruling Ògún tribe in Olori always hated the Olókun tribe. They knew that if Olókun and night united again, a power great enough to change the universe would be born,' the demon explained. 'We Night Creatures were once honoured members of Olori. Mami Wata protected the seas between Olori and our territory against enemies, Àbíkús protected children in both lands who had no one else to turn to.' He began painting shapes under my eyes.

'Hundreds of moons ago we helped Olori win their fight against the outsiders who tried to steal their land. But they turned against us once the outsiders showed them how to steal our magic. The outsiders had stolen some of our power calling it *juju*, a French word for cursed doll, because that is what the outsiders saw us as. Now the Olori insult us by calling our sacred land, Jujuland. In turn, we became the devils they said we were and became the forest of a thousand demons where light never shines.' The demon paused for a moment, inspecting the work he'd done on my face.

I managed to meet his gaze. His eyes looked terrifyingly old – like he saw the world rise and fall with every blink.

'For many moons, I haunted the humans by resurrecting their dead. I hoped that the humans would stop stealing our magic if I ordered the Night Creatures to torment them by possessing their children and drowning their men. But their greed had no end.' The demon's crescent eyes narrowed at me, like he was trying to figure out how I'd feel about the whole ruining-Olori-people's-lives thing.

'So . . .' I cleared my throat. It felt like there were cobwebs chilling there after not saying anything for so long. 'Why did you have a kid with a human if you hated them so much?' I asked.

'Your mother,' he said simply. His voice softened for the first time. My mum's gentle laughter echoed in my mind as soon as he mentioned her. *I wish she was here*, I thought.

'In Olori, it is forbidden to mention my name, which is Lègbá. Tolani was the first human who wasn't afraid to call me by it.'

The demon stopped painting my face and fiddled with a black stone in his left ear. I recognised the symbol of Olókun instantly. The demon wasn't holding me any more, so I was free to move away, but I stayed right where I was, like I was stuck in a spell.

'Your mother was kind to the creatures of the night and wanted us to be accepted by humans.' Suddenly, he didn't look so scary no more. His eyes drooped at the sides the way mine sometimes did when I was thinking too hard.

'Once Tolani and I united, I ordered the Night Creatures to stop terrorising humans. But a human your mother was close to betrayed her, and the Ògún king learned of our union and secret child. He was threatened by the fact that the Olókun tribe and night were uniting. He was terrified of how strong our child might be if it inherited power from both of us. So he tried to destroy both the Olókun people, and my Night Creatures in Jujuland.' His voice turned cold and deadly. 'We were punished for choosing peace. I will never make that mistake again.'

My head was swimming, but a numb feeling in my body kept me standing. My eyes reeled as the shadows surrounding Lègbá rose up into tall, ghoul-like shapes that touched the rocky ceiling.

'We managed to keep you safe, but your tribe was wiped out, including your mother.' The shadows hovering over him drooped as his shoulders hunched over. 'The Ògún king and his men could not kill me, but they were able to trap me in the Crossroads, the portal between living and dead, using *juju*. I need the Night Stone to escape this place, and they know you are searching for it. They will not rest until the Night Stone is destroyed and our legacy is over. They know night is the heart of our land; without the darkness my creatures and I cannot breathe. Our only hope of survival is that no one knows how powerful you are.'

My guy had to be bugging. Like, how could I help someone older than the world, older than Time itself?

'Have you noticed the way that people in Olori use magic by drawing patterns to their gods in the earth or air, or touching objects with symbols drawn on them?' he asked.

I nodded, remembering the Araba's shining white necklace and how the beads around his neck rolled when his eyes flashed white.

'You have night blood in your veins. To us, magic is as natural as walking or running.'

I flinched at the 'us' part but kept listening.

'At the moment, you are still not making the most of your great potential. You are good at focusing and grounding yourself, and your balance has improved, but you are still relying on your crisis to use your real power.'

My cheeks felt warm, though the cave was cold.

So, Lègbá had been watching me the whole time.

I'd always thought my dad couldn't care less about me, but here he was apparently stalking my basket-carrying lessons.

'Let me explain in human terms. You run faster when someone is chasing you because you are running for survival. This is an adrenaline rush and it helps you push past your regular limits when you're in danger.'

I hmmed, following the explanation so far. Science happens to be my third best subject after art and English.

'That is what is happening at the moment with your powers. Your body is protecting you by automatically activating your powers during a sickle-cell crisis. But you don't need to rely on this. Just like how Olympians don't need to be chased to run really fast. They push themselves until moving fast becomes normal,' Lègbá said, as the shadows hovering over his shoulders separated and formed new shapes. A bunch of people appeared out of the dark, sludgy mist before my eyes: greyed-out soldiers, market women carrying baskets on their heads, and old manky dogs that hobbled over my feet.

'Kokumo, you have the ability to do so much *more*,' he said, as I bent down to stroke a ghost dog licking my toes. My fingers felt nothing but cool air as they went all the way through its patchy coat. 'You can conjure darkness as your mother did, but you can also raise the dead – or share moments with them, by touching their possessions. Just as I can.'

Lègbá raised his hand and clicked his fingers. 'Try pushing yourself to your limit without your fear getting in the way.' His dark maroon eyes glittered at me. 'You can't hold back from your power when the time comes for you to hold the Night Stone. You must fight for your own survival and contain the great energy within it.'

My knees knocked together as the ground began shaking. 'Wait, what do you mean?' I yelled, as Lègbá began slowly melting into the dark.

'Kokumo, you are my son,' his voice rang out. 'You are also partially formed from darkness, so you need night to survive. As you are half human, I don't know what would happen to you if the Night Stone was destroyed. But as your father, it is my duty to warn you.'

My blood chilled in my veins as I took in the words – might not survive. I'd heard them before cause I was used to being sick, but for the first time I actually had the power to stop it happening. For some reason that only made me more terrified. Lẹ̀gbá gripped my shoulders and pulled me closer to him. He didn't use his ghosts this time. 'As long as I am trapped here, you must find your own tribe of people you can trust to protect you.'

'You're trapped?' I asked.

Lẹ̀gbá didn't answer, he gave me a long hard look and then folded his giant arms around me. His chest was warm, his musk – palm oil, tobacco, a hint of coconut – burned my nose.

'*O daaro*. I will not be trapped in the Crossroads for ever. Before I leave you, you must know that your most dangerous enemies are not those who are obsessed with power, but those desperate to unleash the darkest secrets of the universe. Once you save the night we will meet again, *omo mi owon*, my son. I am the guardian, and you are the gatekeeper of the Crossroads. Please keep my existence secret from the humans.'

His fading hands roamed over my twists.

'And the horns are a nice touch,' he said, with a wink.

'NO!' I screamed, as he dissolved into the darkness.

A bright light erupted behind my eyes. I sat up spluttering a whole bunch of dirt.

'*Did you see your mother on the other side?*'

It took me a moment to realise it was the Araba talking.

'Nope,' I said, watching his shoulders sink low. 'But I did see the . . . I mean, my—'

'*Kokumo.*' The Araba's eyebrows knitted into a deep frown, his beaded necklace rolled and his eyes flashed brightly at me and then dimmed slowly.

I shivered, wondering if the Araba already knew my secret. I didn't want to hide anything from him, as he'd looked out for me and taught me loads of important stuff, but having a real blood family was something I'd always wanted.

'I saw my . . .' I struggled to get the word out without revealing everything I knew. '. . . father.'

'*Don't worry, Kokumo. The ancestors have spoken. Even an Araba does not need to know all,*' he said. But his voice, normally sure and steady, betrayed a crack.

CHAPTER TWENTY-ONE

The Mark of a Warrior

My cheeks still tingled from where the demon's hands had touched them.

'Koku, how far now?' Osoosi asked, scooping the sand away from me so I could sit upright. It was Olori slang for 'What's up?'

I didn't know what to think or say. I was still reeling from the convo with my demon dad. I still hadn't made up my mind yet. Was my dad a demon? Most definitely. Was he a bad guy? Maybe, maybe not.

It was insane. I had a dad who, in his own really strange and terrifying way, had been looking out for me. I was part of something – I'd *always* been a part of something.

I wasn't alone.

Keep my identity a secret from the humans – my dad's voice reverberated in my head as I cleared my throat to speak. 'I'm just wondering if I'll ever be strong enough to control the Night Stone,' I said, deciding to go with the non-demon related stuff.

'You are the only one with the power to restore night to Olori. The Araba's Oracle no dey lie for mouth!' Osoosi said this with chest.

I shrugged at her as we turned back. I guess we'd find out sometime.

'Koku, are you hearing this *ewuro* smell again? Something is not right somewhere,' Osoosi announced suddenly as we walked back across the Mami Wata's lagoon.

'Nah,' I said. I took a deep sniff and smelled salty water and mulchy earth. But I knew the girl-with-the-nose could sense stuff I couldn't. And the air was rippling, like there was something pushing through it.

Osoosi had a point – something weird was definitely going on. A faint high-pitched whine irritated my ears like when you leave the fridge door open for too long, and I swear I caught a movement from the corner of my eye that looked like a kind of wobbly, transparent shape on the rocky shore.

Knowing she wouldn't be able to hear the whine, I was about to ask Osoosi if she could see anything when the Araba interrupted my thoughts, slapping my back heartily and crying, 'Ehen! *Kokumo! I go give you something.*'

He pulled out a white thing from his baggy trousers that looked like a dead rat.

I inspected the bloated flower warily. 'You really didn't have to,' I said, and I meant that.

'*This is not for you, you hear? It is for Moremi, the one that go make your heart go* tungba!'

He had clearly lost the plot if he thought I fancied Moremi, when there were bare peng Ọṣun girls who didn't have attitude problems back in Olori.

'So, you're the one that taught Moremi about the magic braids, then?' I asked, poking gingerly at the flower where it lay on my palm. I still had loads of questions about her hair. I knew she got the powers for it from that giant tree we saw when we first walked into Jujuland, but that was about it.

'*It is an ancient Babalú remedy but, yes, you are very right – I am the one that introduced her to this thing.*' The Araba sounded like he was choosing his words carefully. '*Kokumo, I know you have plenty questions about this thing. But the only thing you can be knowing is there is heavy price for this power.'*

'What does that mean?' I asked, weighing the flower in my palm. The soft petals had a faint honey scent. It was surprisingly heavy, even though it wasn't even that big.

'*Not everything the eye sees should be spoken by the mouth. Make you run your own race,* abi? *We all have our own destiny to face.'* The Araba's cloudy eyes hovered over my head, like they were staring at something far away.

When we finally got to the hut, Moremi was leaning on the door frame with her arms crossed, silently watching me.

Osoosi's eyes bounced between us.

Moremi disappeared back into the hut and then stomped back out and over to me, a mirror in her hands. She was so close, her eyelashes fluttered against mine briefly before she lifted it up to my face.

My cheeks heated up as she traced her forefinger all the way down my face to my chin. 'This is an *akin* mark. The mark of a warrior.'

I stared at my reflection open-mouthed. I wondered why Osoosi hadn't said nothing about it before.

There were white swirls around my eyes and a long

line drawn down my nose and under my chin. It was the paint my demon father had used during the ritual. I hadn't thought it would last when I returned to the real world.

I was glad it did, cause it actually *banged*.

'Now you are *oyinbo* no more,' Moremi said.

I nodded, even though it didn't feel that simple. I was always going to be in between, no matter what I looked like.

You must find your own tribe of people you can trust. My father's deep voice echoed in my head.

We were a tribe of weirdos when I really thought about it: Moremi had magic braids, I had a demon dad who'd given me his zombie powers, and Osoosi was half-dog or something. But somehow I knew I belonged with them.

It made me want to dead the beef with Moremi. And if I'm being real, I was jealous of Moremi and Taiwo. I'd always wanted siblings so I wouldn't feel so lonely all the time. Osoosi had ten brothers, and Moremi had a whole twin even though they were mortal enemies. But I knew she'd tell me about Taiwo one day, when she was ready.

I shuffled in my back pocket for the *iroko* flower and handed it to her. 'So, yeah, this . . . I dunno, maybe you can use it for your hair or something?'

She snatched it out of my palms and immediately started pouring its amber liquid on to her scalp, gently massaging it in circles.

'So, you ain't gonna say thank you or nothing? You're rude, fam,' I said, only half joking.

She just laughed right in my face. She was lucky she had a nice laugh, or I would've said something. Swear down, man.

*

The next morning there was a weird atmosphere at the table.

Ever since the Araba had checked the Oracle, he kept jumping up at the tiniest noise. 'Did you see a bad fate?' I asked.

The Araba cleared his throat, which was funny as he didn't use his voice to speak. *'There is truth in this saying of our elders: "However fast yam runs goat will eat him, however fast goat runs tiger will eat him, and however fast man runs earth will eat him."'*

'I ain't ever seen no running yam before,' I mumbled.

'Today is the last day before the summer solstice. Now I must tell you the location of the Night Stone.'

He let out a long sigh. '*But first we must break the kola. The* oriki *prayer is yours,*' he said to me, breaking the lobe into four equal parts.

I held it up to the orange light, admiring how perfectly black it was.

'*Orun mo eni ti yoo la.* The sky knows who will prosper.' I recited the prayer to Rùnmí, the god of wisdom, the way he taught me, but the Araba shook his head at me.

'*Today we will say the Olókun* oriki *in your honour!*' He slapped the table, making our *garri* dance in our bowls. '*Goddess of the bright moon and darkest night. We give you praise,*' he said slowly, teaching me the words.

After that, we all said the Olókun *oriki* in unison. A warm glow lit up my cheeks around my warrior mark. Osoosi patted my back, while Moremi offered one of her half-smiles as I brought the kola nut to my lips, preparing myself for the bitter taste.

But before I could chow down on it, the door swung open, scattering the kola pieces across the floor.

'Wetin be dat?' Osoosi asked, sniffing around her.

There was nothing there. I shrugged and looked towards the Araba for an explanation.

'*He wears rags and dances in the night, but soon it*

will be daylight,' he hummed, staring straight ahead as if he could see something clearly in front of him.

The air had changed. It pulsed like there was a force moving through it. We all looked around, trying to figure it out, until we heard slow, heavy steps, and the *clank*, *clank*, *clank*ing of metal against the floor.

CHAPTER TWENTY-TWO

Juju Junkie

A sickening crunch echoed as a kola piece was crushed by an invisible foot. And then the air rippled as an armoured figure slowly materialised in front of us.

The colour drained out of Moremi's face. Osoosi's tongue practically fell out her mouth.

I'd know those dead-fish eyes anywhere.

'*E kaaaro*, Taiwo.' The Araba rose from his stool and, for the first time, moved his lips to speak.

'If you have harmed a hair on my father's head, you are finished!' Osoosi yelled.

The spidery black veins bulging around Taiwo's neck didn't seem to faze her. His eyes were totally black, it looked like the night had eaten his eyeballs, so you could only see holes where they used to be. He let out a tired sigh. 'Of course, our king would never seriously harm a tribal chief, even if he is a traitor to his own kind.'

The knots in my stomach loosened. I squeezed Osoosi's shoulder tight. My guy was being proper rude, but at least now we knew Chief Inaki was okay.

'I see that you have returned using *juju* power that is not your own,' the Araba said calmly.

'I have crossed this cursed land to find you,' Taiwo said, as his eyes faded back to their usual colour. He ran a hand over his neat cornrows and surveyed the room until his eyes locked on mine.

'Why are you tryna end me?' I asked, heart thumping as I peered behind him to see if his iron mandem were close behind.

'*Ki lo de?* What's the matter with you?' He let out a short laugh that he quickly killed in his throat. 'You think I came all this way just for an *oyinbo*?'

I flinched. 'But . . . you've been looking for me all this time,' I mumbled. I looked to Moremi, but she just stood there, her almond eyes unnaturally wide.

Taiwo unsheathed his sword when he caught sight of her. It was the length of his entire arm – long, wide and flat, with a curved end. The shining metal hissed as he ripped it out of its sheath. Glowing, swirling patterns sprawled over its surface and it pulsed in his hands like it was a living, breathing thing. Beads of sweat trickled down Taiwo's forehead as he gripped the handle tight, like it was taking everything he had not to crack the metal over her skull.

'You are confused.' Taiwo's lips contorted into a dry smile as he looked at me, lifting his pierced brow in scorn. 'Good. There is nothing more terrifying to an outsider than something they don't understand.'

This guy was a legit savage. I swear down, it was like it ran in the family or something.

'So, you're *not* going to kill me then?' I asked, ignoring the way my insides liquified when he stared at me.

'The king wants you dead, of course, but I'm actually here on a rescue mission.' He shrugged, apparently admiring the way the patterns on the sword shimmered when it caught the light.

The tightness in my chest loosened the teeniest bit. Maybe he wasn't going to murder me.

'Rescue mission?' I repeated, just to make sure I heard that right.

But then the floor shuddered with the weight of many more heavy, clunking steps, and the knots in my stomach tightened again as a dozen Ògún warriors stormed into the room. They were the same goons that had tried to end us back in Aganjù. Each of them held a sharp spear that pointed to the high heavens.

'Remember if you no act your own, of course this earth go swallow you!' The beads on the Araba's neck rolled viciously as a silent storm brewed in his cloudy eyes.

'Do as I say, and I won't harm them,' Taiwo said, jerking his chin at us.

The Araba's eyes darkened immediately, and his necklace stopped moving. 'For now.'

Taiwo smirked. 'Take him!' he ordered.

We watched as a bunch of guys built like a block of flats crossed their spears over the Araba's chest.

'He has kept himself hidden for years, but your stench made it easy for our friend to track you to this place.' Taiwo's lips tilted. 'A dupe pupo, thanks for leading us to him.'

A movement out of the corner of my eye made me turn to Osoosi. She was drawing an air sign, about to transform into a hyena. 'We no go let you take Baba from us!' she yelled, as her spotted fur spiked up like razor blades.

Moremi's braids, however, stayed still; they hung

limply by her ears. But her eyes hardened as she faced them all with her bare fists.

We were so outnumbered it wasn't even funny. A pair of Ògún guys held the Araba prisoner as the rest of them rushed towards us.

I ignored the way my knees had started knocking relentlessly, like a door-to-door salesman. I closed my eyes and focused. I blocked everything out and used the grounding technique I normally used in a crisis. I concentrated on the sound of the water lapping against the shore. The sounds of the waves washed over me until I felt like I was a part of it. A tingling feeling flooded my body.

When I opened my eyes, I met Osoosi's wide hazel ones.

I'm no good at maths, but I had conjured a dozen ghosts that formed a shield around us. And for the first time everyone could see what I could, as sludgy, glistening forms blacked out the light and confused the Ògún warriors, who were now fighting with dead people.

Taiwo's slightly raised eyebrow was the only sign he was caught by surprise. 'It can't be . . . that is not the power of Olókun. What kind of magic is that?'

'It's something else, fam,' I said, feeling powerful,

imagining my demon father hovering over me with his towering frame and large horns.

Taiwo nodded at his biggest henchman, who had four ferocious tribal marks carved into his cheeks. Clearly hygiene wasn't his priority, as he licked the flat side of his blade with an evil grin as a silver ring flashed over his eyes.

It was the fastest I'd ever seen someone power up. He spread a bunch of knives like a deck of cards and threw them at my phantom army with terrifying precision. Each ghost let out a horrible raspy noise when they were speared with the cold metal and then dissolved into a swirling black mist.

I acted on instinct. Static energy burned through me like a rush of adrenaline. A shadowy arm shot out of my side and knocked the blades away. But then I found myself doubled over, panting madly. I figured that summoning more than one ghost took a toll on me. I'd managed to stop them all, but my energy had run out sooner than I thought.

The smirk didn't leave Taiwo's face as he watched me. I was hunched over, trying to catch my breath. 'Nice try,' he said.

'They go call me No-Miss,' the big guy said, pointing his meaty hands at the fallen daggers. 'Why?' he asked, cause no one else was going to. 'Because I no miss.'

Then the blades zipped through the air again. One moment, we were standing there; the next, we were stuck to the walls of the hut. Each blade with its leopard-form handle had pinned our clothes.

'*Yepa!*' Osoosi gasped dramatically. The shock had forced her back into her human form.

Moremi groaned as she tried to wrench herself from the wall. A thin trail of grey smoke rose from an iron blade that had been thrown in a space right near her face. The single knife kissed her cheek. If No-Miss had thrown it any closer, it would've sliced her nose clean off.

A crackling noise like a hot stove filled the air.

'*Chai!* Wetin be dat smell?' Osoosi yelped.

My nose curled up. A bitter scent turned my nose hairs to dust. The smell was sickening: charcoal mixed with leather being burnt. Moremi groaned in pain as she tried to wrench herself free. And that's when I realised – it was coming from her.

Moremi's eyes were large and wet as she stared at Taiwo, like she was begging him without words. It was mad, cause the Moremi I knew never begged no one for nothing.

'You may leave us; guard the perimeter in case any Night Creatures come to their aid.' Taiwo raised a hand and dismissed the Ògún warriors. They stormed out wordlessly giving us deathly stares. Now it was just me, the Araba, Moremi, Osoosi and a psycho with a soul-swallowing sword.

'Àbíkús are extremely sensitive to iron,' Taiwo said, like it was obvious, looking over his shoulder. 'Then again, I wouldn't expect an outsider to know that.'

Moremi avoided my gaze, which was getting easier to do as the smoke started to cover her entire face like a dark veil.

Taiwo's eyes twitched madly, even as the rest of his

face looked unbothered as usual. 'How stupid can you be? Your so-called friend isn't human!' When he saw my doubt, he continued: 'Why else would she react to the iron blade like that?'

'There's no way . . .' I said, as I turned to Moremi.

But she kept inching away from the blade, her eyelids pressed tight.

'The devil is a liar!' Osoosi piped up, a fire blazing in her eyes. 'I no go believe you! My *oga* no be Àbíkú. She is a great warrior!' When Taiwo ignored her, she continued: 'Do you think you are knowing anything about honour, eh?' Osoosi yelled. 'You shameless, tribeless nobody who does not respect his own roots!'

Taiwo stared at Osoosi with vacant eyes. 'Your *oga* is a parasite that feeds on Olori souls,' he said, matter-of-factly.

The room spun around me. The way Moremi was reacting to the iron blade was the exact same way the Àbíkú had reacted to those iron handcuffs at the festival. As if she was being burned.

'Àbíkús are cunning little parasites,' Taiwo said. 'Normally they swap back around the time the child reaches their tenth year. I waited and waited.' He moved forward until he was inches from Moremi's face. 'But *you* stayed . . . you have been living my sister's days, while she rots somewhere in this cursed jungle.'

It all fell into place: Moremi wasn't scared of Taiwo like the rest of us; nah, she'd been acting strange whenever his name was mentioned this whole time cause she felt *guilty*.

It was a mad ting – Moremi was an Àbíkú, and she'd swapped with Kehinde, Taiwo's sister.

Suddenly the name-change made sense.

'*Tayewo*. It is enough!' The Araba intervened, his eyes flashing brightly as the beads on his necklace rattled noisily. 'What you are doing is against your precious king's orders. What would the king say if he knew you suspected an Àbíkú in your own family and you kept this secret, instead of letting the mighty Ògún handle it?'

'You're not wrong.' Taiwo breathed slowly, like he was resisting the urge to rip us all to shreds. My man really needed do some yoga or take a mindfulness class or something. 'But Kehinde is my sister. My duty to her comes first. This parasite must live until I destroy the Night Stone. Then, once she is freed from this hell and the leech is dead, I'll let the last Olókun descendant and the Aganjù reject rot in Jujuland.'

'So, you would shave the crow's feathers but claim

that the blade is blunt when it is the vulture's turn?' the Araba said.

'You may borrow the words of ancestors to call me a hypocrite if you like.' Taiwo brought out his sword – fluorescent lines spread across the curved metal like it had suddenly awakened. 'But I promise you, my blade will be sharp when it comes to your turn.'

CHAPTER TWENTY-THREE

Kehinde's Wish

The Araba turned to us suddenly; his eyes were glowing white as he projected his voice through our brains. *'Listen well, you must find the Night Stone at any cost. The fate of Olori is depending on the three of you. Don't worry for me, I am a man who carries death in his pocket. I cannot die. The location of the stone is not too far from where we are standing . . .'*

We listened carefully from the wall, feet dangling, hanging on to the Araba's every word. Taiwo followed our gaze to the Araba's sealed lips.

'You must first find—' the Araba started to say. And then in one swift movement Taiwo lifted his giant glowing sword right under his chin.

280

'No more secret mind-reading conversations,' Taiwo said flatly and nodded towards the doorway. 'Now lead me to the Night Stone,' he demanded, walking the Araba out of the hut. We watched our only hope of finding the Night Stone walk away, with our feet dangling pathetically in the air like we were overgrown babies in highchairs. The Araba was the one who protected us, who trained us. We were nothing without him.

Osoosi began kicking her legs, using the momentum to pull the daggers out of the wooden walls.

I copied her and when the knives came loose, I wriggled free.

Moremi's breaths were slow and ragged, and her eyes were closed. She was still shaking from being too close to the iron daggers that had pinned her to the wall.

Osoosi and I looked at each other

and nodded. We were still trying to get our heads around the Àbíkú stuff, but one thing was certain: for the first time ever, Moremi needed our help.

We took out the daggers one by one. We made sure we didn't touch her skin with the metal, or slice up any of her braids. When she was free, she slumped to the floor as though she had no bones in her body.

The tension in the room was so thick, even a chainsaw wouldn't have put a dent in it. I guess we all finally deeped how doomed we were.

Taiwo was gonna find the Night Stone with the Araba and we were gonna be trapped in Jujuland for ever.

Even Osoosi, who was normally a walking talking energy drink advert, slouched to the floor.

'My big brother betrayed us!' she said, cradling her head in her hands. 'He go be the one that led the Ògún to us.'

'Why would he do that? I thought your family needed night back cause of your animals and stuff?' I said.

'*Nawa* for us-oh.' Osoosi sucked in a sharp breath and then let it all out. 'Sebe has always wanted to follow Ògún rules. He thinks if the Ògún trust Aganjù we can become great again, like the days of old.' Her tongue clicked at the back of her mouth. '*Chai!* He must believe the lie that they will share their technology with us and give us all the power to live without sleep like their own warriors. I should have known when I smelled the *ewuro* leaf in the jungle, Sebe is the one teaching me about this thing. That is what the Ògún have been using to follow us.'

I stared hard at the holes the daggers left in the wall, remembering how Osoosi's brother practically decapitated me at dinner back in Aganjù. He must've known I was the Olókun descendant all along, and if he was on the Ògún side, he probably hated me for it.

The room was silent while we all reflected on his betrayal.

Then I turned to Moremi. 'So . . . when were you planning on telling us you're an Àbíkú?' I asked, straight up.

Osoosi blinked in shock, finally breaking her no-blink streak.

Moremi turned. 'Do you remember your life in Olori, before you were sent to England?'

'Nah, I don't remember nothing. And what has that got to do with you being an Àbíkú?' I huffed.

Moremi sighed at my answer. I dunno what she expected. I hadn't lived in Olori since I was three years old. Okay, maybe I faintly remember running around with some annoying kid that flicked my ears, but I didn't even remember what my own mum was like.

'I am sure you are knowing the "stories",' Moremi said. 'Àbíkús no go steal children,' Moremi said firmly, pressing her full lips into a line. 'They only swap souls with permission from the child. Because young children still remember their connection to the spirit world, and adults forget. That is why the Àbíkú can talk to children at night. If the child does not agree, they will not exchange with an Àbíkú.' Moremi fidgeted with one of her braids. 'Àbíkús have a bad reputation, but they are free spirits who just want to experience life outside Jujuland. After all, they used to pass freely between Jujuland and Olori before the war between humans and Night Creatures.'

'Eh, is that so?' Osoosi piped up. 'But why would any child want to be Àbíkú?'

'Àbíkús live freely – they no have worries at all. They live as children in Jujuland, and live a happy life with no *wahala*,' Moremi explained.

Osoosi scratched her head like she was considering this.

'To swap with an Àbíkú the child must make a wish that connects them to the real world,' Moremi went on, now pulling at the purple threads in her ankara cloth instead of her braids. 'Once the wish is accepted, the Àbíkú will take the child's place in Olori and the child will be turned into an Àbíkú spirit in Jujuland.'

'So, what was your wish?' I asked.

'Kehinde's wish' – Moremi's deep brown eyes looked in my direction – 'was for you, Kokumo.'

Osoosi stared, open-mouthed.

'What are you talking about?' I blurted.

'Before you went to England, Mama Oti was your guardian in Olori. She was one of your mother's closest friends. She was looking after you with the twins who were also staying with her – Taiwo and Kehinde.'

I nodded, cause that lined up with stuff my uncle had said about living with some kids in Mama Oti's place.

'Many moons ago, when you were smaller than a piece of yam, the twins took you outside at night. *Abi*, you are knowing that night is the only time where Jujuland creatures can pass over into Olori?'

I nodded.

'The twins wanted to see if the creatures from the stories were real,' Moremi said.

'Wetin dem see?' Osoosi whispered.

'They did not see any creatures of the night, but

they did see an Ògún warrior with powers from the god of iron.' Moremi paused. 'His whole body was covered from head to toe in sharp-sharp knives.'

'*Yepa!*' Osoosi scooched over on the floor so she was closer to us.

'The twins had never seen this strange man before. But he had orders from the king to take the small boy.' Moremi glanced in my direction. 'You.'

'*Aba!* Gods forbid!' Osoosi interjected, with another Nollywood sound effect.

I shut my eyes and tried to imagine this metal guy, but I couldn't remember nothing. He didn't exactly sound chill, so the memory block was probably for the best.

'There was nothing the twins could do to stop the man from taking you. So Kehinde closed her eyes and wished for anything to save him . . .'

Moremi's voice got so quiet we had to lean in to hear her.

'An Àbíkú.' I whispered the words at the same time as she did.

'Protect Kokumo.' These go be the first words I tasted when I entered the human world,' Moremi said, looking up to meet my gaze for the first time in ages. Then she looked away again. 'The truth is I don't remember anything before I became Kehinde. But I remembered all of her memories and how much she cared about protecting Koku and her brother, Taiwo.' She sighed. 'I knew of Taiwo when he was good. But I never understood why Kehinde used her human life to protect this boy. It made me confused and angry. So I wanted to continue the twins' bond, even if Taiwo does believe in finishing night and getting rid of all the Night Creatures for good.'

Moremi's braids stirred as she drew her knees up to her chin. 'Taiwo was never the same after that day. He does not know that Kehinde wished to be an Àbíkú to save you, Koku. He is thinking his sister has been stolen by Night Creatures and now he will not rest until she is returned. This is why he wants to destroy the Night Stone. He thinks that when all the Àbíkú spirits die the children they swapped with will be returned.'

Osoosi's face screwed up. She was scarily silent for a few moments, and then she leaped up from the floor. '*Oga*-boss! You are a great warrior. I no care if you be creature of night, or you be slice of bread!' she declared, passionately. 'In Aganjù we have one saying – the thing wey mata be your true heart, no be the thing wey you fit see for eyes, or talk for mouth.'

Moremi's braids crawled over Osoosi's shoulders, but instead of strangling the living daylights out of her she pulled her into a warm embrace. Then they both turned to me, expecting me to join in or something.

I shifted. Part of me wanted to join in. I looked around the room instead.

The Araba's stuff had been mashed up; glass, broken pieces of clay pots, peacock feathers, cowrie shells, pins and stuffing from the voodoo dolls were all dashed on the floor, along with the iron daggers. The two dolls I noticed earlier were the only ones left standing on the Araba's shelves. They looked exactly the same, like twins: two unsmiling faces on long-necked bodies, one with a red necklace and the other with a blue one. Taiwo's hollow eyes flashed into my head. They were empty cause his sister had been taken from him. That's probably how he got rid of his feelings and controlled the Ògún sword so easily.

'What Taiwo said is still true, though.' I shrugged. 'You're here instead of the real Kehinde.'

'Koku, Osoosi, I should not have lied to you,' Moremi said in quiet voice, 'But I swear to the goddess, I am the same Moremi you have known. At first all I knew was Kehinde's own memories, and my duty to protect you. But then I made memories of my own.

And I made a life of my own with Mama Oti, and both of you,' she said earnestly. 'We don't have much time left. We need to do whatever we can to find the Night Stone together.'

'I gotta go for a walk. I'm done with all this. The Araba was the only one who knew where the Night Stone was and he's with Taiwo now.' I cleared my throat as I got up from the floor and dusted my knees. 'It's over,' I said, as my throat squeezed painfully tight. That would be the end of the Night Creatures for ever, and that meant Moremi wouldn't survive and if what my dad said was true, maybe I wouldn't either.

Moremi didn't say nothing when I got up to leave. Her eyes shined over, but she nodded understanding what I meant. I was giving up on both of us. I couldn't bear to look at her no more.

It was almost unbearably hot outside. The moonlight that shone down was so bright and perfect it turned my eyeballs to mush.

As I walked along the coast, I was felt totally numb. The Night Creatures were doomed. I'd just reunited with my real dad only to let him down epically. And Olori was finished for sure.

We had *failed*.

I had failed.

And the worst part of my brain kept replaying everything I'd just learned. But I couldn't hate on Moremi for being an Àbíkú. I remembered the Àbíkú kid from the festival's weird clicky noises and giant eyes. It didn't just look like a kid, it acted like one too. I knew it wasn't evil. At least, not in the way we'd been taught.

And the burial ritual had showed me I was just like Moremi in a way: I was half spirit.

What it all came down to was that Moremi was just trying to protect me. She had a funny way of showing it, but she'd always had my back, no matter what. But, I dunno. Soul stealing seemed wrong.

I stopped walking and looked up at the night sky. My whole life I didn't notice the people who had given up stuff to be around me, not just my new friends: Kehinde, the Araba, Mama Oti, my uncle, Jollof . . . plus my parents, who I inherited my magic powers from.

It was a lot when I thought about it. As hopeless as it was, I didn't want to give up.

CHAPTER TWENTY-FOUR

The Gatekeeper of the Crossroads

My thoughts were interrupted by a jarring, whining noise. It made me want to rip my ears off and then light them on fire. It was hard searching in the dark, even with the light of the Jujuland moon. I searched the ground under a canopy of glowing leaves until I found a half-transparent Àbíkú lying on its side. Its eyes were closed, its long lashes fanning out over its inky, round baby cheeks. It was twitching violently, blinking in and out of existence.

I brought down a branch so I could see better and inspected the dark purple kid carefully – it was kinda hard, cause it kept disappearing every five seconds. And it was then that I spotted the mosquito-bot lodged in its small neck, its glass wings still flapping. There were swollen veins around the bite. It looked painful.

I swivelled around, checking behind me. If there was a mosquito-bot on an Àbíkú, Taiwo could be stealing its invisibility to walk around the jungle.

Moremi's skin had burned just from being close to iron; I had no clue how long the Àbíkú had been stuck like that. But every time I tried to yank the mosquito out, my hand went straight through the Àbíkú's neck, just like when I tried to pet that ghost dog my dad summoned. It was like trying to grab hold of a shadow.

I knelt down next to it and focused on the tiny silver buzzing dot. I tried to use my power to summon ghosts to reach out and grab it, but every time I tried I felt dizzy and shaky. My powers must have still been weak from the Ògún attack. So, remembering the Araba's teachings, I closed my eyes and meditated.

Moments later, cool metal grazed my fingertip. I pinched the mosquito's tiny metallic body and gently pulled the thin needle out of the Àbíkú's neck.

As soon as the Àbíkú kid was free it got up and looked up at me with giant black eyes. Its neck was still bruised but less swollen. I recognised its unblinking stare – I was pretty sure it was the Àbíkú from the festival.

I took two steps back and so did the Àbíkú. I pointed, and it pointed right back at me.

It felt so different from when I first arrived in Olori. I couldn't help wonder if a kid's promise brought it here. And if it had, who was the kid the Àbíkú swapped with?

'Er . . . Yoruba? *Se o le so o?* Do you speak it?'

I knew my Yoruba was peak, but I had to try.

'ꝊꝋꝊꝋ, Ꝋ Ꝋ‼ ‼, ꝊꝋꝊꝋ, Ꝋ Ꝋ‼ ‼ ‼Ꝋ Ɪ ‖Ꝋɪ ‖' The Àbíkú released a whole bunch of strange sounds. The clicking noises it made echoed along the shore. It sounded like a car backing up, like *skrrrrrrat,* then *pap-pap ka-ka-ka boom*! It sort of had a rhythm to it, like a good Trap beat.

Then it did a weird and totally random thing.

It reached out and flicked my ears.

I used to know a kid who did that.

'Wait . . . who are you?' I said, as it started to get all misty and blurry. I stood on the shore trying to figure out who that kid from my memories was until the Àbíkú completely disappeared.

But I didn't have time to think as, just then, a large wave crashed on the shore and a glistening figure emerged from the water. It was a Mami Wata in their human form.

I craned my neck, expecting to hear a smooth velvety voice, or catch a glimpse of a sparkling tail, but Yemaya was nowhere to be seen.

'Honoured chile of Olókun,' the Mami Wata said, bowing her head as she walked towards me in a glittering dress that looked like it was made out of water droplets. She was the leng Mami Wata who was always by Yemaya's side, with cowrie shells braided in her hair. 'Or should I say son of Lẹ̀gbá, di guardian of di Crossroads?' she asked, with a full-lipped smile.

I stared at her in shock as she winked at me with her violet eyes. The thing was, I didn't remember telling the Mami Wata about my demon dad. But I guess it wasn't a bad thing for Night Creatures to know I was the son of their leader.

'After yuh left wi prayed tuh Lẹ̀gbá an 'im answer wi prayas. 'im say 'im trap now but 'im a send 'im sone from di land of outsidas tuh save us,' the Mami Wata explained. 'Yuh our only hope.'

'We?' I tilted my head in confusion.

And, in a blink, the shoreline was teeming with Night Creatures, rising up out of the earth or crawling out of the water, hanging from the trees or coming in to land from the sky. Àbíkús appeared out of thin air;

young kids with grassy skirts and shining purple skin painted with neon white skeleton paint. The one I'd just helped was still glitching a little and couldn't disappear fully like the others. Three-headed crows flew over my head, along with flying fish and firefly people who swung their lamps, bathing me in a warm amber light.

'*Kabiyesi!*' The Mami Wata started chanting, 'Your Majesty!' at me.

Then the Mami Wata with cowrie shells in her hair spoke to me: 'Di iron people – dem av used dem wicked mosquitos an take wi leader fi *juju*,' she said, her head bowed low.

That explains why Yemaya is missing. I clenched my fist tight, remembering the last mosquito attack in the lagoon. If I was there I wouldn't have let that slide. I would've summoned the maddest ghost hand to slap up those metal parasites.

'They planning fi get rid of night tomorrow. Wi need yuh help,' the Mami Wata said. And then, every single Night Creature, from the ginormous two-tailed alligators down to the teeniest firefly followed her lead: they all bowed to me in the *dobale* pose and chanted, '*Kabiyesi!*'

*

295

It was hard to feel like I deserved to be called *Kabiyesi* when I had just stood by and done nothing as the Ògún stole the leader of the Mami Wata and the Araba away.

The Jujuland mandem were still counting on me to save night, but now that the Araba was with Taiwo I couldn't do it – my guy hadn't even told me where to find the Night Stone before he got captured. And even if I did miraculously find a way to confront Taiwo before he got to the stone, he had a soul-swallowing sword and a bunch of of knife-throwing goons.

All I had was a couple of ghosts and an incurable disease.

There *had* to be another way.

I ain't gonna front or nothing. I was scared. I'm scared of my sickle cell and the psycho *juju*-powered assassin tryna end me, and I sometimes get scared of the barber who doesn't like me pushing my hairline way back. But I'm even more shook of what I'm made of and who I might be.

That's why I've always felt weird whenever someone said my full name. *Kokumo. Don't die any more.* Cause it isn't just my name. It is a prayer. But it isn't for me.

I looked around at all the strange Jujuland faces that were becoming familiar.

It was bigger than me. It was for all of us.

'Alright, we got this,' I said, trying to make my voice sound calm. 'You say you're the oldest creatures in Olori, so one of you lot have *got* to know where the Night Stone is, you get me?'

The Mami Wata shook her head, making her braids bounce against her shoulders. 'Only di Araba knows using 'im Oracle.' She paused then, looking at me with misty lilac eyes. 'Many moons ago dem sey one English explorer located di Night Stone. But 'im tek di knowledge tuh 'im grave.'

'Took the knowledge to the grave, you say?' I said, a big fat grin on my face. 'Yeah, I can work with that.'

I don't have too many skills, but communicating with the dead is in my top five.

I walked up to the largest rock on the shore and stood on top of it. I looked out at all the Night Creatures surrounding me. 'Okay, guys, I'm gonna need you lot to collect the stuff from the boats and bring me anything that looks like it might've belonged to old timey British explorers,' I said, remembering the convo I'd heard when I touched that mouldy fedora.

It didn't take too long until I had a massive pile of stuff that had been flown, dragged or swum from the other side of the lagoon, gathered from the wrecked boats. The pile by my feet contained a fancy-looking quill pen, a broken globe – and the once beige, now bogey-green fedora.

I placed the hat on my head and got to work – but not before the Mami Wata set me up with a satin bonnet to protect my twists.

As soon as the damp felt touched my head, I began to hear whispers.

Maybe this was a bad idea, I thought, as my knees wobbled and I almost buckled. But the Mami Wata formed a circle around me and held me upright.

It was totally different from the Araba projecting his voice in my head. I felt like I was right there, just before the boat crashed: I could hear it creaking, icy wind slapped my cheeks, leaving me breathless, and salty air burned my throat, launching me into a mad coughing fit.

'*According to the rumours, the natives have hidden the precious stone in a cave at the very top of a waterfall named Olumo Rock,*' a man's voice said.

'*The savages call it Born and Die Cliff because they believe there's a demon spirit guarding it that will turn you to stone if you try and climb it,*' another replied, with a low chuckle that sounded like tin cans getting recycled.

As I took the hat and bonnet off, fireflies buzzed over my head, Àbíkús crouched near my feet and the Mami Wata stroked my twists.

'I think I know where the Night Stone is . . .'

*

I made my way back to Osoosi and Moremi. They were asleep, curled up together in an exhausted heap. Osoosi drooled over Moremi's shoulder, while Moremi looked like she was beefing someone in her dreams.

I gently shook Moremi awake. Something fuzzy tapped the back of my neck. I met Moremi's steady gaze as she retracted the braid.

'Look, at the end of the day yeah, we ain't too different.' I let out a sigh I had been holding for time. 'I don't care if you're an Àbíkú or not. I just thought we could be real with each other. But I can't even be too mad at you,' I said, crouching down. 'I ain't supposed to talk about it cause I'm the last descendant of Olókun and all that, but my real dad turns out to be Lègbá, the demon guardian of the Night Creatures. And I got his powers and everything . . . I just can't use them too much cause it's like, really draining, you know?'

I sucked in a breath and stared down at my hands. I bet she would think I was a massive hypocrite and hate me.

My eyes widened when a thick, heavy braid rested along my shoulders and squeezed them tight. I felt warm. I slowly turned to Moremi, her dark eyes glistening like almond oil in the low light.

I exhaled slowly. 'Can you tell me the reason you chose to be human?' I asked, carefully.

'I don't remember being an Àbíkú,' she admitted, quietly. 'But I remember wanting to be part of something. Àbíkús live for ever, but they are not connected to anyone or anything. They just live free. But I wanted to bond with others. I wanted a real family. When I became Kehinde and I got the task to protect you, I had a purpose. But I couldn't protect you from the Ògún. And they are still after us.' Moremi looked at me. 'And if we don't have the Night Stone then it was all for nothing.'

I was about to open my mouth and speak, but she continued: 'I have lived a thousand lives I don't remember. The worst part is not dying. But Mama Oti is my family here, now, and she knows my secret and accepts me for who I am. She is working so hard to keep her plants alive so she can heal the sick in Olori.

I don't want to let her down.' Moremi sniffed. 'And Taiwo is still my family. He thinks all this will bring Kehinde back, but our lives are connected now – if I disappear when night ends, Kehinde is finished.'

As she spoke, I noticed a thin line on her cheek – it must've been from the dagger that got too close. Moremi caught me staring at the scar and immediately covered it with a thick braid.

'You ain't gotta worry about that promise to protect me no more,' I said, firmly. Now that I had my own tribe, I wasn't gonna stand by and watch them get hurt. 'You helped me accept my destiny and do the stuff I was born to do. I ain't gonna let nothing bad happen to you. Now it's my turn to protect you,' I promised, feeling the energy spark in my veins.

'*Mo dupe pupo*, Kokumo. Thank you,' she said, eyes widening like she was really seeing me for the first time.

My cheeks heated up when she used my full name. It hit different that time. It was probably something about the way her voice curled around it like a song.

It made me want to hear her say it again.

CHAPTER TWENTY-FIVE

Born and Die Cliff

'*Baga!*' Osoosi woke with a start. 'We think this boy finish himself! We are even thinking of digging grave. But look atchu! You are doing well-oh.'

'Thanks, man – I think,' I said, deciding to take the backhanded compliment. 'Now, look guys . . . I think I know where to find the Night Stone.'

Osoosi scrunched her nose up and took a deep sniff. 'Even my nose cannot track the Araba any more. How can we find the Night Stone?'

'Well, it's kind of a long story . . .' I said, and clued them up on how I could hear voices from beyond the grave. 'It's hidden in a cave at the very top of Olumo Rock. It's not too late – the Mami Wata told me we've got until midnight, and the Night Creatures will guide our way to Olumo Rock.'

'Them say anyone who enters Olumo Rock go decorate the place with their own head,' Moremi said, knitting her brows together. 'And before you get there, you must face Àgbákò, the man-eater,' she warned.

I flinched when she mentioned Àgbákò and turned to Osoosi instantly.

The edges of her lips were twitching. 'Even the great Chief Inaki no wan carry himself there,' Osoosi whispered. Her mouth stretched into a crazy smile, '*Chai!* This one na flavour adventure-oh!' And then she quirked a brow at me, reminding me of my promise to distract Moremi while she fought Àgbákò.

The Mami Wata had warned me about how dangerous Àgbákò was and how many people he'd munched up. It was hard cause I didn't want to snake Osoosi, but I didn't want her to get hurt either. 'We ain't even food to Àgbákò, you get me? We ain't even a snack, or a side dish. We're the toothpick Àgbákò uses after he's done with his lunch,' I said, trying to get her to see sense.

'I no go gree, make you listen well-well, na me, Osoosi Ashagidibi, go make Àgbákò taste fire!' Osoosi announced. 'My people dey fear too much.

303

I no go fear Àgbákò. Anything wey Àgbákò wan do me, I go do double, even *treble* for am!'

'Osoosi, it is enough! If you face Àgbákò, you go die o!' Moremi protested, her braids whipping around her head angrily.

'If I die . . .' Osoosi went quiet, and then gave Moremi a smile. 'Wetin be this thing you are calling I? I am Aganjù, there is no "I" there is only "we". If we don't protect our own, no one else will. That is the meaning of tribe.'

My jaw fell open.

'We are knowing Aganjù for people of honour,' Moremi said. 'You must give us your word that you will avoid fighting the Àgbákò at all costs, and help us return night to Olori.'

Osoosi licked the tip of her finger and held it in the air, making the Olori promise sign. Moremi's braids shrank back to their normal size.

'Now, we must find a way to avoid this thing if we no wan provide meat for Àgbákò's soup,' Moremi said.

'Does Àgbákò have any weakness?' I asked.

'Àgbákò used to be my big grandfather, Osanyin Ashagidibi. My father tell me that I get my hearing problem from him. His own was even worse than mine – he could not hear anything *patapata*!' Osoosi wiggled her ear for emphasis. 'But he get very powerful sense of smell *sha*. If Àgbákò's nose catches us we are finished!'

Moremi poked around in my backpack and pulled out a bunch of leaves. '*Ewuro*. This bitter leaf go help us hide our smell. But we still need to find a way to pass Àgbákò without him looking us for eye.' She scratched under her chin with one of her braids.

'And Àgbákò go have sixteen of them,' Osoosi added.

That gave me an idea.

I remembered the way the Àbíkú had put its hand in mine, making my hand disappear.

'Alright, so what we're gonna do might sound a bit mad but listen up,' I said, laying out the plan.

It was totally crazy, insane, and only a desperate madman would even consider it. But I hoped they'd give it a shot.

It was our only chance of saving night, after all.

Once we'd rubbed ourselves with the bitter *ewuro* leaf, the Mami Wata helped us return to the mainland.

We set off in the direction of Olumo Rock.

It was the darkest part of Jujuland we'd ever been

in. The bright oversized Jujuland moon was hidden by a towering rock face. As we got closer we could hear water gushing over rocks – it sounded like a giant gargling mouthwash. It drowned out all the sounds of the jungle so we couldn't hear nothing.

Then we peeped the sparkling water through the thick, overhanging vines.

I'd never seen a waterfall in real life. But it was not like in the movies; here, the water ran bubbling over stones that looked like a thousand faces twisted in silent screams.

I was glad it was dark enough so that I couldn't see what they were screaming about.

When we got to the base of the waterfall, the spray was so thick I couldn't see my own two hands in front of me. But then a tiny spot of white light appeared, flickering pathetically in the pitch-blackness: Moremi had pulled out the ancient Nokia Uncle Tunji dashed me. The torchlight cast twisted shadows on stone walls.

Rushing water sprayed over our heads. It was only a thin spray of water now, cause we had a rocky ledge hanging over us, but soon we would have to climb it. I gritted my teeth while the cold water sprayed on me. It was only a matter of time before the cold water triggered a crisis.

I distracted myself by summoning an Àbíkú to help us find our way in the dark: 'Hey, Àbíkú kid! Remember me? Koku, the guy who saved you from that mosquito robot thing back at the festival? Well, I need your help, bro,' I shouted.

Moremi and Osoosi stared, mouths open, as shimmering forms rippled in the air, peppering the darkness like stars.

I held out my hand to one of them. A prickly feeling burnt the edges of my fingertips as soon as they made contact. I squeezed the Àbíkú's palm gently and watched my skin fade away. I made sure to grab on to Moremi and Osoosi so we could all share its power.

Now we were nothing except faint fuzzy outlines poking out from the night.

As we walked onwards, the ground shifted to rising moss-covered rock. As we made our way up the incline, our footsteps slapped against it, echoing back at us.

Then a low sigh echoed in the total darkness.

The sudden noise made me stumble, and I let go of the Àbíkú's hand for just a second to sort myself out.

Moremi swung the torch ahead of us. I saw her and the Àbíkú in the dim yellow light.

Which meant whatever was making that weird noise could clearly see *us*.

Osoosi tugged on my pinky finger tight and then released me from her grip. And that's when I knew something was off. 'Oi, hyena breath!' I whispered, hoping she wasn't planning to confront Àgbákò.

The tiniest sounds echoed loudly: Moremi's shallow breaths, my thumping heart and the *scratch*, *scratch*, *scratch*ing of something scraping against the wet stone.

'Osoosi, you better respect yourself and come here before I make your backside chew pepper. We don't have time to waste!' Moremi shout-whispered, her voice was cracking all over the place.

I knew Osoosi was half-deaf and all that, but there was no way she didn't hear that.

The sigh returned. It was an awful, moaning sound, the dying howl of an animal I couldn't name.

'Do you think that's Osoosi?' I asked hopefully, as the sigh stretched into a weak, trembling voice.

Moremi's braid wrapped tightly around my wrist, cutting off my circulation – but that was the least of my worries. Her voice quivered so much I barely made it out, until she whispered the word I'd been dreading.

'Àgbákò.'

CHAPTER TWENTY-SIX

Àgbákò

'So, you think you can rubbish my people, eh?' Osoosi's strained voice echoed, but she was nowhere to be found. My heart thudded as Moremi walked away from the rock face and swung the Nokia torchlight in the direction of her voice, trying to catch a flash of orange, or an afro puff. It was too dark to see anything when we looked around us except for the huge waterfall. Everywhere I looked I saw oily black water gurgling through white stone.

'Where is this foolish goat?' Moremi asked. 'We don't have time for this nonsense.'

Guilt hit me like one of her braided slaps. 'I got a pretty bad feeling about this,' I whispered back.

'What are you talking about?' Moremi squinted at me through the dark. 'She would not go and face Àgbákò alone! Osoosi does not have any sense for head, but she keeps her word. She promised that she would help us save night . . .'

'Yeah, about that . . .' I started to say, deciding to come clean about the deal I made with Osoosi.

But Moremi frowned deeply and held a braid to her lips to shut me up.

'I am O-osoosi Ashagidibi, f-future chief of the Aganjù. Y-you are my ancestor . . . a-and it . . . and it is only r-right that a child of Aganjù go f-finish you today.' Osoosi stuttered, tripping over every other word.

Moremi and I shared a horrified look.

The ground thundered under our feet. Clawing steps grew louder and louder. Something was there. Waiting. The low, sickly moan returned again in full force. It slowly elevated into a wrenching howl that made my teeth chatter. My eyelids blew back with the force of it.

All I could see was black. Osoosi was done out here. And it was all my fault, cause I agreed to that stupid pinky promise.

Back then, all I'd cared about was getting rid of my sickle cell so I could feel better. I hadn't cared who I had to throw under the bus to get to the Araba. Now my stomach churned thinking about what Taiwo was doing with him.

I hadn't even cared about what would happen when Osoosi actually faced the massive man-eating monster. Osoosi let out a battle cry before charging into the unknown. The low moan intermingled with the sounds of her heavy breathing and quick footsteps.

Then came hard, thudding noises, that had to be Osoosi's small body being slammed against the rocky ground, and sharp cracks that were the unmistakable sounds of her bones being rearranged.

Then I heard the slushy, liquid sound of something feeding. It sounded like a bunch of guts sloshing around in a giant wet sack.

Moremi waved the light about and called Osoosi's name. I joined in until my voice was hoarse. Osoosi had to be out there somewhere. She just had to be.

As we ran forward, the weak light illuminated an enormous, oblong shape in the darkness.

We both had Àgbákò's name trembling on our lips. A fuzzy grip tightened around my wrist and pulled me in close. Moremi stared at me with hollow eyes. The weak light lit up her face at a terrible angle so she looked like a sad Halloween pumpkin. But to be honest, I don't think catching angles was her top priority at that moment.

'Don't do follow-follow for me-oh,' Moremi warned, handing me the phone. 'You stay here, Kokumo. I am counting on you to live up to that name of yours. Carry your leg and go and find the Night Stone. You must find a way to Olumo Rock without fighting Àgbákò.'

Before I could answer she had run off to find Osoosi. The phone flashed feebly and died as soon as I got my hands on it, plunging me into darkness once more.

I heard Moremi yelling in the distance. Then I heard those awful wet groaning sounds. That had to be Àgbákò! I didn't know what I was moving towards, but I hoped my feet would move me closer to my friends. I knew I desperately needed to find the Night Stone, but I wasn't gonna leave my friends behind . . .

It was so dark, I didn't know if I was going forwards or backwards, but I had to keep going. I pressed myself into the wet rock, trying to find my way in the total blackness.

That was a mistake.

The cold waterfall rushed over me. It stabbed my eyeballs until they felt raw and pink and fleshy, while my body sent shockwaves of pain through my joints.

I bit the insides of my cheek to stop myself from screaming aloud.

Every distortion in the darkness could be Àgbákò. Every harsh breath could be Osoosi or Moremi's last, and time was running out.

Terrifying images of what Àgbákò looked like shot through my mind. All I knew was that it was part scorpion, part elephant and part snake. An insane combo. What if I accidentally bumped into it? I felt totally useless. I'd promised to protect my friends, but I couldn't do nothing to save them.

I kept tripping until my feet sank into wet marshland. I tried to pull myself out, but stopped when I felt steaming saliva dripping on to my neck.

My heart thrummed as the air shifted around me. A sharp light blinked on and off. I crouched right down, shaking the Nokia around, hoping that it had come to life again. But the screen was still dark.

My insides turned into mush. I turned around slowly – and saw a floating skull blinking in and out of existence.

I let out the breath I'd been holding as soon as I saw it. When it materialised, its fluorescent skeleton paint highlighted the outline of everything around me.

'It's *you*,' I said. I thought the Àbíkú had run off when I let go of its hand.

313

'❘ ❘ ! ‡?' the Àbíkú kid replied.

I copied the greeting, which made its mouth stretch upwards. It pressed a muddied cloth into my palm.

'Erm . . . thanks,' I muttered, stretching the material out. It was soaking wet but I recognised the familiar fabric of Moremi's ankara, which she usually had tied around her arm. I knew she would never leave it if she had the choice. I brought the cloth to my nose: it smelled like blood.

A shivery feeling crawled up my spine and my eyes burned. The force of it made me gasp aloud. But I didn't have time to deal with a crisis right now.

I shoved the cloth in front of the Àbíkú. 'Àbíkú, take me to them,' I pleaded. My breath was running out after every syllable. The pain from the crisis made it hard to talk.

It tilted its head and I nodded, hoping it could sense what I meant.

'Ɵ‡Ɵ‡Ɵ, ‡❘ ‡❘!! !! , Ɵ‡Ɵ‡Ɵ, ‡❘ ‡❘!! !! ‡!!❘ ❘ ❘❘Ɵ❘ ⊩?' The kid released more weird sounds. But then the murky air turned glossy as other tiny figures appeared.

My guy had called for backup.

The Àbíkú kids started running ahead of me. It was pretty easy for them, since they could pass through trees and boulders and that.

314

They led me away from the waterfall and deeper into the jungle. I dragged my feet back through the brambles, not caring about the sharp sticks digging into me. Even though we hadn't known each other for that long, I knew Osoosi and Moremi were meant to be in my life. I *had* to save them. I wanted to see Osoosi become the chief of Aganjù; she was loud and stubborn enough to make a great leader someday. And I wanted to tell Moremi that she was a savage, but she could be alright sometimes. I wanted to protect her like how she'd always looked out for me.

The Àbíkú led me to a deep ditch. They circled around me and clicked excitedly.

'*E gba mi o!* Help me! I could make out a weak, pained cry followed by a high-pitched screeching noise.

I traced it to a slumped-over creature whining in the wet soil.

I recognised that spotted hyena fur immediately. 'Osoosi?' I whispered. And then something pulled me down into the soil. A braid. I caught the sharp angles of Moremi's face – her cheeks were shiny with sweat and her bottom lip was puffy and swollen.

'What happen—' I started to say.

'*Shey* you get any sense for head?' Moremi whispered fiercely. 'Instead of "Don't die any more", they should have named you "Please kill me always".'

'Whatever,' I said, turning to Osoosi, who was still whining.

'*Ehen*, well done, very good-oh,' Moremi hissed, but this time she was looking at Osoosi. 'I am telling you we no want Àgbákò's *wahala*. Now because of you we go enter Àgbákò's stomach.' Then she screwed her eyes and winced, like it hurt to talk.

But if Moremi was a car crash, Osoosi was a ten tonne lorry pile-up. It looked like one of her paws was bent badly.

I was about to ask her if she was alright, when Àgbákò's raspy howl stole the words out of my mouth.

We sank into the wet soil, hoping it would swallow us before Àgbákò did.

Olori people are known for being extra. But even Uncle Tunji's wildest dreams couldn't have compared to what Àgbákò actually looked like. If I could have scraped my eyes out of my skull I would have – but once you see something, you can't unsee it.

First off, it was *huge*. It was supposed to be part elephant, part snake and part scorpion, but so many animal parts had been mixed up to create it that it basically looked like many rotting animal corpses all stitched together. And these weren't even fully meshed with its body. Added to this, Àgbákò's elephant body was stretched so thin it was practically translucent. You could see all the arteries and muscles underneath. It turns out I was right before: the weird liquid sound *was* a bunch of guts sloshing around in a giant sack. And you could also see the creatures it had swallowed fighting for dominance inside it: arms and tails were shifting around in its middle like drowning things trying to get to the surface, before being pulled down by others. Some of them had human shapes . . .

Every time it took a step you could hear dry bones creaking with the weight of its gigantic mass. It had sixteen glowing orange eyes in a sharp scorpion face that was surrounded by lots of silky, stringy hair.

Clearly whoever hooked Àgbákò up with that Brazilian lace front did him dirty.

When it unhinged its snake-like jaw, I could see multiple rows of sharp teeth – but that wasn't the worst of it. It released the garbled noise of a thousand dying animals. Including human groans.

I had thought it was Osoosi crying out for help when I heard '*E gba mi*.' But it had been Àgbákò all along.

CHAPTER
TWENTY-SEVEN

E gba mi

'*E gba mi . . . E gba mi . . . E gba mi . . .*' Help me.
Help me. Help me. Àgbákò kept butchering the word
as it dragged itself towards us. It moved with grudging
steps, like something was driving it forward against
its will. Àgbákò's breath even kicked differently:
the raw stench of rotting flesh hit the back of my
throat. It made me seriously consider going veggie for
a hot second.

Each time it spoke, steaming hot spit rained down
on our faces. As Àgbákò staggered towards us like a
drunk, Moremi sucked in her breath.

And I ain't even gonna lie – I was holding mine too.

It was like we secretly hoped not breathing would

suddenly make us invisible, or something.

Osoosi, of course, had other plans.

'Àgbákò, I go defeat you today!' she yelled, rising to the Gidigbo martial arts pose.

At her words, Àgbákò bent down and studied us with its sixteen eyes. Its clapped face was so close I could practically kiss the space where its nose should be. Its scorpion face was oddly pale like its outer shell had been ripped clean off and it had enormous pincers that twitched revealing a pale, thin wound of a mouth. I noticed it had a furry clump of animal hair dangling around its neck.

A feverish shiver rose inside me as Àgbákò's mouth twitched above Osoosi. I squirmed. It was the worst possible timing to have a crisis: I didn't have time to use one of my grounding techniques.

Osoosi threw a punch at Àgbákò's giant scorpion eyes. It just blinked like an eyelash got trapped in it. Then its pale, fleshy claws circled around her.

'Osoosi!' Moremi roared as Àgbákò lifted her high into the air, like a forest offering. Osoosi kicked in Àgbákò's clutches, swiping desperately at its neck. 'You no go finish me-oh! I go fight for Aganjù!' she yelled.

But it was no use. Àgbákò unhinged its gigantic

jaw, revealing those rows of terrible teeth. Its enormous stomach shifted and morphed in front of us, like it was making space for her.

Moremi stood up in the dirt and faced Àgbákò directly, her braids flying around her shoulders like whips.

'Remember your name, yam head. *Don't* die! You hear?' Moremi spoke to me with her back turned. All I could do was watch and let the sickle-cell fever run its course through my body, crippling me.

Moremi's braids formed a massive fist at her shoulders. Then she leaned over, sinking her hands into the wet earth and launching herself towards Àgbákò, delivering a hook to its huge jaw.

Her blow connected with a sickening crack. Àgbákò released a harrowing howl as it reeled backwards.

You would have thought it would have released its hold on Osoosi, but its pincers only tightened around her, muffling her screams. Moremi began delivering kicks and jabs in quick succession, targeting Àgbákò's stomach.

It almost worked. The thin skin rippled and shifted with each blow, like there were things inside fighting to get out. *Living* things.

Àgbákò let out a screech as it whipped its scaly,

slimy tail around with horrible precision, hitting Moremi square in the chest. The force sent her flying through the bush. She lassoed a single braid around a tree branch to stop herself falling to the ground. But then a wet, hairy limb from some half-digested animal burst out of Àgbàkò's bloated middle and ripped a single braid clean off her scalp. It snapped back into the stomach like a broken rubber band.

'E gba mi o . . .' Àgbákò crooned as Moremi fell. Her body thudded as it connected with the hard rocky ground.

Silver spears of pain ran through me as the damp air brought the full force of the sickle crisis on, but that was nothing compared to the terror that ran through my bones with each step that Àgbákò took towards me.

It stared down at me with glowing orange eyes, like it wanted me to bow down and worship its mighty ugliness. Its fleshy claws twitched.

They were empty.

Not only that, but the chorus of wailing voices had changed slightly. They had a high-pitched tone when they said 'E gba mi' that sounded exactly like Osoosi's voice. I couldn't believe it.

Osoosi was . . . inside . . . Àgbákò.

The demon spirit surged through my veins, lighting my blood on fire. '*E gba mi o* . . .' Àgbákò pleaded, as it rained its acid breath on me.

A dozen appendages shot out of its middle and reached towards me.

I summoned a few shadow arms to protect me from Àgbákò's blows. I was so exhausted that all I could create were thin, bony limbs twisted beyond recognition. I couldn't even keep those up for long. The shadows disintegrated each time Àgbákò shoved through them, fading away into a dark mist.

Àgbákò's hard claws clamped around me. Its rancid breath made me want to throw up in my own mouth. Now I had an image I couldn't scratch out. And to think that would be my last one.

Àgbákò lifted me mercilessly into the air, way above the treetops. Then it let out another gut-wrenching howl.

'*E gba mi o!*' Àgbákò roared, its voice sounding more human than ever before. And it let out another pained howl and then let me fall.

I have never been so happy to have a mouth full of stones and dirt.

I shook my head to clear it, and then crawled

towards a lanky arm that belonged to Moremi.

Her face was so bruised I could hardly recognise her, but she was alive. I let out a breath so deep I could feel my ribs all up in my chest.

Àgbákò released another ear-shattering moan that blew the trees back.

Moremi and I gripped each other tightly to avoid being tossed around in the air again. Àgbákò pulled its ugly head back as its stomach churned like Mama Oti's famous *okra* stew.

And then we heard a booming *bang* as it exploded.

Pieces of Àgbákò were scattered everywhere. A shimmering black liquid sloshed over us, along with fleshy chunks that used to be Àgbákò. It was pure carnage. I blinked, and the next thing I knew there were unspeakably horrible things chilling in my eye sockets.

Moremi stared at me with stony eyes, flicking animal innards out of her braids.

A bright glow of orange flickered in the darkness. I traced it to a small, gooey figure limping towards us. Slowly, Osoosi's tribal patterns sank into her skin and the bright rings around her eyes faded.

'What happened?' I asked, proper confused. 'How did you make Àgbákò explode like that?'

'Ehen . . . I go tell you and *oga*-boss everything, *na*

everything!' Osoosi punched a wet, slimy fist up in the air. Her fingers clutched a damp, furry object.

'Go on then!' I examined the fur ball in her hands – it was the same one Àgbákò had been wearing. It was a large black paw with a bright orange symbol on it.

'But first' – Osoosi swayed from side to side – 'I go rest small.'

And she fainted right in the middle of a giant, gooey puddle of guts.

CHAPTER TWENTY-EIGHT

Ancestors

I thought Osoosi would be hyped – defeating Àgbákò
had been her all-time dream. But when she came
round, a frown crouched between her brows like she
was doing a Moremi impression. And she whimpered
every time she had to move her foot.

'So how did you finish off Àgbákò?' I asked again,
hoping Osoosi would go into all the grisly details.
Osoosi gripped the furry paw in her hand so hard it dug
into her flesh. 'This is the Aganjù talisman! Àgbákò used
its power to swallow every kind animal in Jujuland and
Olori. So I allow Àgbákò to grab me while I thief the
thing from its neck,' she explained, as Moremi pulled
out the medicine Mama Oti had stashed in my bag.

'When I enter Àgbákò's stomach I use my power to transform into every kind animal you go read for book. Àgbákò cannot contain this so him dey finish.'

'You better respect yourself!' Moremi kissed her teeth as she wrapped herbs on Osoosi's ankle. 'Do you not have shame, eh? Have you forgotten our duty to is to find the Night Stone, not to go and find our own original trouble?' Moremi got up at once – she was so angry she was shaking.

'I defeated Àgbákò to return honour to my own people. Whether there go be night, or no night in Olori, as long as the Ògún rule over us the Aganjù tribe go still suffer.'

Osoosi glared at Moremi with hardened eyes. 'We used to be a mighty nation of our own. Things fell apart when the first Ògún king created Olori and united the tribes. Now my tribe must bow before the ones who call us animals in human skin.'

'What about the animals who are dying in Aganjù because they no get rest from the sun? Will this power save them?' Moremi shook Osoosi by the shoulders. 'You made a promise to your own father to save night. And you go promise me say you no go fight Àgbákò.' Moremi shook Osoosi by the shoulders. 'Don't you know that without night I . . .'

'Yeah true talk, we were properly worried about you, broski,' I interrupted. I didn't want Moremi to say the last part aloud, in case she gave my secret demon heritage away. I already figured that if night was gone for ever no Night Creature would survive including all the Àbíkús, which meant Moremi was done out here.

I had a fifty–fifty chance thanks to being half human, but with my luck I was probably doomed already. 'Can't believe we almost got cheffed back there,' I said. 'But now we gotta focus on getting the Night Stone – and the Araba – and then facing that Taiwo madman.' Then I added, 'No offence,' for Moremi's benefit, since he was her brother. Sort of.

Osoosi held up the talisman with trembling fingers – the symbol drawn on the black spotted paw had an orange glow reminding me of Àgbákò's rotting eyeballs. All of a sudden Osoosi's bottom lip wobbled. She nodded. 'How can I wear the talisman while breaking my promise, *oga*-boss?' Her voice sounded like it scraped the sides of her throat before it came out. 'If I wear this thing I become a monster like Àgbákò,' Osoosi said, as she drew a flashing orange sign in the air.

'What are you doing?' I asked as bright orange

sparks lit up our greasy, Àgbákò-bin-juice-stained faces. 'We ain't got time for that, we've got to find the Night Stone!'

'I am needing a moment.' Osoosi's back hunched over and her smooth skin turned into prickly fur. But her hyena form looked even more mangy than usual – I doubted she'd be able to keep it up for long.

'I go give you five minutes. The sky is getting lighter,' Moremi warned. 'That means we don't have long until the solstice, when night is weakest. That is when the Ògún will attack the stone.' I craned my neck upwards; the sky wasn't pitch-black no more, it had a dark blue tint to it. 'Don't go anywhere my braids cannot reach, you hear?'

Osoosi nodded her furry head before scampering away. While Osoosi had her moment, we walked back to the waterfall and de-slimed ourselves. Moremi stuck her body under the rushing waterfall to get the gunk off, but I had to just splash it around as best I could, so it didn't trigger another crisis.

One of Moremi's eyes had almost swollen shut and she had a bust lip; worst of all, she was missing a chunky braid on the right side of her head. I caught her shining eyes for a moment. She let out a shaky breath before she spoke.

'We no get much time. You and I both have night blood inside of us. Maybe we get one hour, that is all.' Moremi squinted up at a slab of stone rising above us. 'When the time comes, leave Taiwo to me, you hear?' Moremi said.

I nodded, trying to ignore the twisty feeling that clogged my lungs whenever Taiwo was mentioned. 'I'll get Osoosi to hurry up,' I suggested. Moremi's braids gathered into a giant finger and pointed to her left.

Even in the dark, it didn't take too long to pick out Osoosi's afro puffs among the bushes. She was chanting in Yoruba in the dim moonlight while kneeling, using a palm leaf to flick drops of water everywhere.

'Oi, Osoosi, what are you doing?' I asked, glancing over her. 'How can you be chilling when we haven't got long before night gets destroyed in Olori, forever ruining all our lives?' I paused to watch her do her little ritual. She had arranged orange ankara strips from her clothes around a dirt mound that had cowrie shells from her hair surrounding it, and she was burning camwood mixed with lemongrass. She fanned the incense so the smoke rose in thick spirals.

'We've got to go, fam!' I repeated, leaning over her. Your people in Olori and the Night Creatures who helped us get here are counting on us.'

'Osanyin Ashagidibi, I salute you!' Osoosi intoned, her eyes closed. 'Great Leopard, I return the talisman to you.' Flick. 'Son of Aganjù, I salute you.' Swish.

I felt my eyebrows peel off my face. 'Man almost got done out here just so you could return that hairball to your tribe. You could've used that to help us fight the Ògún mandem, you know. Don't you *want* us to save the Night Stone?'

Osoosi set down her palm leaf and finally looked up at me. 'My father is a great chief because he go do anything to save his people. *Oga*-boss go talk true talk, my people are suffering in Aganjù because they no get rest from the sun. Our animals are dying. Maybe one moon a warrior worthy of the talisman will arise,' Osoosi said with wet, giant eyes. 'But for now, I must give my all to bring night back to my people and bury this thing so it no go harm anyone.'

'Well, the talisman is actually bare ugly anyways,' I chipped in. 'And your tribe would be lucky to have a chief like you, man. You're brave and you got like mad fighting skills, you get me?' I was gassing her up, so she would see how cool she was.

Osoosi grinned.

'May your soul join the ancestors in the great beyond,' Osoosi whispered, laying the palm leaf down gently over the altar. I fixed up my posture and bowed my head. As soon as I did the air rippled around us. I swear I saw a hazy shadow with a wide-toothed grin that was too big for its face.

'I hope my big-grandfather go hear our prayers today,' Osoosi said, getting up from her knees. I stared at the dark space where the smiling shadow had been watching over us. 'Yeah, something tells me he totally did,' I said.

CHAPTER
TWENTY-NINE

The Horror!

Moremi didn't waste a single moment climbing up the waterfall. She managed to find holds that she could grip on to with her braids, even with the water rushing over her.

I hoped Osoosi would be as bad at climbing as I was, since her ankle was all busted from fighting Àgbákò. Annoyingly, she was pretty good at scaling the rock.

I stared upwards and gulped hard.

Moremi dangled a braid in front of me. I gripped on to the rock and made my choice. I was tired of being the weakest one in the group just cause I had sickle cell. My friends had their own stuff to deal with. Besides, I had real powers now.

'I'm good,' I said, lifting one of my legs on to the wet, rough surface. Moremi got the message and went on without me. I scrambled up, spitting out the water that gushed over my head. I tried to focus on placing my feet in the right places so I could haul myself up, and not think about the massive distance between us.

The rock was lumpy, like a hardened sponge. After a bit I realised it would be easier to go barefoot, so I finally parted ways with the uncle sandals the Araba lent me.

'You know why they are calling this thing Born and Die Cliff?' Osoosi yelled down to me. The name was kinda familiar so I grunted in reply which was all the encouragement Osoosi needed to go off on one. 'Dem go say the Demon of Death cursed this waterfall to protect Jujuland from outsiders. If body dey too long you turn into stone.'

With Osoosi's warning about my dad's curse in mind I started climbing in earnest.

As I climbed higher, the air felt colder. It felt like I was chugging a bucket of ice each time I opened my mouth. I wouldn't be able to hold back a crisis for much longer.

Looking down to check on a foothold, I realised I could see the water crashing on to the rocks below. And reality hit me. Hard.

If I fell from this height I would be dead.

The rushing water suddenly slid beneath my fingertips, turning them to ice. My joints locked so I couldn't even bend my fingers to hold on.

'Yam head!' I'd know that insult anywhere.

Moremi threw down a braid to save me. I felt it in my hand for a moment, then it slipped through my fingers. A sharpness in my chest sliced me into ribbons and I saw nothing but white, then I lost everything.

All the colours faded out as I fell.

A whisper thumped in my ears like a fading heartbeat. Before I could figure out where it was coming from, an ice-cold splash of waterfall water brought me back to life.

Now I finally understood why the rock was so

uneven and lumpy in places. Osoosi wasn't chatting air, she was telling the truth: the cliff was made out of stone-covered skin and bones.

I had been saved by a skeleton, a *human* skeleton.

Bony arms had caught me in their grip. I slapped them away as hard as I could.

The rest of its body jutted out of the rock with its mouth wide open in a final scream. 'I should never have tried to find that stone,' a voice said in a harsh, choking breath. Then I heard a dying cry: '*The horror!*'

The skeleton was still clothed, with a waistcoat and pocket watch and everything. I could even make out a neat inscription on the back of the watch: *Victor Frobenius*.

It was the explorer guy we had learned about on our museum trip. That was definitely him. Frobenius. I remembered his name cause it was weird, it had a soft sound at the beginning, with a puff in the middle and a slither at the end.

Water rained down, piercing my skin like knives, but I couldn't move. Each step I took would bring me closer to Frobenius's fate. I didn't know exactly what had happened to him, but now he was nothing but a stack of grisly bones.

'Koku, you better carry your leg-oh! We are waiting

for you to join us!' Osoosi's voice yelled from somewhere above me. I craned my neck and saw the blurry outline of my friends waiting at the top of the waterfall.

When I finally reached the top, Osoosi gave me a thumbs-up and Moremi patted me on the back so hard I nearly coughed out my lungs.

*

The air was thick and warm again, but there was still a weird chill in the air. I got a strong sense of déjà vu. I looked up and saw an archway of stony teeth hanging above us, splashing drops of water on our foreheads.

'I dunno why, but I got the feeling I've been here before,' I said.

Moremi wrinkled her nose at me. 'Quiet your *yansh* before the Ògún come and pepper us with their swords.'

It was dead quiet. We could only hear loose stones shifting under our feet and the patter of water droplets.

We found ourselves in a maze: there were narrow passages marked by giant rocky pillars. Each one looked exactly the same as the others.

The walls were made out of crystal, which glittered

like fairy lights. I guided my hands over the cool walls to steady myself and felt patterns carved into the stone. I pressed my fingertips into the grooves and saw a whole line of markings sparking to life, bathing the entire cave in a luminous blue glow.

Moremi let out a quiet gasp. Osoosi craned her neck in wonder.

I turned to look at the rest of the cave. To be fair, it was a massive upgrade on the waterfall. Mainly cause it wasn't made out of human body parts.

I could totally see why all the explorer mandem had tried to climb all this way to find it. It felt like we were up in space, watching a sunrise on Mars, or something.

When the glowing patterns faded out, we walked towards a single spot of blue light in the far distance. As we got closer to it, Moremi silently clutched my arm.

The light we could see was coming from a crystal-like stone on the top of a hexagonal column. It was totally black and yet a blue light reflected off its surface, as deep and rich as the colour of an Àbíkú's skin.

It was kinda obvious how it got its name: it looked just like someone had ripped out the heart of the night sky.

CHAPTER THIRTY

The Night Stone

'You knew all along . . .' A flat voice suddenly echoed around the chamber.

I shivered. *Was that Taiwo's voice?* I thought, listening to snippets of rising conversation as we crept deeper into the cave.

Shimmering light danced on the cave walls like something was coming to life with a vengeance. And we breathed out a collective sigh of relief when we saw the Araba.

Until we realised we'd walked right into the middle of a fight.

'*Boju ri enu a dake,*' the Araba said, shaking his cuffed fists. 'Not everything the eye sees should be spoken by the mouth.'

The warrior had a strip of purple cloth between their armour – Taiwo.

'I'm tired of hearing your irrelevant proverbs, old man,' Taiwo retorted.

The Araba paused for a moment, and his chest heaved as his eyes roamed over Taiwo's body as if he was trying to meet his gaze. 'Even though Rùnmí has gifted me with the power to see the seeds of time, I cannot pretend to know the mind of the gods themselves. That is why I cannot tell you about Kehinde's destiny. The unknown must remain unknown. Even an Araba must bow before those who created our world,' the Araba explained.

'Destiny again . . .' Dark clouds inked into Taiwo's eyes as he clenched his fist tightly. 'So it's my destiny to have my sister taken from me? Is it my destiny to be unconnected to anyone or anything?' he spat out. 'I refuse to believe that.'

'If you look inside yourself, you can see that Kehinde has never left you.' The Araba spoke softly. 'Nothing' is what we call something we have forgotten the name of; but 'No one' is the name of someone who has forgotten who they are.'

Taiwo paused, and then turned slowly. He looked

towards us, raising his pierced eyebrow at us. '*E kaab o.*' He welcomed us drily, waving a hand that made thundering steps echo around us.

His goons emerged from the dark.

Osoosi went on all fours as Moremi flung her braids back and balled up her fists. Just as I was about to use my powers to summon some phantom help, Taiwo held a single finger up, instantly stopping his guys from attacking.

'They are here for the man who wears his title like a thief in stolen clothes.' Taiwo's finger ran idly down the blade of the giant sword. It had a roaring leopard etched on to the handle with ruby eyes.

'You are cursed person with a bad destiny, an *oloriburuku* that rebukes the ways of their ancestors.' The Araba held his head up high.

'*Aba!*' Osoosi flinched. Even I knew that was a violation still. According to Uncle Tunji, it's the worst thing you can ever say to someone in our culture.

Taiwo's eyes were totally black, but he didn't even blink. I was desperate to cause some serious damage to his face for violating the Araba like that. But we'd agreed that Moremi would talk to him first, while Osoosi and I figured out how to get the Night Stone and return darkness to Olori.

No long ting.

'Tayewo.' Moremi took a step towards him. 'The Ògún have been feeding you lies. I did not take Kehinde from you. The Night Creatures are not the monsters you think they are.'

'I know the truth,' Taiwo bit out, stepping down from the rocky ledge he was on.

His flat voice was totally on brand, but his eyes kept twitching. Moremi had told me not to get involved, but I closed my eyes and focused on the darkness behind them, just in case she needed some ghostly backup.

'I shared a womb with Kehinde! Did you really think I wouldn't notice that her soul was different?' His voice rose – and the shimmering metal sword *pulsed*, like it could sense the change.

Taiwo gritted his teeth so hard we could hear scraping. But he had still managed to calm down somehow. 'We shared one soul. When twins are born, their parent keeps the soul in a pair of *Eji Ogbe* dolls. You have to keep both as they say you never know which twin has the soul. Since she went, I've felt nothing. Now I know I was the one that was born empty . . .'

'Taiwo, please! There's something you need to understand, *ma binu*.' Moremi took a last step towards him. She was right between him and the Night Stone.

It would take no distance at all for him to plunge the sword through her chest.

My palms tingled as I concentrated hard, making sure my undead army was on standby.

'Goddess Ọya is my witness.' Moremi licked the tip of her finger and held it in the air. 'Let her mighty wind strike me down if I lie for mouth. Kehinde chose her own fate. I did not steal her place.'

'She would *never* leave me,' Taiwo said, stroking his purple ankara cloth with his free hand. The more he touched the cloth, the more his eyes shined over till they looked like pools of almond oil. 'You *took* her from me!'

The sword started vibrating in his hands. It looked like Taiwo was actually struggling to control it. He used both hands to grip the hilt, but the sword jerked madly in his grasp like it had a life of its own.

'My dear student, you see yourself?' The Araba's eyes had storm clouds in them. '*Ayanmo ni iwapele, iwapele ni, ayanmo. Abi*, you know this one, or have you forgotten everything I have taught you?'

Taiwo breathed slowly until the sword stopped humming and turned into dead metal again.

He brandished the iron like it hadn't been trying to end him a couple seconds ago. 'Destiny is good character, good character is destiny,' he said, mechanically. 'The truth is destiny doesn't exist, you take what you want, or you get what you are given.' His dead eyes roamed over the three of us. 'Destiny is for the pathetic, the desperate and the stupid.'

Taiwo raised his sword over Moremi's head.

Her eyes shrivelled so they looked like two glossy ants burrowing into earth. Beside me, Osoosi took a shaky breath. I prepared for the worst, the air shifting as I summoned every sorry soul that was unlucky enough to have died in this place.

I shut my eyes tight and focused on saving Moremi. Precision was key: one wrong move and she was done out there. Hot lightning built up behind my eyes as a phantom arm shot out towards her.

It was too late. Taiwo plunged his cold metal sword . . . into dark rock.

The Night Stone cracked with a deafening noise. Each splinter tore into my heart. Moremi doubled over like she was rearranging her intestines.

'*Yeparipa!*' Osoosi shrieked, as blackness swirled into our eyes like a night sea.

CHAPTER THIRTY-ONE

No-Miss the Blade Licker

Peach light bled through the cracks in the rocky ceiling. It was the first time I'd ever seen sunlight in Jujuland. We didn't have much time until night disappeared for ever. *Maybe no time at all.*

I watched helplessly as Taiwo used the sword to slowly carve into the rock. The top of the diamond had already been severed and it kept cracking. I winced sharply, clutching my chest, trying to steady my footing. I had a pretty high pain tolerance cause of my sickle cell but it felt like someone was hitting my heart repeatedly with a bat, and throwing my thoughts into a blender while they were at it.

'Tayewo!' the Araba's voice boomed as I struggled

to stand straight. A tornado raged in his marble eyes. 'I taught you to be an *Emi o ola*, an honoured child.' His forehead gleamed with sweat as his white eyes flashed brightly. 'But it seems that you have chosen to dine with the eaters of leftovers.'

'Baba, no! You no get enough energy for this!' Osoosi called out.

'I have plenty!' the Araba cried, his necklace rattling across his bony chest, the patterns on it glowing brighter than ever before. 'Don't you know that I am an old *iroko* tree? I cannot die!'

With this, the Araba shone his white flashing eyes in the direction of the Ògún guards. Their eyes clouded over, and they dropped their spears with a loud clunk. Their eyes stared glowing white and they had no pupils in them just like the Araba's.

'Taiwo, are you content to send pigeons to do the job of the eagle?' The Araba flexed his newly freed hands as one of the mind-controlled guards uncuffed him.

Taiwo's pierced brow twitched as he drove his sword deeper into the heart of the Night Stone.

The white ring around the Araba's eyes waned and the matching white rings that had appeared in the guards' eyes disappeared.

The Ògún wasted no time in trying to get back at the Araba. I recognised one of them – No-Miss, the blade licker from before. He had ferocious tribal marks carved into his cheeks like a wonky hashtag.

He chucked a shank at the Araba. It sliced the air in a smooth arc.

'You think the Ògún have accepted you, Taiwo?' the Araba called out as he caught the No Miss's blade deftly between his thumb and forefinger. 'No! You are not one of them.' The blade fell to the ground with a loud clatter.

'The Ògún have accepted me as one of their own, unlike my tribe, which abandoned me when my parents died, or that Babalú witch, who let an evil spirit take my sister away from me,' Taiwo bit out, releasing his grip on his sword.

As soon as he let go, the Night Stone released blue waves of energy that spiralled around the blade.

'That is enough. Leave us,' Taiwo ordered, simply. The Ògún guards stepped back. It was crazy how the teen commanded a whole bunch of adults.

Blade Licker's face fell, but when he clocked us, the corner of his lips slowly curved. Now we had six of Olori's deadliest goons trying to shish kebab us. *Just great*.

'You do not need to steal magic to be strong, Taiwo. The power that allows you to use this sword comes from those who stood before you,' the Araba said.

Taiwo faced him directly. 'And the point of that power is to move beyond where they were standing,' he retorted. 'Humans with power from the gods will one day be legends of the past. They make up a fraction of our population, and there are fewer being born. To progress, Olori must embrace new sources of power.'

'*Oho!* Is *that* why you use stolen magic?' The Araba creased his forehead in Taiwo's direction. 'Our lessons are not finished-oh. Your mind is not balanced. Since you will not learn by words, let us talk with fists as it is the only language you understand well-well.'

The Araba slowly approached Taiwo with fisted hands.

Taiwo focused on upper body moves in close combat. His armour rattled as he delivered a flurry of jabs, elbow strikes and uppercuts. Blades extended from his hand armour. If he landed one hit on the Araba he'd be giving him a brand new set of tribal marks.

Each time a white ring appeared around the Araba's eyes, they quickly dimmed. Taiwo's eyeballs were entirely black, like they were filled with blood.

'So, you are now using your *juju*, eh?' the Araba asked, with sweat raining steadily into his cloudy eyeballs. 'How many Night Creatures have you killed for this?' he demanded, narrowly avoiding one of Taiwo's punches and delivering one of his own.

'Not enough,' Taiwo replied. 'But don't worry, Baba. I'm here to remedy that.'

While they beefed, we fended off the overgrown Ògún mandem. Ever since the Night Stone had cracked, it had been getting harder to just stand upright, let alone fend off seven-foot warriors decked out in bone-crunching metal gear. I ignored the pain in my heart, to summon a shadowy shield to protect us from the Ògún guys. My breaths got shorter and harder as the stone broke away piece by piece; I knew I wouldn't be able to hold it for long.

Osoosi drew the most complex air sign I'd ever seen. Then she started to transform. Soon we couldn't see nothing except a pair of eyes surrounded by inky blackness. The sunlight that filtered through the cracks exposed a faint smattering of spots. It was a madness.

I couldn't believe that the majestic black leopard that started prowling towards the Ògún crew was the goofy kid that chewed her braids.

'Make I show you what a daughter of Aganjù can do,' Osoosi growled, as the Ògún attacked.

She squared off with the hardest looking guys: a meathead whose ginormous forehead grazed the rocky ceiling, and a hench woman who had so many piercings in  her face there was no way of knowing where her skin stopped and the metal started.

'See me? You go see trouble!' Meathead said, before swallowing an entire spear whole. His skin slowly went silver as he transformed into a metal shield. A fierce leopard mask rose over his face.

The two big cats circled each other: one silver, one black. They sized each other up like they were trying to establish who would be predator and who would be prey.

'You are a thief! First you thief the leopard from Aganjù, then you try and thief night from us and leave us with a barren land.' Osoosi let out a deadly snarl. 'I go take everything you have stolen by force. This go be for the chief you disgraced in Aganjù; this go be for all the people of Olori!'

Meathead's eyes turned into bullets as he bulldozed towards her. Pin Cushion made things about ten times worse by flinging darts in the air. Her aim wasn't on Blade Licker's level, but Osoosi had to dodge her attacks to avoid ending up with the maddest piercings.

Osoosi drew a quick sign in the air and jumped. Orange sparks blazed as she shrank in mid-air, transforming into a gliding lizard. Now she could weave between the flying darts and focus on ambushing Meathead.

When she landed on the big guy, she grew ten times bigger. I wish I snapped the look on his face when he got smacked with an alligator tail.

The strike would've ended a regular person, but his massive bulk was only pushed a couple of steps back. There wasn't even a dent in his armoured skin.

'So, you want to dance the dance of death, *abi*?' Meathead cracked his neck, while Pin Cushion pulled out a whole bunch of insane ammo: ring knives, throwing spears and razor-sharp discs that made *Grand Theft Auto* look tame.

'Na you go dance the dance of death today!' Osoosi yelled, as spotty hyena fur replaced her alligator scales. Pin Cushion used the distraction to chuck a bunch of darts her way. Osoosi leaped over them, but couldn't avoid crashing into Meathead's outstretched fist.

Her back smacked against the wall with a thud. The impact changed her back into her human form. She slumped to the ground.

Before Pin Cushion could finish the job, a fuzzy black braid swiped past my eyes. The braid whacked against the darts, making them whoosh across the room. Pin Cushion stared over at us in shock.

'*Oga*-boss!' Osoosi yelled.

Moremi was taking a massive risk fighting around a bunch of iron that could touch her at any moment *and* with the effect of the Night Stone cracking, which was making both of us feel slower. Not to mention that if her braids got sliced up in the process, she'd be done out there.

I wanted to step up and protect my friends, but it didn't look like Blade Licker was going to give me a chance. I flexed my hands and powered down the shadow shield, cause I knew I'd have to focus all my attention on him. He was kinda obsessed with me.

Now I could see his face in crazy detail. It was peak,

honestly, cause the oblong pointy head and flaring nostril combo wasn't that cute.

I fought off the pain in my chest and the dizziness subsided for a moment. I was used to dealing with pain and a body that didn't work. My sickle cell gave me a higher tolerance than most, and now was the time to use it.

I breathed slowly as I focused on my surroundings; the muggy air that smelled like damp socks, the gurgling sounds of the rushing waterfall outside and the way the sunlight burned through the cracks in the rock. Static energy bubbled inside me as I stretched my hand out towards his blades coming my way. A long shadowy arm shot out from the centre of my hand. It deflected the blades but it only lasted as long as a breath before fading into a dark mist.

Blade Licker wouldn't give me a break. There was an artistry to his movements: his daggers danced in the air before skimming towards me. I had no time to think; the most I could do was conjure the ghosts as temporary shields.

'*Ki lo de?* What's wrong with you?' he remarked, as he levitated another knife that my shadow army deflected. 'You know all this fighting you *pikin* are doing is senseless. Daylight has broken in Jujuland.

The stone is finished. Night will soon be no more. You should accept your fate, as the Olókun did before you.'

That did it. He had no right to talk about *my* tribe. I was so mad it was spiritual.

'As long as I'm around they ain't gone nowhere,' I said. A dark fog began hovering over my shoulders like a phantom cape, and a glowing pair of eyes burned out of my skull.

The effect on Blade Licker was instantaneous. His daggers dropped to the ground with a loud clang. 'But . . . the king said the demon of death is finished!' His eyes grew with fear as ghosts surrounded me, adding a few extra feet to my height so I towered over the poor guy. 'H-him say Ògún sword swallow him m-many moons ago . . . !' he stuttered.

'You don't know nothing, fam.' I could see my reflection in his eyes: I had black, hollow eyes, and a skeleton face decorated with half black and half red painted designs and my hair transformed into two ginormous curved black horns that looked like they were made of a black shimmering fog.

Blade Licker's silver skin melted away as his fear took over.

Thankfully, Moremi knew exactly what needed to happen next. She faked a high kick and then aimed for his ankles, swinging her legs in a low arc. Without the metal protecting him, the kick actually connected. His gym gains didn't work in his favour, cause when he fell, he fell hard.

As he fell, Osoosi thwacked him across the chest with her hyena tail. Her aim was scarily on point, cause she knocked him right into Pin Cushion. It was peak for both of them since he weighed a thousand tonnes, and her spiky face wasn't exactly cosy to land on.

'You see, Koku? *Oga*-boss? We go dey wound dem like that!' Osoosi punched the air, her furry paw transforming back into a smooth fist.

But even though we'd somehow managed to finish No Miss off, the rest of the Ògún mandem was barrelling towards us.

They didn't look too happy that a bunch of kids had made wastemen out of two of their crew.

We were so outnumbered it wasn't even funny. Osoosi had run out of juice, Moremi had pushed past her limits, and I'd relied too much on my powers and now it was backfiring. Big time.

Phantom voices thumped loudly in my ears. My head was crowded with the undead. Their voices were driving me crazy; I couldn't hear myself think, let alone command them to help me.

But just as my face was about to get remixed, the Ògún guys stopped in their tracks.

Something was off.

CHAPTER THIRTY-TWO

The One Who Holds Death in their Pocket

The Araba seemed to be leaning on the Night Stone.

And it was only when Moremi let out a strangled sob that I realised the sword blade was sticking out of his stomach.

'Baba!' Taiwo yelled, like he'd been jolted out of a dream.

Everything slowed down for a moment. And then silver lightning started spewing out of the sword, whirling around the Araba's chest in a deadly force field.

We all stared in shock as the Araba's necklace shattered to pieces. Taiwo tried pulling the sword out of the Araba, out of the Night Stone, but it was no use. It wouldn't budge.

My ribs strangled my chest as the Araba's arms and feet melted in a swirl of black dust. He was disintegrating before our eyes.

The Araba's white flashing eyes spun slowly until their gaze settled vaguely on me. I felt like he was seeing me for the first time. His voice rang clear and true in my head, his lips firmly closed as ever. '*Kokumo, the ku in our names will always connect us. I have danced to the tune of my own ancestors; now it is your turn to fulfil your destiny and save night . . .*'

And he crumbled away.

A whirl of dust spiralled around the sword for a fleeting moment before getting absorbed into it. The sword pulsed once, as if the Araba was still fighting inside it. Then it was still.

CHAPTER THIRTY-THREE

Mad Goddess Energy

The Araba was gone. He was the only person that made me feel connected to my tribe, the only one who reminded me I was part of something. The only one who had a half-decent shot at reversing the impossible. My eyes burned from holding back the pain of losing him.

I felt totally useless. I was tired down to my bones. My chest felt like it was getting ripped out of my ribcage slowly; it was way worse than the pain in my heart caused by the cracking Night Stone and it was way worse than any sickle-cell crisis. I stared pathetically as the Ògún sword fell to the floor with a loud clatter. It had sliced its way through the Night

Stone, splitting it into two halves that were starting to get blurry, like they were fading away.

There was no light radiating from it now; it just looked like a normal diamond. You would never have guessed that it was once the heart of a mighty goddess.

Sunlight flooded the cave, bright enough to reveal shrivelled creatures, chained to the cave walls, reaching out towards us. Wailing voices rose, and their gasping breaths became shorter by the second. With a start, I recognised one face: one of them had a rainbow tail and faded violet eyes. It was Yemaya, the Mami Wata leader. And the rest of them were all Night Creatures.

I had to do something. I turned to Moremi, to see if she was getting affected. She was a Night Creature, after all.

She was leaning against a rock to steady herself, clutching her chest so tight her knuckles turned grey. Her skin was becoming translucent, and it had a purplish tint to it. She looked like she was fading away too.

Some protector I was.

'The Àbíkú will be finished now that the night is gone. Sort out the hyena girl, I'll take the *oyinbo*,' Taiwo ordered his warriors, picking up the sword from the floor and clutching it tight.

Osoosi grimaced as she drew a quick air sign, spotted fur spiking across her shoulders.

'So the rumours are true . . .' Taiwo said, pointing his giant sword my way. 'An Olókun woman *did* have a forbidden child with a Night Creature.'

I gulped hard as the sword sparked up, luminous veins spreading across the shining metal like it was getting ready to devour me whole. I shut my eyes tight and forced myself to summon a few shadows to shield me. But I was so exhausted I could barely stand upright any more, let alone dodge any of his attacks.

Taiwo looked at me as black veins tattooed his entire face. His knuckles were still gripping the handle of his sword so hard I thought they'd burst. 'Your eyes go black like mine when I use the Night Creatures' magic from the *juju*-mosquito. That must be where your power to summon ghosts comes from.' His eyes widened slightly as he figured it out.

I didn't bother denying it. The distraction was keeping me alive, giving me a few more moments to figure out how to survive.

'That means everything I lost . . .' Taiwo said stiffly, his eyes narrowing again, ' . . . the war that took my mother . . . all those Olori lives . . . was because of *you*.'

'I lost everything in that war too, and you took the Araba away from me!' I choked out. 'Away from all of us.'

'The Araba knew about the Ògún sword.' Taiwo tilted his head up and let the sunlight warm his cheekbones. 'In the end, he chose to surrender to his feelings.' He smoothed his blade against the purple ankara cloth that he wore tied in the middle of his armour. 'He was once an honourable man. But, as they say, life ends when honour ends.'

My body moved without me thinking and I lunged at him.

He side-stepped, extending his metal claws. 'Nice try.'

Taiwo's brown eyes bled to black as he raised an armoured fist towards me. Now I was up close, I could see Taiwo wasn't the perfect warrior everyone thought he was: whenever his eyes turned black and veiny from *juju* he got ultra-paranoid and jumpy, slashing around, anticipating attacks.

'Look here mate, I don't want my face remixed, I like the original, fam,' I pleaded, dodging one of his fiery punches.

'No more tricks, *oyinbo*,' he said, rushing towards me.

No matter how much I concentrated, the ghosts wouldn't appear no more. They'd disappeared along with most of the darkness. I had no choice but to get personal.

'Your little Ògún cosplay ain't gonna impress me, you get me?' I said, as I used Moremi's signature Gidigbo move: I faked an uppercut, forcing Taiwo to protect the chiselled jawline Olori girls loved so much.

I reached for his torso instead.

Taiwo's eyes practically bust out of his head when I yanked the purple ankara out of his armour. A whole load of memories flooded into my brain. For the first time, I could actually *see* them flickering through my mind, and not just hear them.

I saw a tall, thin woman with the rigid face of a seasoned warrior, and warm almond eyes. When she spoke she had a low, ringing voice.

'*Tayewo*, omo mi owon, *listen and listen well, my son. Your sister is one of the few to receive the gift of the goddess of the wind. She thinks she must use her power to protect everyone and everything. But if I ever have to go away, make sure you protect her.*'

Seeing Taiwo's memories made me feel bad, cause it's not like I checked with him first, or nothing. But I had to. It was the only way to figure out his weakness.

In the blink of an eye, I saw his most important memories: his mother getting the twin dolls as a gift from the Araba when the twins were born. And then there were brief snippets of the twins growing up: their constant bickering, mainly about Taiwo being jealous of his twin, and her retaliating by flicking his earlobes.

It finally made sense. That hazy memory I always had of a kid that kept irritating me and messing about with my ears.

'Is that Kehinde?' I said, not realising I was speaking aloud. Next thing I knew, Taiwo's fist was right in my face.

Lying on my back, my head spinning, I opened my eyes and saw a purple-black figure standing over me, blinking in and out of existence. The Àbíkú had stopped Taiwo from carving a new face on to mine.

It had giant black eyes and a wide gummy smile. It was the one that had been following me around this whole time. It did a weird thing where it flicked at my ears – like it was its way of saying hello.

Taiwo saw it too. The Àbíkú started to morph – its paint faded away, revealing skin that was glossy and smooth. A random yute materialised, wearing purple ankara.

There was no doubt about it.

'Kehinde,' he breathed her name.

Kehinde clicked around herself in confusion. She may have been a normal kid once, but she was an Àbíkú now. The dark veins sank back into Taiwo's skin and his eyes returned to normal.

Kehinde spread tiny fingers over Taiwo's face – it was wet with silvery tears. She clicked rapidly like she was trying to tell him something. 'I ‖ ! ǂ!' Then she went all misty and blurry, before she started fading away.

Now I finally knew what that clicking noise meant. *Goodbye.*

Taiwo opened his mouth to say something. But it was too late. His sister had gone.

Moremi used the last of her strength to pull me away with a braid as a blinding light burst from Taiwo's side.

He had showed emotion. The sword would have its reward.

Taiwo pulled out the Ògún sword and it ignited immediately, a giant forcefield spewing out of the shimmering metal and surrounding him in a prism of light. The ground quaked under our feet.

Taiwo let out a gut-wrenching cry as the light struck him. It sounded like he was being burnt alive. First, the hand holding the sword ignited, then he started breaking away, piece by piece.

'Kehinde never left you, Taiwo! She was only trying to protect me!' I shouted to him.

'Protect *you*?' Taiwo's voice was steady, even as his own sword turned his body to dust, ravaging his body before getting sucked into the shining metal. 'I was supposed to be the one to protect . . . her.'

His armour clanged against the floor. Taiwo had gone.

There wasn't a second to waste. I acted on instinct. A sharp jolt electrocuted my fingertips as I grabbed the two halves of the Night Stone and slotted them together.

Up close, it had a salty, earthy smell to it, like the sea.

Am I really worthy of the Night Stone? Yeah, sure,

my ancestors may have been able to use it in the past. And I wasn't from these parts. I was an outsider. But I had a connection that went beyond my upbringing. It was spiritual.

I started thinking about all the stuff the Araba had said about the emotional core of Olókun. Death. Mourning. Grief. My mother and now the Araba. Then there was my father, the demon who wasn't dead, but trapped. We'd never had a chance to spend proper time together. They were all important losses. But they weren't exactly negative. They were still a part of me. Like the Araba taught me, I was finally beginning to understand something that was bigger than me. The connecting thread in all of our lives. This was the land of origins, where the world began. There was sky inside us, earth inside us, night inside us . . .

I emptied my mind and focused on the truth inside me. I guess I must've done something right, cause the Night Stone started waking up.

It started with a tiny dot of blue light. And then a whole load of colours burst in front of my eyes: magnetic purples, electrifying reds and fiery oranges . . . until my eyes were flooded with black.

Blacker than black. It was strangely comforting.

'Kokumo . . .' A thousand voices echoed my name.

But one stood out from the rest: it had a gentle melody to it that I recognised instantly.

'*Iya mi*,' I responded to the call in Yoruba.

I felt a warm, solid touch. A hand in mine. I could finally see her.

My mother.

'*Omo mi owon*.' Her voice soothed me instantly. Her smile was just as radiant as in my photo, her twists piled on top of her head like a never-ending stream. 'The Night Stone is your birthright, the heart of Olókun beats inside you,' she said, as ghostly forms started appearing before me.

Majestic-looking mandem in blue ankara print took shape before my eyes. They proudly wore the symbol of Olókun around their necks. I saw everyone who had ever touched the Night Stone. I could even peep the exact moment my parents touched it: my mum with trembling, worshipful fingers; my dad with the confident grip of someone who'd lived a hundred lifetimes.

And then I saw further back into the darkness. Before the beginning of time. Just for a millisecond, I glimpsed an impressive figure: constellations in her indigo eyes, wrinkles like the path of a winding stream.

'Kokumo Akanbi.' I pressed my chest to the floor in

the *dobale* pose as soon as she called my name. I didn't know what I was supposed to say to the goddess, but I figured bowing was a good place to start. 'Child of Olókun and son of Lègbá, blood of my blood, *Iwo lo ye*. You are worthy.'

When I opened my eyes, the Night Stone didn't have a single crack in it. And it was glowing like nobody's business. So, yeah, it was a mad one still, but I did it.

The sky was dark again. The night smothered everything like a comfy blanket.

The shimmering forms of Àbíkús danced in the moonlight. Kehinde was there, blinking in and out of focus, hovering over me. Which meant . . .

Moremi had to be okay. She had to be. But before I could make sure, I heard a bone-rattling, '*Baga! Koku*, you have done it-oh!' from Osoosi as she practically strangled the living daylights out of me.

Moremi rolled her eyes at Osoosi's antics, and punched my arm, which I translated as '*Thanks for saving my life and all the Night Creatures, not to mention all of Olori.*'

'You're bare rude, you know.' I laughed, partly cause it was true, and partly cause I liked her anyway.

The Ògún goons tried to dip once the night returned.

But the Night Creatures we had just freed weren't having that. The Mami Wata made sure the Ògún didn't leave without golden souvenirs sticking out the sides of their necks.

Just before we left Olumo Rock, I heard a shuddering groan. I turned back and saw the Ògún sword briefly flicker to life. Sounded like my man Taiwo wasn't too happy about being trapped inside his own sword.

But even though no one had ever escaped it, I got the feeling it wouldn't be the last I'd be hearing from him.

CHAPTER THIRTY-FOUR

Deathless

Yemaya made sure that the Araba's funeral was insane. It was basically two full weeks of constant partying. All the Night Creatures attended. There was singing, dancing and feasting – all of the Araba's favourite dishes were passed around by the Mami Wata: *egusi* soup with pounded yam, along with glow-in-the-dark salt fish and hairy caterpillar dumplings.

Everything smelled delicious, but they were mostly uneaten; even Osoosi wasn't hungry no more. The grief of losing the Araba was worse than any crisis I'd ever had. It felt like someone was using my organs as a punching bag.

The dark sky glittered as we made our way through Jujuland for the last time.

'*Ki lo de*, Koku?' Osoosi nudged me in the side with her elbow. When I didn't answer she translated: 'What's wrong?'

I had understood the Yoruba, but I had no language left to describe how I felt.

'Dem fit dash Araba flesh, but dem no go fit touch him spirit!' she reassured me.

From the corner of my eye I saw Moremi look around at us. 'She is right-oh. The spirits survive as long as they are remembered by the world.'

It was moments like those that reminded me that Moremi wasn't quite human. I followed her gaze to the purple evening that stretched out above.

Dead leaves rattled and scraped under our feet as we walked. We finally reached the *iroko* tree with the giant hole in it that had brought us into Jujuland in the first place. Then Moremi started to sing.

> '*I am an old iroko tree;*
> *Mo dagba iroko.*
> *I will not die;*
> *Mi o ni ku.*
> *I am a thousand hills;*

Mo digba oke.
I cannot be moved;
Mo duro gbon-in.'

There was a hushed silence as her voice vibrated through the whole jungle. Tiny firefly people danced around her. Osoosi and I watched in silence. And I swear down, along with Moremi's voice, I heard a gruff old man's voice singing all the wrong notes to the same melody.

Moremi's braids stretched out as high as the tree itself. There were two chunky ones missing. I knew she'd lost one from the Àgbákò fight, but I hadn't noticed the other one. She'd probably lost it when Pin Cushion got trigger-happy with those darts.

'You want chop fly for mouth?' Moremi snapped, when she caught me staring.

'You never told us the secret to your braids,' I said, honestly. Moremi's braids quivered. 'You ain't gotta tell me nothing, you know,' I said, quickly. 'It's like the Araba used to say – it's alright if you don't know everything, cause you can't unknow something once you know it, you get me?'

'Even though you were raised in the land of the nameless, you have swallowed small sense, *sha*,'

Moremi replied.

'Wow, thanks, man.' I rolled my eyes while she laughed. 'So, you're good, yeah?'

'Taiwo and the Araba may be with the ancestors now, but you are here, and Osoosi is here, and as long as the spirits of the ancestors live inside us, we are deathless.'

I let the words linger as her braids twisted around me.

Deathless. Yeah, I liked the sound of that.

Before we had left, Yemaya had given us stuff that the Araba wanted us to have, since he didn't have any kids of his own.

''im want yuh and yuh likkle friends fi av dis.' She handed us a bunch of stuff wrapped in a white lace cloth. Her voice was as smooth as ever, but her smile was bittersweet. I couldn't even imagine how she felt, being the Araba's wifey and all that. 'An neva forget, yuh always welcome pon mi shore.' She winked, before slithering back into the deep folds of the dark forest.

Moremi put herself in charge of handing out the goods – even though Yemaya gave them to *me* – with a look on her face that suggested that if Osoosi or I dared to disagree, she'd shove one of her stupid braids up our nose or something.

'Osoosi, the Araba is giving you the leopard amulet that belongs to the highest chiefs on the land.'

Osoosi squealed with delight, '*Yepa!* This thing dey sweet well-well-oh! I go wear this when I become chief!'

'For my own . . .' Moremi pulled out a pair of matching wooden sculptures. Osoosi and I almost headbutted each other trying to get a look. It was an *Eji Ogbe* twin set. They looked exactly like her and Taiwo – they both had constipated facial expressions. Yeah, she could keep them. 'Yemaya also give me the divine Oracle to return to the Rùnmí people in Olori so they can be choosing the next Araba.' Moremi showed us the tray wrapped in layers of lace cloth. 'And Kokumo?'

'Yeah?' I answered, low-key interested to see what I would inherit.

'The Araba is wanting you to have . . .' Moremi bit the inside of her cheek to stop herself laughing as she unceremoniously threw the Araba's ratty old flute to me.

'Rah, are you dizzy, fam?' I said, hoping I wasn't touching the part the Araba lipsed. As soon as I touched it, the Araba's gruff voice busted my eardrums singing '*Omi o lota o*' and all the B sides of all the off-key hits he'd been torturing us with since we met him.

'Also this . . .' Moremi handed me a carefully folded piece of blue ankara cloth.

I opened it up and I ain't even gonna cap – my eyes stung as I studied the intricate designs I had spent years endlessly tracing with my eyes in my mum's photo.

Now I had it in my hands, I could not only hear her voice, but all my Olókun ancestors calling me home . . .

We'd all three of us known it was finally time to go back to Olori.

I stared into the giant black hole in the middle of the *iroko* tree. Moremi went first, like before, then Osoosi let out a loud Aganjù battle cry as she jumped. I went last, swinging my legs over the twisty bark and letting go.

When I opened my eyes again I was greeted by an inky night sky. Staring up at the total blackness felt like home. The *iroko* tree wasn't so ugly any more. The giant trunk was dark brown and shiny smooth, it had loads of bright green moon-shaped leaves and its fat white flowers were in full bloom.

We lay under the stars for hours just drinking it all in.

We stayed until the sun crawled over the horizon and then made our way back through the ruined Olókun district. I put my hand on my ankara and let the sounds paint a picture in my mind. I didn't see crumbling buildings no more; I saw gleaming houses with tinted blue windows and mosaic tiles sitting on tangerine sand beds facing the water. I imagined faces shining with paint as men and women built magnificent sculptures with blue, glowing patterns trailing down their arms. I smelled the sweet aroma of crayfish and *tilapia* frying. I saw Olókun women wheeling rickety food carts in front of the swimmers playing on the shore. I imagined my mum laughing with her mouth open, just like in the photo.

'There's something I gotta do, guys,' I announced, as I folded down to the ground, pressing my knees into the warm sand.

After a moment's thought, I ripped the cloth into two, keeping the second one. Moremi wordlessly handed me some incense so I could add it to my shrine. Osoosi chipped in too, handing me all the seaweed dumplings she'd yammed from the Araba's funeral, to use as offerings.

I spread out the stuff neatly and burned the incense so it rose in tall spirals. 'May your soul journey safely to the land of origins,' I prayed the Olókun *oriki* that the Araba had taught me. 'Goddess of the bright moon and darkest night. I give you praise.' I tied the rest of the ankara around my wrist, looping it around in a double knot that resembled an infinity sign.

Now I could always remember my roots, no matter where I was.

Once I was done, Osoosi let out a long, ear-splitting whistle. In seconds, two dark furry outlines prowled towards us. My airways shut down as a massive furball plopped over my face and gave me a long, prickly lick.

'Ah-ah! Moin-Moin, you are too much-oh!' Osoosi laughed as Gizdodo cosied up to her knees. I noticed both panthers were back to a healthy weight and their furry coats were glossy and thick all over, and as black as the midnight sky.

I was glad we were travelling by panther. The dusty harmattan wind made everything look hazy, but I saw red cliffs in the distance, huge boulders and steamy clouds. Antelopes, giraffes and zebras roamed in tall green grass. They had lush furry coats that sparkled when they caught the sunlight.

*

'Ah-ah! *Wahala* has returned-oh!' Inaki yelled at us once we arrived in Ekundudu.

He was alright after all! I thought, watching Osoosi give him a massive bear hug. Then she ducked into her yard with her tail whipping behind her.

She didn't even say bye or nothing. And I thought Moremi was the rude one.

Osoosi re-emerged with an iPhone between her teeth. 'Koku, are you having WhatsApp?' she asked.

CHAPTER THIRTY-FIVE

My Tribe

Mama Oti and Moremi dropped me off at the airport. I'd arrived at Olori with an old backpack, and was leaving with three tanks of luggage, and a pot of steaming *okro* soup. I had no idea how I was gonna get that through Customs.

I tried to dash it before I went through Security, but Mama Oti gave me that dangerous Olori look that told me exactly what was gonna happen to me if I tried it.

'*Eh-hen*, there go be plenty meat in this stew. So tell your uncle that he does not need to worry himself,' Mama Oti explained, nodding so hard her multiple chins danced.

'Yeah, whatever, man,' I said.

When Mama Oti brought me in close, I almost suffocated from her flowery perfume. 'I am giving you small-small Babalú medicine in this stew. You hear me?' She probably thought she was whispering, but she might as well have been using a megaphone. 'Chop small before you enter plane, eh? Rùnmí officials remove selected memories, so the outside world will not know our secrets. This go help you remember, so you will be knowing who you are when you are in your England.'

I had no idea how I was going to do that, but I'd find a way. There was no way I was gonna forget this. It had been the adventure of a lifetime.

Moremi and I shared a quiet look. Her lips tilted into a sideways smirk.

Then Mama Oti patted her softly on her back and they both turned to leave.

'*O daabo*, Kokumo,' Moremi said finally, waving with her braids. I waited until their silhouettes dissolved into the crowd before I turned away.

*

Thwack! Man had literally just arrived in the UK and some random just shoved into me.

'Oi, do you mind?' a girl around my age wearing baggy white clothes said. Her voice rang loud and clear, but her lips didn't move. Weird.

'Are you dizzy, fam? You're the one that bumped into me!' I insisted, a moment too late. She'd already disappeared into the crowd. Her London accent threw me off, cause she was wearing Olori clothes: a long, white hooded robe and a matching ankara headwrap.

I pushed the strange encounter to the back of my mind when my uncle arrived. 'Kokumo! You have arrived, my boy!' he cried, giving me a bone-crunching pat on the back. Then he reached into his pocket and pulled his phone out and tapped hard on the glass screen.

'Say sheez!' he said, as a blinding white flash burned my eyeballs.

I let him get away with it cause he actually looked pleased to see me. He was even more pleased to tell me about a new aunty he had met while I was in Olori. I ignored his nonsense, and gratefully snatched my iPhone back out of his hands.

The first thing I did was add Moremi and Osoosi as contacts.

*

It's funny how it all turned out. I still get shook by the ghostly mandem, but as long as I practise the stuff I learned on my trip, I know I'll be okay.

I even got a C+ for 'creativity and enthusiasm' on my holiday homework when I got back to school. It was on African History and I had to answer the question, 'What is a tribe?'

My first paragraph had just one word: 'Everything.'

Then I added sick drawings of Moremi's magic braids and Osoosi transforming into a hyena and crazy details and all that. Miss Adebayo really liked my artwork. She showed the whole class, and even Atticus Sharp gassed me, saying my drawings looked 'rather splendid'.

Course, Miss Adebayo thought all the stuff about the mosquito-bot was a bit mad, and she didn't really like me calling Frobenius a thief instead of an explorer, but it was the best grade I got all year. She put, 'You're a star! Very creative work!' at the bottom of the page. I usually get sarcastic ones like when Mr Stokes writes, 'You should get the dog to eat your homework next time instead of writing it', when he *knows* I'm a cat person.

After that, I signed up for Art Club for the first time. I never bothered with clubs before cause I thought my illness would get in the way, but I've been drawing a lot lately. My grounding technique that I now use during a crisis makes me so good at noticing stuff I figured I might as well put it down on paper.

But the best part about getting a C+ was when Miss Adebayo called Uncle Tunji to tell him about it.

'Mr Tunji?' Miss Adebayo said, giving me a comforting smile.

I felt sorry for her – she was making a rookie mistake holding the phone so close to her ear.

'So, this boy wants to kill me, eh?' Uncle Tunji yelled, when he answered. He must have seen my school's number come up on his screen.

I tried not to laugh when Miss Adebayo blinked in shock. 'H-hello, Mr Tunji. This is Miss Adebayo speaking, Koku's history teacher. Actually, I would like to—'

'Ah-ah, when will sense open in this boy's big-for-nothing forehead. Eh? Hello, ma?'

'Hello . . . Mr Tunji? I feel as though you might've misunderstood me. I'm calling because Koku—'

'Don't worry, ma, he must taste fire today! This *oyinbo* method is not working-oh; in fact, I am coming there myself. Today-today this boy will learn by *force*!'

'I'm calling because Koku has been well behaved

recently. I just thought you should know. I'm not sure what magic that trip to Olori did to him. I believe he's a talented artist with an amazing attention to detail.'

'Eh?' Uncle Tunji's voice lowered to a normal speaking volume. 'Is that so? Well, of course now, that is my nephew, after all.'

I couldn't believe my uncle was actually proud of me.

'He will even be a doctor or a professor!' Uncle Tunji said, brightly. Which was mad, cause he knows I have a sparkling career ahead of me as a manga artist.

Even Miss Adebayo couldn't hold back a laugh at the sudden enthusiasm. Her tortoiseshell glasses bounced on her nose.

When she moved them up, I peeped a tiny Olókun symbol on the outer rim.

'Yes, I'm sure this C+ is just the beginning for Koku. He would've gotten an A* if it was an art assignment. There's no limit to what this boy can do.'

'C what? Koku, are you hearing me?'

I rolled my eyes. *How could I not?*

'Go and read your books, *jo*! How can you be disgracing me like this, ah-ah?'

I had to go home early cause I felt a crisis coming on.

My uncle came up to get me, and when we got home, a giant orange furball was waiting for me on the doorstep.

Jollof had gotten kinda heavy still. My uncle figured out I had been keeping him and looked after my guy when I was in Olori. So now he's three times bigger than when I left. He headbutted me as soon as I reached the door to say wagwan as usual, and I bent down to scratch behind his ears.

'I had to feed this demonic rat when you were away. This thing can chop for England!' I smiled when my uncle shook his head as he turned the key to let the three of us in.

As soon as we got into the flat, my uncle laid out some premium wet cat food for Jollof. Then he *forced* me to save the moist airport photo as his screensaver.

His full cheeks widened at the glass screen with our squished faces on it. 'Now hurry and pass me the remote. *Kiakia!* I don't want to hear any argument,' he ordered, letting out a fat yawn.

'No problem, man,' I said, raising my hand towards the TV stand. While my uncle was distracted with flinging his slippers off and stinking up the yard with his expired toenails, I summoned a ghost hand to pick up the remote and drop it into his lap.

No long ting.

'There you go!' I said, watching him blink at the remote that had suddenly appeared in his lap.

'*Ehen*, that Olori trip has turned you into a useful somebody. You must return to that place every summer,' he remarked, jabbing his fingers into the rubbery buttons.

'Okay, sounds good, man,' I said, and I meant that.

I still got a lot to learn about my powers and my tribe. Linking up with Osoosi and Moremi would be cool, especially now that night exists in Olori and I can get some proper shut-eye. Plus I would get to have some of Mama Oti's *okro* soup again. It's even better when it's not dripping into your eyeballs.

I don't even care how crazy they all are. No matter what, that's my tribe.

Dear Reader,

Disappointed by the lack of diversity in my university course, I centred my dissertation around postcolonial Nigerian literature. Through this I actually became quite curious about pre-colonial Nigerian history. I was amazed by the things I found out, like the incredible and highly sophisticated Benin and Oyo kingdoms that were never mentioned in school.

Once I graduated I knew I wanted to write a novel that would speak to children straddling British and African identities and make them proud of both. I've always been frustrated with the lack of children's literature featuring black protagonists. I know that this is steadily increasing, but we have a long way to go when it comes to building a canon of children's literature that reflects modern Britain.

As a child I was especially drawn to fantasy and adventure stories; reading them as an adult was disappointing as I began to realise how inherently racist they were – which naturally takes the fun out of anything. They were genres black people have historically been left out of, or worse still, been positioned as the object of ridicule.

Adventure books were explicitly racist (*Heart of Darkness*, *King Solomon's Mines*, *Treasure Island*, *Robinson Crusoe*, *Tarzan* etc . . .), fantasy books (such as *The Lord of the Rings*, or the Harry Potter series) simply didn't include any important characters that looked like me. The only books in which I found myself represented were American novels that dealt with black trauma.

The few children's novels that did include black protagonists were often very gritty; they generally spoke to an older audience and the themes were stereotypically around poverty, living on a council estate, drugs or fighting against racism. They distinctly lacked the whimsy and magic I sought in literature, which is why I often felt like I had no choice but to relate to white protagonists who were allowed to explore their childhood and go on amazing adventures to far-away exotic places.

I had never quite managed to write successful stories about people who looked like me, and *Koku Akanbi and the Heart of Midnight* is my first attempt. Koku Akanbi speaks to the authentic experience of being Black and British with a dose of adventure and magic that could be enjoyed by a child of any background.

I feel that we are living in a time where a lot of non-fiction is coming out to help us navigate our identity as people of colour such as *The Good Immigrant* and *Why I'm No Longer Talking to White People About Race*. However, there's a huge gap when it comes to literature that centres around the coming of age of black children, specifically black boys. When I think about the stories that had a profound effect on me growing up between the ages of 9–16, I think of coming of age stories with male protagonists such as the *Alex Rider* series, the *Percy Jackson* series and *Artemis Fowl*. In fact, I cannot name a single black child that I could relate to growing up and that's appalling.

Koku was initially created out of the frustration that came with being constantly excluded and misrepresented in literature. As Audre Lorde says: 'if we do not define ourselves for ourselves, we will be defined by others – for their use and to our detriment'. But Koku's spirit broke out of the confines I set for him. It has been lovely to explore his emotional vulnerability and to define him outside the boundaries of what black boys are 'supposed' to be. Koku Akanbi is not a martyr, or a freedom symbol, he is a thirteen-year-old, smart-mouthed kid with a morbid streak, who is very sensitive at heart.

Maria Motúnráyọ̀

ACKNOWLEDGEMENTS

I want to first acknowledge my late grandfather, Thompson Kokumo Tawose, who owned a little bookshop in Ibadan Nigeria and loved reading, tennis and eating beans.

Of course, Koku Akanbi wouldn't exist without my little sister and best friend, the one and only Emmanuela Oludara Adebisi. Thank you for supporting every writing endeavour I have ever had with patience, kindness and a scarily thorough understanding of what children actually want to read.

I'm endlessly grateful to my mentor and dear friend, Jane Robinson, who championed the novel when it was just an idea and encouraged me to keep going after each painful rejection. Thanks for speaking to me practically every week and breathing life into my work.

I also want to thank my delightful mother, Yemi Oluwatoyin Tawose Adebisi, for encouraging me to choose a Black British protagonist and for actually selecting the name Koku Akanbi and helping with all the original Yoruba translations. You are my biggest inspiration and I love you to the moon and back, *iya mi*. I'm lucky to have been raised by a larger than life, proudly Nigerian father so thanks for being you, Adekunle Adebisi.

Adedayo Adebisi thanks for being the best niece anyone could ever ask for and for providing me with support and confidence throughout. I am so grateful to have you in my life. I am blessed by a wonderful group of ridiculously talented women – Priscillia, the BGG and my Greenford High School day ones (you all know who you are) and my 'house of abundance' – thank you all for being so amazing, generous and hilarious.

Thank you Aunty Yemisi for educating me on so many aspects of Nigerian history and being supportive during a difficult time for my family. I'd like to shout out my favourite cousins Richie and Kemi Ayodele for giving me a lifelong addiction to anime, and for your encouraging words after I wrote the very first version of the book.

Muchas Gracias to my Spanish family Ximena and Pol who kept me alive during the pandemic, and made sure to cook me delightful treats while I worked on my second manuscript. I especially want to thank Timothy Black for suggesting having an excitable kid as part of the Jujuland group, and Jordan Rose for listening to endless rambling voice notes while I fleshed out my magic system.

The children's writing community has been SO supportive. Thank you for embracing me! I especially want to recognise Rachel Faturoti for reaching out to me first when I was a budding nervous writer struggling with imposter syndrome. Thanks Tomi Oyemakinde for your fierce intelligence, razor sharp insight, great advice and being a sounding board for the Orisa magic system at very random times.

I also want to recognise all my friends and colleagues at Beam, who have been so kind and understanding while I balanced work and writing commitments, while also delivering amazing case work to people who need it most.

Dupo pupo Olayinka Bakare, my Yoruba tutor for being the most patient teacher and for providing amazing translations for the Yoruba and Pidgin English in the novel. I am also grateful to Annabelle Steele for your brilliant work on the Patois which has really helped bring the Mami Wata to life. I have so much gratitude to Dame Elizabeth Anionwu for your incredible contributions to destigmatising sickle cell and conducting life-changing research into this condition. I'm super grateful for you letting me interview you over a hot steaming bowl of ramen.

I have the privilege of having an agent who really understands the book and has been a huge *Koku* fan from the very start. It has been a pleasure working with Lydia Silver and the structural work we did together was a HUGE gamechanger, even though I was reluctant at first. Even though we only worked together for a brief time I want to thank Tig Wallace for commissioning *Koku* and getting the essence of who he is instantly. Thanks Polly for all your editorial work on *Koku* – your keen eye is so impressive and it has definitely taken the book to new heights.

Simone! Your INCREDIBLE illustrations brought Koku, Moremi, Osoosi and Jujuland to life; they are better than I ever could've hoped and I am in awe of your insane talent. I have been given such an innovative team at Hachette and I especially want to thank the PR & Marketing team who have provided so many opportunities for the novel to get into the hands of as many readers as possible.

Finally, I want to say a HUGE thank you to all English teachers and Librarians for encouraging creativity and providing a nurturing space for imaginative children.

Maria Motúnráyọ̀ Adébísí graduated
from the University of Oxford in 2017
with a degree in English Literature. As part
of her degree, she focused on post-colonial
literature from Nigeria, and on graduating
she realised that she wanted to write a
novel that would speak to children
straddling British and African identities
and make them proud of both.